CW00820362

Sid Falconer

GOODNIGHT, SWEETHEART

Proudly presents a collection of short stories

AUSTIN MACAULEY PUBLISHERS™

LONDON · CAMBRIDGE · NEW YORK · SHARJAH

A CIP catalogue record for this title is available from the British Library.

ISBN 9781788781015 (Paperback)
ISBN 9781788781008 (Hardback)
ISBN 9781788781022 (E-Book)

www.austinmacauley.com

First Published (2019)
Austin Macauley Publishers Ltd
25 Canada Square
Canary Wharf
London
E14 5LQ

Another One Bites the Dust

Over thirty years, I've protected folk at venues and punished violent thugs! I'd KO'd many. A boxing colleague, suggested the punch line, "another one bites the dust!" This story begins on the 4th of September, 1962. I joined the army as a junior leader and bandsman! Later, at York railway station, a soldier gave me grief, so I bashed him, and he bit two cobbled stones! One occasion, my right hand connected with the jaw of general duties corporal Michael Langthorne, and hey presto, I say, this fable is getting a tad violent!

Joined the regimental band in Berlin, West Germany and a staff sergeant, Moose Riley, angered me so I've blotted his copy book, and another one bites the dust! I was dismissed from the band then assigned to B Company, where a corporal, Ron Rosenquest, punched me in the face whilst present were four NCOs to make sure he wasn't knocked out! Outside the Silver Oyster bar in Colchester, I KO'd one of them vile corporals, and another one bites the dust! I joined the company boxing team! Later, in an inter-company bout, I cut Rosenquest to shreds and at ringside was my brother, Dave, which pleased me immensely and secured one's revenge, and now, in my mind, he's a mere remnant!

1965/66, one did a tour of active duty in the Middle East! Whilst on one's leisure time, I've thrashed a non-commissioned officer and booked myself into the guardhouse! Major Robinson cried, "There's a vacant position at HQ ration office, go and apply as I'm fed up with you knocking out my NCOs!" I went over and applied for the post and was successful! A corporal replaced me in B Company, 7 platoon and later died in an ambush along the Yemen border! Finally, returned to England where I went absent without leave, then 586 days later, I've returned to my unit! 23/2/69, I was court-martialled for desertion, and June 10/06/69, I was discharged! Later, I was awarded a pugilist license! December 1970, after four debatable defeats, I suffered a fractured spinal column, canal, cord and broken pelvic girdle!

Throughout the night, a flash of light kept invading my sleep, then I awoke with a loss of memory and paralysed! A year passed, then I returned to the gladiator arena and continued with the boxing career! In 1972, I was informed a punch to my head could prove fatal! Well, reader, at this time, I was flat broke, so I boxed until 1978 and became a top-ten contender at light-heavyweight and heavy! Fought, in Calais, France and in Norway! My wife, Lorraine, and I supplied door staff to work at public venues, clubs, wine bars and restaurants! One Sunday night, I was attacked with lead truncheons, but in the end, I put two men in Poole, hospital! Now, is the backbone, style and sheer nature of this saga wetting thy insatiable appetite?

1984: lightning flashed, alerting me and awakening my keenness to jot down notes of a dream! Come to think of it, something strange occurred in dreamland as you will read in due course! I called Lorraine, and she remarked, "Yes, dear!" I told her a tale of an island named headache and of encounters with evil pirates and by the grace of God enveloping into the humbled body of Longjohn Silverhead! I rode upon splendid dolphins in shark-infested waters, visited a loony bin and witnessed murder, most foul! Now, I am writing stories about the heartiest little Irish leprechauns one could possibly imagine! Well, pal, there is nothing much more left to say except have I dangled enough carrot for you to be wanting more?

Wee Folk Orchestrate My Life

In my opinion, there's more to life than an eye can envisage, because supernatural spectre, I firmly believe, does exist, and we live in a mere speck of the enchanted universe where weird explosions, far beyond our creative ability to understand occur! Are dreams factual or not? That's the question everyone asks, but nobody knows! Are there dimensions where illustrious fiery dragons roam and demented leprechaun reside? Did Jack climb a huge beanstalk that reached the white fluffy clouds where a giant lives? Now, let your creativity flow, and you'll, maybe, drift where a pigeon-toed Walt Disney intended and unnatural occurrence come with utmost delight!

Is the kingdom in heaven pure blarney or does utopia exist? Could our series of thoughts, images and emotions which occur in sleep be fiction? I believe in miracles! Now, reader, sit back, and take pleasure in reading this fiddle-faddle fable! Hopefully, you see this nondescript I'm about to stage in the same light that I do, in which case, hurray, as that's what I aimed to achieve! Most of my life has been spent at one's word processor, typing novels, especially when a storm gusts! I let my imagination flow, and rolling waves echo, and magical, scenic views mingle with extraordinary characters!

Old, marauding bandits who strive to warm the cockles of one's heart! "And I say," exclaimed an elf, "terrify, imagination!"

"I must stress, you wee folk have taken over and orchestrate my life!"

"We pencil in the background of what ye visualise, and that is all!"

"Next, I'll be talking to rabbits and rodents."

"Like field mice?" cried Muskrat.

"Vermin have left droppings!"

"They are burrowers!"

"Good thinking, Moss."

"Bog Roll, I know!"

"Us house guests tidy up our excrement," exclaimed Peat Bag!

I distinctly remember, as though it were yesterday, an extremely dangerous situation being unleashed in the heart of Poole! The day was the 21st of June, 1988. I'd say about six-thirty in the evening. I was driving towards the centre, approaching a roundabout opposite the main dolphin complex. If one's memory is correct. A quick glance to my left revealed a row of taxis positioned on a forecourt, in front of a wide entrance, thus projecting a cosy welcoming scene! A couple of articulated lorries on the inside lane rushed by, so I decided to continue driving round in the outside lane until reaching Wimborne road, intending to drive towards Oakdale and the pottery, public house, on Ringwood road!

I noticed the George Hotel, a white building capped with a tall, dark roof like Abe Lincoln's hat and a large signboard swaying in an easy breeze; suddenly, a loud, deafening explosion sounded from across the far side of a long bridge where the old section of this Dorset town stands! I continued around the roundabout for another circuit when a monster explosion rang out! I turned onto the bridge and ascended to investigate the incident when a thunderous explosion sounded, followed by an incredible series of terrifying eruptions; simultaneously, plumes of black cloud, like an American-Indian smoke signal, billowed as barrels zoomed three-hundred feet into the air!

At the top of this hill, I realised it was in fact coming from the BDH Chemical Works on West Quay Road! I then noticed raindrops falling upon the windscreen and thick clumps of debris; suddenly, silver cylinders escalated into a darkened sky as Satan unleashed his awful, psychopathic wrath!

Tudor Fox

Juggernauts, large motor vehicles and cars were stopped at the bottom where another junction is positioned! The fire brigade, ambulance and police service would soon be arriving, and this congestive traffic was now clogging up the only route to the chemical plant! The road finally cleared, and I was travelling around the roundabout when, holy smoke, even greater explosive matter discharged! This was becoming nightmarish!

Adjacent to the BDH Works, somebody fell to the ground! For several split-seconds, my thoughts were, an elderly person was slumped by the wayside, so I continued around the roundabout circuit until finally, returning almost to the same spot then, I turned left and drove towards the Chemical Works' main entrance and to my surprise, noticed a badly injured fox! I left the car and picked up a little lame brown vixen! A loud explosion shook me to my core, and I literally beat a hasty retreat; finally, I was travelling round the dolphin roundabout and heading up Longfleet Road! This fox was unconscious and her frail body was bleeding and covered in glossy liquid! I didn't have a clue what this substance was except, to my touch, it was greasy with a thick slimy coating!

As I drove home, this ragged fox never stirred and appeared totally lifeless! I suppose, according to the law, I should have taken this vixen to the police or vets, but, at this point, my concern was her safety! Lord only knows what I was thinking! The car came to a halt outside mother's abode, where I live. Inside, I quickly grabbed a coloured towel with thin stripes, reminiscent of a red and black bumblebee, before returning to the car as rain became foul and fell in abundance and an old wind howled like a deathly wolf cry!

I folded the towel, then gently placed it over and round a frail, bony animal, and for the first time, this lady became slightly disturbed! Next, I picked her up and walked slowly like one carries a new-born child into the house and along a wide corridor into the kitchen, at the rear. I gave her a bath, then attended to her wounds! She was conscious yet never flinched! I put cream onto parts which were almost bare and tiny clumps of brown hair appeared, scorched! There were plenty of signs of scar tissue amongst fresh cuts, and I thought, this captivating vixen, has already seen her best days then. I noticed she was in the early stages of pregnancy!

A feeling of emotion, which is natural, overcame me, and for a few moments, I thought this poor little animal must live, and I said a small prayer asking God to save her life which, at this precise moment in time, hung in the balance! The prayer, I would say, lingered! I picked the fox up and carried her into our sitting room where a warm, radiant fire burned gaily! As I entered, several fiery embers cracked, as though our precious lord was signalling, and I assumed everything was going to be just magic, and that was like the distinct sound of music to my ears and at this moment in time, exceptionally welcome! Next, it became dark, then lightbulbs flickered! "My lord, what have you got there?" exclaimed mother. "A small fox!" I remarked, as one laid her upon a colourful lounge carpet!

For the next two days, it was touch and go, but I knew, deep in my heart, this little, innocent vixen would survive her ordeal! Couple of days later, she aroused and by the end of a week, was moving and drinking liquids! Early the next morning, our latest addition began chewing solid food! So, I named her Chew and was overjoyed by her progress! It was amazing, watching her walk across the room until she'd disappear out of the back door into an enchanting garden, full of wonderful flowers filling the air with a scented fragrance! Our little rabbit would come out of her burrow which I'd made beneath a concreted section where our cars parked, and while the fox, was intruding, upon her play area, she would retreat into her apartment, beneath ground level!

A few days and Chew grew stronger, then I noticed her body development as milk increased; then, late one afternoon, I looked around, and she was gone! In, the next garden, situated at the rear, two service engineers from a local sewerage works were busy emptying a septic tank. "I say, gentlemen, has anyone seen a small fox?"

"Yes, over here, several minutes ago," came a reply.

"Bitch has gone," exclaimed another workman! I hopped into our sunbeam rapier, parked out front, and began a search of the vicinity! All to no avail, and for at least two weeks, I widened the search, looking in areas located near West Quay Road where I first set my eyes upon this magnificent animal!

In my sleep, thoughts entered one's mind as though she was calling me; simultaneously, alarm bells rang, and my heart beat rapidly! What happened next is best left to one's own wild imagination! Something inside told me to drive along Victoria Road, turn right at the lights and head towards Poole centre! Each passing second, the vehicle gathered speed, and for a few moments, the direction appeared simulated, as though I was now being controlled by alien forces! Left, down Constitution Hill, where an elegant viewpoint overlooks the natural harbour, and over the brow towards a small island!

The main traffic lights up ahead were on red but one instinctively knew the signals would automatically change as I approached which indeed happened, allowing me to continue my journey! I drove on past the Shah of Persia, a newly painted public house, over the brow of a hill and down a long, narrow, straight road, typically named Longfleet, onto Parkstone Road! I distinctly recall swinging around the roundabout at the old George Hotel and bumping over the bridge. Now, the next several lines are pure fantasy, as there are other foxes occupying, the den, and so, whereabouts of their habitat is a secret known only to me! With an extremely vivid imagination, there stands a tall, green street-lamp where light casts a majestic silhouette, standing forever beside the bleak water as a monument of respect for the early days of Poole.

Somehow, I sensed something was wrong! Eventually, I reached high street, which ghastly buccaneers once frequented! This morning, my brain became extremely active and memories, where crazy, mindboggling effects lurk, emerged as Prince Eddie Albert, alias Jack the Ripper, throttled prostitutes in the very heart of London, and Diana is murdered, and millions of pounds from Oxfam vanish, and heads of British soldiers found along the Yemen border are fixed on poles! This voice inside, one's equilibrium, cried as the air stilled! "Sid, hurry, I'm slipping away!"

I stopped the car and directly ahead was a signpost, and beneath an old-fashioned gas-lamp was my cunning foxes' lair! I walked past an illustrious street-lamp, where raindrops formed a drinking pool, and for some unbeknown reason, over to the water edge! Light from over the far side of the harbour cast upon this embankment and lit up a pathway down which I descended! A trickle of rainwater upon the heavy ground made the going exceptionally arduous as dirt underfoot became quite slippery; finally, I came to a small cave set into a bank! In my hand was a torch I'd somehow acquired! I flashed a beam into this secluded hole, simultaneously climbing, inside!

In a corner, barely alive, lay Chew and beside her, dead, newly born cubs had been breast feeding at the time of their untimely death but one, I presume the runt of this litter, was curled up and alone! This cub may have drank some contaminated milk! I moved over and picked up this illustrious reddish ball of fluff and felt the faintest of heartbeats! By a miracle, this little creature was still alive! Chew sighed, and in the darkness, her soul departed! This beautiful fox was now dead! Precious tears of tender emotion welled up inside for this thin vixen whom I had now become attached to! The smell was overbearing, putrid and increasing with each passing second. Was this cub, that I named Tudor Fox, destined to survive?

A few moments later, I placed this adorable mammal inside my damp shirt and left! There was nothing more I could honestly do! Outside, a frosty morning welcomed us! Not the brightest of beginning of life for a small cub! I drove home, put a cupful of milk into a microwave oven and switched it on, and suddenly, this circular platform twirled and old mother time lapsed whilst I searched for something to enable me to feed this animal. In a cupboard, beneath a kitchen sink, I found a yellow sponge. When wetted, it was able to absorb! I opened a large microwave oven and withdrew the cup but the milk was piping hot! I added sweet sugar! I must have inhaled fumes, because I was now feeling ill.

Some time lapsed before emptying the contents into a bowl and adding fresh milk! "Drink this, little fox, and I'll promise, you will survive." Suddenly, I saw movement and to my sheer surprise, a small tongue appeared! Outside, thunder cracked like a wounded animal and lightning flashed across a dusty sky! A storm arose and ferocious winds broke away from its harness and panes of glass smashed! Massive trees quaked under such burden, swaying to and fro before uprooting. "Hell is nigh," came, whistling on the wind!

"My God, this storm is cyclonic," cried Lorraine.

"Newscaster stated we were in for a wicked storm, but this is terrifying," said mother.

"I think we should go into our cellar; hopefully, it will be quieter!"

"And safer!"

As we passed the main windows, torrential rain, like a drum, beat hard. "I'm very glad we're insured," cried Lorraine, quickly grabbing our two sons. Down, in the basement, I switched an old electric fire, which had an acorn of energy compared to modern systems, on and shortly, a warm glow and heat projected forth. I sat beside my wife and cuddled our fox! Later, I ascended the stairs and popped into the kitchen! Outside, this nightmare worsened. I returned. "Pal, feed, and you'll grow into a fine fox, like your late mother!" This statement was short lived, because Tudor also died and is buried along with his beautiful mother and family in the lea of a hill somewhere in the new forest.

Satanic Nightmare

Prior to working as head doorman at the infamous Neptune Bar in Boscombe, Bournemouth, back in early December, 1970, when I was involved in a car accident at the junction of Owls Road and Saint Johns, leaving me paralysed for the night and early morning, I had dreams, some pleasant but one, satanic! In 1967, I dreamt of some horses winning famous races which, at a later date, actually happened! One vision was a horse named Highest Hopes! The next day being Saturday, I went across Denmark Road to the bookmakers owned by Terry Sims and for some unknown reason, told him of my dream! At the time, he was totalising old bets and took no notice! The following Monday, I picked up the newspaper and front page headlines was Highest Hopes, winner of the arc! Also, Humble Duty, another horse I had mentioned! I'd said Highest Hopes, was quoted either 8/1 or 12/1, maybe even 14/1, but at this date, I cannot remember, but this horse romped home at a staggering 28/1! Shame, I didn't know Mark Wheeler, who runs another local bookmakers shop, at that present time!

Terry checked the previous Saturday's papers and one's price was quoted! Also, I remember saying Humble Duty won at the odds-on figure of 100/30, which was also the case! Umpteen years passed; then, I dreamt Rainbow's Quest would win, and sure enough, it won the arc de triomphe in 1985! In a pub in Weymouth, I told everybody to put their money on Rough Quest for the 1996 Grand National at 10/1 and stated it would win and sure enough, the horse won and my pal Tony Carpenter, who is the manager of the Conservative Club in Boscombe won four-hundred pounds! Hey Tony, what happened to my cut? At a later date, my worst nightmare occurred! I dreamt one was dying in Poole Hospital with my mother and brother, Barry, whom I hadn't seen in a few years, looking down at me! Someone once said, "You can't dream of oneself dying!" Later, out of the blue and unexpected, Barry came home! After several weeks of working together, purchasing and selling roadworthy cars and heavy vehicles, he collapsed in my arms after a fantastic night out with Dublin Bob and a month later, died in exactly the same circumstance, in Poole Hospital! I had told our mother of my dream and she promised to wait in the corridor until I came out of the intensive care unit but when I was standing at his bedside and turned, mum was standing there and I knew, without doubt, Barry, whom our other brother, David, and I shall always cherish, was going to die! This situation was in reverse order and our world was forever shattered!

Barry died in 1973, and still, after these years, tears swell and I get upset. Then, in early June, 1974, I met Lorraine and have sons, Sidney John, named after Barry, David and my stepfather and Matthew. Nobody will know what occurs after death but there have been millions of puzzling cases of unexplained phenomenon and I have had umpteen unimaginable dreams, so I keep an open mind! Oddball, I may be! If that is what you choose to think, well, who on earth can blame you? Certainly not me, and that's for sure! Reader, I've witnessed what I have stated! If one is uncertain, pop along to Boscombe and ask Tony about a certain evening at the Victoria public house in Weymouth! Now, it's up to you to read my account and if you think one's old mind was unbalanced, that's your prerogative! I wouldn't mind a few more horses winning a stately race again and pray to our lord I never experience another satanic nightmare!

The Dormouse Derby

I went across to Ireland where it's claimed leprechauns be; suddenly, a pocket-sized, citizen sporting a green jacket, grey knee-length socks, leather britches and black shoes with chrome buckles looked up at me and sprinkled a bag of powder into the air! Sparkling flakes of diamond-shaped dust floated upon the wind! Minute particles entered my bloodstream! Next moment, I felt on top of the world! Unexpectedly, I'm watching oneself becoming smaller! Now I'm pintsized and still descending! Next, I'm tiny and sitting inside a dugout or sheltered accommodation with a miniature man! "Hello, I'm a wood cutter! Gnome who chop logs and this be where we midgets dwell!" Now, would anybody believe I can see and hear a transparent, winged fairy yodel?

Well, I sat upon a rock whilst she yodelled! Climbed a mighty beanstalk with a sweet, scented fragrance and visited a big friendly giant's castle and met the sweetest pixie named Shamrock Dixie in a toadstool cafe! "My dear, the truth is, the little people inhabit woodland!"

"And notorious wee folk, state I, Kilkenny Imp, wear tartan kilt and drink alcoholic beverage rarely seen potcheen!"

"Irish imps are folklore!"

"Harry Elves, be that me?"

"Tom O'Flynn, I'd be guessing!"

"We walked in the Cooley, and I kissed blarney stone!"

"Storyteller, eat emerald bullfrog, be most divine!"

"The vertebrate with a deep, booming croak?"

"That be him!"

"Sprite, what a delight!"

"Cup Cake, do fairies drink dandelion tea?"

"Trick O'treat, we do!"

"In that case, white sugar, three lumps!"

"O'Flynn, you are no taller than five inches yet you're towering above me!"

"Indeed, I am!"

"Now, wood cutter, where's the pot of gold?"

"I say, over the rainbow!"

"By the way, red dwarf, whom are you?

"Sunshine, my loyal subjects call me King Louie!"

"And there's more!"

"Jimmy Cricket, like snakes and spiders?"

"No!"

"Writer, ye danced in a fairy ring and met a bucket load of dwarves."

"Including cobbler, Job Hobbit!"

"I feel sozzled!"

"Eat, brawn!"

"We feed on vegetable, nuts, raspberries and barbecued rodents!"

"And rabbits!"

"Stubble Face, sitting upon a stately mushroom, come on down and meet our noble guest!"

"Bog, would ye like a humble toad's testicles in white sauce at lunch?"

"No, thanks, I've already eaten!"

"Musci, like a cuppa snail vomit?"

"One Thumb, change their subject and stop licking dormouse!"

"Ok, Fairy Cup!"

"That rodent's live," I remarked.

"Them urchin be very tasty," exclaimed Sean O'Marley from Headache! A well-known part of this magical domain where pirates roam and King Egghead rules a mighty kingdom, but that's another fabled tale!

"I am sure that mouse is edible," I replied, feeling quite sick! "How can anyone enjoy eating such an awful rodent!"

"I say, plenty of folk eat hedgehog and grouse," called another mini man, name of Finnegan! "Don't they, Yodeleahee?"

"Gentlemen, let it be known, humans!" Pointing a narrow, elongated finger towards me! "Ye beggar eat pig head, don't ye?" Leprechauns, green goblin and hobgoblin, wearing hobnail boots and snail eaters, sniggered at mention of piggies! "Sid, would ye like roasted lizard or juicy bullfrog?"

"Fairy, jingle thy magical wand and let us fly!"

"There be plenty of froggies, I state, in stream!"

"Sorry, I've already eaten!"

"I shall fetch ye a wee emerald amphibian later!"

"I'll starve before eating reptiles or warty beasts!"

"Please yourself, but I tell ye, frog leg be delicious cooked in garlic and dipped in buttermilk!"

"Tom Foolery, stop gasbagging, collect spawn and fry frog legs, gently!"

"Louie, what did you say?"

"Tommy, talk all the time! Now, sunnyjim, spawn be the magic, X factor ingredient!"

"I thought it was Simon Cowell," whispered thumb, prodding my ears!

"Sire, how long does the fairy dust last?"

"Storyteller, the bewitching fungi be forevermore!"

"What?"

"I'm afraid that be!"

"Are you joking?"

"That I am! Now, friend, write a little fairy-tale, because we enjoy reading!"

"When I'm home, I shall begin, but when will that be?"

"I cannot say but when the dew fall, ye will know by then, ok, pal?"

"For a wee time, ye'd be gobbled smacked but ye'll understand and realise what a funny bunch of urchins we be!"

"Matey, I do feel tipsy!"

"Drink, dance and yodel be my motto," remarked Harry Elves!

"In the meantime, pixilated feeling will wear off and that be me final statement!" As the evening faded, I drifted into slumber land that giant trolls frequent and where buccaneers roam! My word, this elf is an ugly little oaf!

"Writer, I am not!" I was not speaking yet Cutter heard every word I was thinking! He must be telepathic, and now, I know one hundred percent I'm not dreaming! "We take a supply of dust to ward off stranger lurking in this neck of the woods!"

"Paddy O'Tool, them people be vagabonds!"

"Upset us, and ye'll pay dearly," exclaimed Sean O'Marley.

"From a village somewhere in headache!"

"That, mate, be another wee tale, yodeleah!"

"My goodness, friend, I'd love to yodel!"

"Shamrock Dixie, come over here and teach sunshine to yodel like me, ok?"

"I say, Paddy, that would be majestic!"

"Sing along, ok?"

"Pixie, let's yodeleah!"

"Potful of gold coin be over rainbow!"

"Cobbler, Job Hobbit, be right!"

"Gold be at end of bow guarded by Pandora gorgon!" A silent hush fell and the infamous leprechauns, green goblins, hobgoblins, trolls, elves and dwarfs as well as tender fairies wearing a pair of angel wings cowered in fright at the mere mention of her name! This sent shivers down my spine, and my immediate reaction was to go over the intrepid rainbow and slaughter a frightful, "What is a gorgon?"

"A huge serpent covered in green scales and pure evil!"

"Job Lott," cried King Louie. "There be seven wriggling snakes on her vile torso and at top of each shapely form be this man head! Cut one off and another, it be stated in ancient history, grows!"

"My word that is truly unbelievable!"

"Known only to us," said Shamrock, dressed entirely in white silk. "Pandora's box is where her notorious treasure is stored and the way to this evildoer's cave is to locate the tapering end of the magical rainbow where a narrow, rugged, twisting tunnel winds deep into the bowel of mother earth!"

"One Thumb, this tale's frightful!"

"Shoemakers and household cobblers, come. We be off to take her precious jewels," said O'Tool. "This path be ours for the taking and we'll catch her when she's fast asleep which be in the morning sunshine, ok, yodeleah?"

"You are good at yodelling!"

"Magnificent be me interpretation," he replied, somewhat surprised at my lack of knowledge!

"Most of us wee folks in enchanted emerald isles be yodelers," exclaimed Wood Cutter. "Pandora's gold and precious jewels be deep underground, but we be used to living beneath ground on account of wicked searcher looking for us!"

"River Lace, ye old windbag, didn't I tell thee to repair leather britches not gasbag!"

"Wee folk, ye'll not go near the cave where pandora be," commanded King Louie! "She'll gobble up ye lot, do ye understand? Ogress be invincible! Many goblins have attempted to steel her divine treasure, but none have succeeded, because nobody ever returns to tell tale of their encounter with evil she-devil," remarked his royal highness!

"Brave heart, I am aware of your loyalty and bravery, but it would be pointless to seek the fortune in jewels and coinage that be secured in pandora's box, for ye and an army will never return," stated Queen Lizard!

"Money bag," shouted Commander Wellington Boot! "Put out the garbage this instant, and where in the dickens is Tinkerbell?"

"Sir, pixie is working in the living quarter!"

"I see! Is lavatory attendant drinking that dandelion tea again?"

"Nobody be cleaning ablutions, so can I be of service?"

"Lime juice, my dear cordial, our public demand clean toilets, and I say these ablutions be absolutely filthy!"

"Boot, the bogs were cleaned only several years ago," shouted Money Bag, in defence of the entire cleaning establishment and comrades in sanitation department!

"It be like a smelly pigsty," retorted the head of sewerage, inspecting his workplace! "He is a right old pig head at times," said Lady Bird, recently promoted to first cleaner! A position respected in this trade, yodeleah!

"If Buckingham Palace had toilets like these, you'd all be hanging at execution dock by now! Understand me, if them ablutions ain't cleaned within the next eight months, I'll have ye guts for garter, understood?"

"He's a right sod," replied dawn light as daybreak intervened! "We'll teach big-headed buffoon a lesson," remarks dawn, directing her full attention towards her friends, yodeleah! "A lesson boot won't forget! Don't mess with us cleaners!"

"Oh my god, next they'll be staging a wee protest or striking!"

"Old chap, do you think?"

"Light has been flickering all morning!"

"That be really dastardly," exclaimed O'Marley who meantime, arrived from headache! "That be, says I, Pixie Lott!"

"Be another amusing tale," interrupted cutter!

Evening arrived, and I still felt slightly pixilated!

"Would ye like rainbow pizza and wildflowers?"

"Our Lott be sharp as knife with her tongue and long hobnail footwear to boot but not a chef!"

"Sweet pixie, I will be mowzeeing along on my own merry way!"

"Job Cobbler, I have been having dreams of the small folk and a wonderful island since 1984!"

"Sid, how fortunate you are to be lucky enough to see us, don't ye truly think?"

"I guess I am!"

"You see, buddy, wee folk be reality!"

"Thanks, Job Hobbit!"

"Darn, elfin, call me odd job on account of me being elder shoemaker!"

"How many years are you?"

"I'm a hundred! In maybe six years' time or thereabouts!"

"Whom are 'elfin'?"

"Why they be youngest elves," snorted a lively green goblin singing yodeleah, yodeleaheedee!

"There be bluebirds over the white cliffs of dover," sang a fairy!

"Cupcake and sister, Strawberry, are always singing," remarked shamrock!

"Lillies be spread out like a huge designed carpet and mushroom fairy ring!"

"Later be where we'll drink and dance!"

"Sounds fabulous!"

"Imps as well as gremlins will be there!"

"Long blades of thick green grass feel rough to my touch, and the fragrance of flowers are over powering!"

"Chaps, let us yodel, ok?"

"Playmates, who'd believe I am sitting here in Ireland with a group of infamous wee leprechauns, yodelling!"

"Teller of tales, have you visited our kinfolk in Lilliput?"

"O'Tool, in the back of one's mind, there's the faintest, I say, recognition that I may have!"

"Layton Gulliver, I recall, is a gigantic human who saved our brethren long ago in the town of Bottleneck from an enemy who travelled far across ocean, so it be written down in our archives!"

"I remember there was a film produced with Joe Black as Gulliver!

"Hey Sid, bless my cotton socks," exclaimed an elderly sprite! "That be me old pal's name, yodeleah, yodeleah, yodeleah!"

"There be many tales of mysterious leprechauns with evil intent but this ain't true and they give us devil some problems as seekers come a looking for the truth, which we supply, but nasty searcher come for wicked intent! To catch us and steal our jewels and to rid the world of us poor urchins! Now, tell the true story of our simple lives and maybe some of us will visit ye, be ok?"

"Quite, whenever, ok?" The evening drew close, and in the distance, a yodelling party began suddenly; these wee folk sprang to life!

"Come, let us drink, dance and yodel!" I walked into meadow lane, finally, reached an orange tree where partygoers were riding on mighty field mice, or so I believed, but no, this was the dormouse derby!

"Come on, writer, it be time ye rode in our rodeo," remarked Paddy!

"I'd love to," I replied very sheepishly, for the giant monster seemed very ferocious!

"They be gentle as a lamb?"

"I hope you're right!" I'm afraid now; I was in a close compound with a barrier keeping this untamed beast tightly secured but when this bar is raised, all hell shall be unleashed! I knew instinctively this was an experience I'd never forget! "So be it," I cried as the heavy reins were placed into my hand! The next instant, thunderous snoring and threatening use of a few choice words awoke me, and I'm back home!

"Diminutive gnome, I'll dirk ye and slit thy gut from ear to ear!"

"Wake up, Longjohn, you're dreaming!"

"Storyteller, William Bones, better known as billy, sailed the mighty oceans with the Caribbean pirates!"

"Aboard the jolly roger!"

"And the Magnacious Hispaniola captained by yours truly, bound for an enchanted Skeleton Isle!"

"I say, that's another fabled saga!"

"I knew that," replied Silverhead! "Infamous leprechauns, funny bones and his shipmates, elbow grease and taut wrench unloaded cargo when the hispaniola docked in the lagoon!"

"Back bones be youngest kinfolk," said old john. Suddenly, I'm marching into a field and through new blades of slender green grass where bluebells grace the meadow; finally, we arrived at the famous toad hall where the ever-popular toad welcomed us!

"Sidney, nice to meet you!" cried squire Trelawney!

"I remember you in Treasure Island!"

"There I was!"

"This is great," I replied but not before sitting upon a comfortable seat! As we rested, heavy rain beat against window panes! The next moment, I awoke to a warm reception! An angelic choir of house martins tapping against the bedroom window, singing merrily, and I was finally back home in bed! All six-foot one-and-five-eighth inch! God, my bones felt heavy and one's slender fingers were, I'd say, tender, and dark shades of long green grass were between each toe! Friends, until this very day, I haven't returned and still yearn to wander through the Cooley and ride in the old notorious dormouse derby, and I say, Jimmy Cricket, there's more!

1984

"Hello, I'm Wendy Winks!"

"Sweet talking imp, you're extremely beautiful!"

"Friend, I am a pink-eyed pixie!"

"My lady, I'm awfully sorry!"

"Human, did you know you're a changeling and have power to alter appearance like the chameleon?"

"Have I?"

"Comrade, look in the mirror!"

"Great Scott, I am a troll!"

"Writer, you're a sprite!"

"Fairy, that's fantastic!"

"Tell me, did this saga begin at Macdonald's farm?"

"Yes!"

"This universe is where small animals, mammals, human beings and vegetable folk dwell!"

"I say, Winks, I've visited this galaxy before!"

"Have you? When?"

"Back in 1984, I dreamt the sun rays beat down and I became imbued! Overhead, a quartet of splendid guillemots and a sea breeze sang softly, then I woke!"

"That's magic!"

"Outside, a snowstorm erupted, then rain fell! Inside our ornate hallway, a rainbow became manifest and pirates emerged!"

"That's monster!"

"Later, I drifted into unconsciousness, then I was headed towards a mythical island surrounded chiefly by red coral where many inhabitants voiced delight!"

"Author, that's quite feasible!"

"Citizen, this fairy-tale is based upon encounters with local merrymakers and stored in my mind is knowledge implanted by residents without whose support this story wouldn't have been composed!" The sound of a parrot disturbed my sleep! I awaken as rays of untamed sunlight radiated into our bedroom! A time elapsed before I told my wife about Wendy and the notorious island located in mysterious water of celestial earth! "I say, living there is a mighty dormouse with a long snout and bushy tail named Doctor Watson! Badgers, Sherlock and Thomas Holmes, also, a pig-headed captain!"

"I be stubborn?" remarked a rogue with an artificial hand and leg!

"Longjohn, I never said you!"

"Ye implied!"

"Hook, change the subject?"

"Ok, novelist!"

An hour passed, then Lorraine said, "My goodness, all that from a single dream?"

"Yes," I replied, and she remarked, "No wonder you're always tired!"

In 1992, I let this literature work lapse, then after a lengthy discussion, I resumed writing! I've experienced jovial encounters with dwarves and buccaneers, dug up bullion, travelled on voyages, met a bunch of vicious, bloodcurdling renegades! "Sidney, ye rode upon a subsonic plane and sailed across an ocean of tranquillity," interrupted Wendy! "You voyaged to sacrifice! Better known as old treasure island where fractured skeleton bone and bloody, rotting flesh, I dare declare, lay!"

"Gasbag, dung chafer, keep nose out!"

"Barbecue, leave him!"

"Sunny, welcome to headache!"

"Thank you!" I turned away from our desk and sprawled across one's bed lay Winks!

"Let us pray this loony bin stuff kickstarts one's imagination!" I then said, "What borough is this?"

And a small long-eared mammal whispered, "We're on Uncle Tom's farmland at Flaghead, and I'm digger rabbit burrow!"

"And I am underground technician Botaney, his brother!"

"Friends, why are we talking quietly?"

"Because farmer Tim Giles has rifles and don't like cabbage crunchers!"

"Rabbit, how do I begin this fantasy?"

"Thy magic is happening as we speak!"

"Shipmate, did you see a small green alien disembark a space craft and pink elephants dancing amongst wild daffodil down in sweet meadow lane?"

"I did not."

"Neither did I; now listen to these flesh-eating polecats!"

"Cap'n Morgan!"

"Iggy Biggles, what is it?"

"Our informant said gung-ho, catweasel and them long black-tipped tail stoats, cherry, plum, and red tomato have been arrested by bow-street, runner beans, and are due to attend court this very morning!"

"Magic Eye, look into thy enchanted horoscope, pal, and tell me, whose the bigwig?"

"Cap'n, I've a vague idea!"

"Richard Dunne, me darling," interrupted Victor McLaglen!

"Who be the beak?"

"Data bank identified a judgemental turkey hen, Madame Falcon!"

"Not the gobbledegook turkey buzzard?"

"Quite and guinea fowl don't take prisoners!"

"And predatory hawk won't tolerate turkeycock," voiced Vestal Vulture!

"Dunne, keep me posted!"

"Batty Cricket, Jump Locust, what's next?"

"Fable teller, we don't know!"

"Narrator, use the home telephone and ask for me Bunny! Talk to that fetid skunk Mister Pickles, Booby Trap and Danger Mouse; all reside in cloud-cuckoo-land!"

"Bugsy, I will."

"Sparrow Hawk, Wrinkled Imp, 'ave ye seen my peacocks?"

"Nope!"

"Jiggery-pokery, a news flash," cried Botaney!

"Jumping jeepers, jackrabbits are butchering mammals!"

"Governor."

"What, Cabbage Muncher?"

"They be kin!"

"Flat-footed fleabags are murderers!"

"Killer Hares be cannibals," replied Fredrick Ferret!

"Writer, there's plenty of blood and guts in booklet!"

"Bunny, is that Brooker?"

"Sufferin' succotash, Batty, it's the ghost buster!"

"I say, Furry, he's phantom driver and ticket salesman!"

"Sparrow, I state Tony pilots, an airborne craft, hover train, a super jet, limousine, super-duper Swan Vesta tram, smart car and peddle cart."

"Plant-eater, that's monster," remarked the hawk!

"As a child monumental earth shifter, my parents told me stories of audacious swashbuckling escapades!"

"Pardon me, Monseigneur."

"What, monsieur Locust?"

"This historic classic began in earnest with an army of elves and greenhead goblins."

"Yes, pal, and their magnificent leader awarded me an insight into a culture I've only read about in books!"

"Hello, playmates, I'm Mick Chitty!"

"Michael, I like your grey beard!"

"Who is knocking at the door?"

"Teller, has anyone seen my wee peacock?"

"Ask William Flasher at stroke club!"

"Before it crows, I'll introduce oneself, Cap'n Longjohn Silverhead! Ye may call me Barbe on account, I roast enemy! Hook or Peg, an amputated hand and leg! Hook be handy but when I forget, nearly hooked me eye out!"

"Pegleg, I be speaking!"

"Chitty, leave it!"

"Pooka, shut it or I is jerk a dirk in ya belly boyo!"

"Bucko, ya words be fighting lingo!"

"Hobbledehoy schizophrenic!"

"Peg, I'm a leprechaun!"

"Oaf, ye be sailing close to the wind!"

"Novelist, I'm Dawn Ormerod."

"Hallelujah, an attractive Musquash!"

"Red Elf invited you to tell noteworthy adventures!"

"This is the goofiest tale!"

"Our story consists of a time-machine, buccaneer treasure, enveloping into a body of a savage thief!"

"Ye rode upon great dolphin and voyaged to sacrifice isle!"

"And witnessed murder, most foul," remarked pirate Jack Straw!

"Unimaginable, but I did!"

"Shiver me rotten timber, Wood Louse, I see another carrot cruncher!"

"Quartermaster Warren Burrow at your service!"

"Ahoy!"

"Who be ye?"

"Blow me, it's Troy Tungsten and Take Potluck!"

"Writer, what is wrong?"

"Troy, when I type, words keep disappearing."

"That's most bizarre!"

"I'd say it's extremely annoying."

"Bewildering."

"Shocking."

"Disruptive!"

As darkness gathered, I drew my thoughts! "Tungsten, this is serious!"

"Sunshine, keep your shirt on; don't you know who is responsible?"

"Of course not!"

"Grape Juice, tell us," cried Longjohn!

"Give me time to get my head, oh yes, let me begin this chapter and verse! One may say those tampering with the typing are three loathsome, devious little critters who would stoop to any level, like jesters!"

"Godhead, give me strength!"

"Who has been erasing typing?"

"It could be matured muskrat Musci Moss from tiny hamlet of sweet cow-dung and his devout, pint-sized followers, beady-eyed rogues, bog roll and peat bag!"

"Cut their heads off," cried Shawn Winks!

"I'd like to teach these jokers a lesson!"

"Perish the thought," said Musci!

"Peat, storyteller's a sourpuss!"

"Roll, I totally agree!"

"Moss, towering tyrant called us eccentric misfit?

"Bog, I got ears!"

Obvious, aquatic rodents are adorned with a scaly tail and webbed feet and wacke lugs unlike us mice! "Governor, is there any beef, cheese or pickle you'd like us to dispose of?

"Sorry, Musci, we haven't!"

"Sid."

"What, Peg?"

"I say, everyone has a book in them."

"Quite true! Each tale a silver lining!"

"Belay, there!"

"Author, it's the sea dog, poison, toxic, Philip Taylor!"

"Would ye bigoted ogres say, be rooted inside me, an angelic spirit?"

"Guardian, what about an Easter Bunny?"

"Underdog, forget tooth-fairies; writer, I could murder a pint!"

"Peat, vamoose, heathen, toxicologist has committed an unlawful killing!"

"Bog, skedaddle."

"Ok, bag!"

"Musci, paint him black," cried Clint Eastwood.

"That's all, folks! Bugs, it's over! I think muskrat has jumped thou gun!"

"Musk-rose!"

"Hey, that's me?"

"Ye feeling lucky?"

"Nope!"

"Moss, ye dirty, pig squealing punk, make my day!"

"Boss, look on the next page."

"It is full of juvenile script like the introduction," called Peat!

"That is true," roared Silverhead!

"Domesticated birds tasted fowl," exclaimed Hans Fondle, a tall Norwegian whippersnapper, ready and exceptionally keen to register penny worth in this fable!

"Holy Moses, unblock sewerage pipes."

"Pesky polecat, I will endeavour!"

"Rat, watch out."

"What for?"

"Plumbers freed this obstruction!"

"Rat bag, the waste matter has been flushed!

"Bag is imbued!"

"Meanwhile, mongoose, Jamaican black and plant ginger breezed into town!"

"My fowls are lost."

"Female, taste lovely and peacock!"

"Chitty, don't rub him up the wrong way!"

"Bunny batten down hatch."

"Right, rabbit!"

"What time is it?"

"Eight bells!"

"Botney, fix up our shelters before that wicked mongoose arrives!"

"Dawn Ormerod, your request is our command!"

"Prepare to gudgeon, hostile invaders," advised rabbit!

"Polly, put the kettle on!"

"Sugar lumps, juicy teacake is creating a mouth-watering flavour," said teabags, licking his tender lips full of cultivated, brownish leaves!

"Rabbit burrow, would you like a cuppa tea?"

"Teasel head, minister of plant and leaf manufacture, no, ta!"

"There's far too many characters in this saga," said Ann Puzey!

"Frankly, precious princess, I don't give a damn!"

"Storyteller, are those dustmen, Char Cole and Brian Bolder delivering coke?"

"No, why?"

"Because it's cold!"

"In that case, rodents get out of my old freezer!"

"Everhard, shut that door," cried Grumpy Beaver!

"Ye heard him, put bung in hole," hollered teasel bag! In the bar, tony, ships, carpenter made a bolt for an exit as press-gang bosun kingfisher blue entered!

"Absent without leave, Anthony, from the Hispaniola?"

"Nope!"

"Detachment, arrest guttersnipe!"

"One-Hung-Low, close the windows before that infested racoon, Big Alan, arrives and fills airway with over-ripened odour!"

"Alleycats, shut them vents," as two muppets zoomed in!

"Tarby, this home is full of old fruitcakes."

"Davison, I quite rightly remember you saying you lodged here, once!"

"Tarbuck, that was Kermit, my brother!"

"Hello, screwballs, I've been on a wild -goose chase, anyone seen a peahen?"

"Nope," came the reply!

"If ye like plenty of codswallop, you'll love this fable; it's full of it!"

"Chitty, you are clever!"

"Us leprechaun be quick of mind!"

"Mick, has there ever been evidence to support that claim, and are miniature mortals true fact?"

"Simple logic tells me we sure do exist!"

"Ok!"

"My gracious colleagues be of many creed and range from thy cheerful illustrious gnomes to them great Irish thingamabobs, little notorious spritely people with a grey beard!"

"Michael, me darling," enquired an amused Victor Mclaglen, "be ye describing ya self?"

"Loafer, be a quiet man!"

"You've a tongue like the common viper and who bedevil be ye?"

"Heavyweight boxing champion of leprechauns, including ye!"

"Oh dear, I've just put my foot in raw sewerage again, haven't I?"

"I'm off," cried Warren.

"Where?" said Rabbit!

"I'm visiting Sire Graham Hobbs, he's having a hip-hop hobbit bash!"

"Hey, Harvey Burrow, is there many carrots?"

"No but bed mites be having a ball."

"Where?"

"In our double bunk!"

"Errol Flynn, why be devil be ye here?"

"Mikey, what do ye call an Irish elf with half a brain?"

"Flynn, pray tell me!"

"Michael Chitty!"

"Ha-ha, that's good!"

"Inland revenue be taxing brains, Mick, you're due a rebate!'"

"Flynn, is the income from taxman?"

"I'm joking."

"That's hilarious," remarked Toxic!

"Furry tail, fetch me crutch!"

"Silverhead, my name is builder burrow!"

"Boss, tell Sid about Mary Celeste!"

"Bog, fresh droppings on floor!"

"How disgusting!"

"Governor, it's much cleaner than our gaff," stated roll!

"Musci, we'd better leave."

"Restauranteur, don't look pleased!"

"Peat, we're not forsaking ship when the going gets tough!"

"He won't, get rid, of us; we're his bread and butter!"

"Won't I?"

"Into the hideaway, lads!"

"Pesky, blooming vermin, be here," shouted Peg!

"Bigot don't you realise, man, we are the rich cream on your fruit cake! Without us critters, what's this story got? Answer, a bunch of bananas!"

"Actually, there are quite a number of citizens yet to be mentioned, such as Eddie Kilkenny, and I won't be forgetting that fine Bucco, Johnny Mad-dog Jagger, without whose help this saga would not be completed!"

"If I see your wild fowl I'll eat it, understand?"

"Ok, humorous Tudor Fox!"

"Bog, remember when we were binge drinking and Peat fell off the toilet seat into that bowl which was chock-a-block and there was Christmas spirit, twenty-four-seven?"

"Boss, I'm thinking!"

"Don't over exert ya brain!"

"Teller wants a verbal!"

"I say, chaps, you are a talkative trio, full of joy!"

"Anyone tells me, mischievous elves, enormous trolls, angry, giant ogres don't exist, I'll tell them they surely do!"

"This book be just what I need," cried Poison!

"We may be real or not, who knows except yours truly; now, 'ave a good day," bellowed Peg!

"Or I'll hang ye, from nearest yard-arm," yelled Taylor!
"This fable is real hogwash," shouted Dartist!

"Pal, you're an insane bumpkin!"

"In which case, you're the lunatic!"

"You're short of a ducat!"

"Pegleg, I'm sane!"

"A bonehead!"

"Bona fide," replied Phil!

"And I have this letter, which proves it!"

"Imbecile, be quiet or I'll stick crutch where sun don't shine, know what I mean?"

"I say, dipstick, don't know much because, Peg, you've nowt under ruddy bonnet!"

"Swabber," roared Silverhead! "I understand pal, now, don't take it personal, but if ya reading this loada twaddle, ya either on wacky baccy or sprinkling magic mushroom dust on ya grub!"

"Silverhead, ye makes me laugh!"

"Chirpy cricket, louse have infested our bedding!"

"Terminate," growled Zapdem Dalek!

One moment, I was sitting in the lounge, the next, I'm standing in the hallway; outside, a snowstorm; suddenly, the weather changed and what happened next was spooky, because this cock-and-bull testament, may be without foundation but loud voices registered!

Firstly, close by our cloakroom, a ghostly shadow gradually became manifest! Like a kindergarten tale, this huge rainbow materialised simultaneously, a tunnel and ill-tempered pirates emerged, then darkness engulfed! A voice hollered, "Destination," thus returning me back to reality!

"Utopia," shouted, an elfish critter!

"Excuse me, are you a manikin?"

"Yes, I am!"

"Where am I?"

"On this airbus travelling main highway to Fantazia; now, enjoy the journey!"

"Are there any girls?"

"Nope."

"Why?"

"Why not? Just creatures with scrumptious wizardry!"

"Who are you?"

"I'm Anthony Brooker; soon, you'll be meeting an elite brigade of unstoppable pranksters!"

"Tony, for Pete's sake!"

"Matey, let me tell you, small dwarfs are a finicky race of time bandits, notorious mischief-makers."

"No way!"

"They be time-travellers."

"That's illogical; who would believe this?"

"Folk who never saw gnomes and greenhead goblins sitting astride mushrooms! Fluorescent imps, creating glowing visibility in darkness and fairies waving magic wands!"

"Am I dreaming?"

"Of course, you are; now, let me continue! Hobbits, mischievous, leprechauns, sparkling sprites and troll!"

"This is fascinating!" This morning kicked off with a tumultuous snowstorm, completely covering rooftops, roads and alleyways, like magic fairy-tales often began! Darkness arrived, and wearisome tiredness graced my aching bones! Outside, a storm, then ghastly buccaneers, reeking of stale tobacco, and I'm aboard an airbus; next, I am strolling across a rocky mountain range when an enchanted island became visible, then, out of nowhere, these talking animals! Later, a red elf said I'd been chosen to be their storyteller and suddenly presented me with a pen-feather and tiny inkwell supplied by a pot-bellied wizard named Ian Doe! Next, I showed Lorraine a quill-feather and ceramic pot containing black fluid!

Morning duly arrived and whilst the grumpiest storm snored, I attempted to draw some frumpy chaps and kick-start this plot, which is from that never -ending fable but failed! Again, with my feather pen fixed firmly between three fingers, I place the tail feather into an ink pot; hopefully, on this occasion, one's English grammar improves, and I finish a page!

"Use a dictionary," remarked Brooker! "It lists fact and fictional material, ranging from cyclopaedia to Satan!"

"Reader, keep an open mind and maybe this novel will be your cuppa tea; now, comrade, what should I write?"

"Never underestimate one's own natural ability," stated Tony! "You simply lost the thread; it is all inside your head, and for spiritual guidance, dial Anthony!"

Now, I'm fully committed to writing, this fable like my friendly colleague, Sean O'Marley! A flamboyant leprechaun and admirable spinner of yarn would, with a flip-flop flapdoodle and pop, invariably say, "Modest writer, use flare, bold imagination; that'll be my final word. I should know, keep ya peeker up and be upfront, tell 'em fairy-tales!" He'd laugh wicked, then vanish! This pure, fact-finding tale of one's vivid imagination consists of a dragon, dwarfs, buried loot, a witch riding upon a common broomstick, and I've spent the best part of three decades visiting mind -boggling haunts! "Once again, ye fable, unravel!"

"Longjohn, never mind, now tell me, do one's readers want to read more?"

A Monster Within

Back in around June, July or maybe August, 1986, I was in Poole Park, Dorset, England with my two young children, Sidney, aged ten, and Matthew, aged seven, and a couple of their mates, knocking a football around! All of a sudden, one's eldest child kicked the large football into the lake where the water was covered in green plankton or spawn! Seeing this ball was near the edge, I attempted to retrieve it; suddenly I over-reached and in the next instant, plunged headfirst into the water and was completely submerged, and liquid entered each nostril! The salt water, at this precise moment, I believe, was full of fish algae and a variety of small crustaceans and of course, tiny eggs; well, they just laughed, and I chased them to our car!

The years rolled over, then I began to have what I would term a summer hay fever and was constantly blowing one's nose! Eventually, one morning, I decided it was time to squeeze brown vinegar up both nostrils to see if I could cure the problem, then, a slimy, dead thing composing of, I'd say, a clear mucus, jelly format, or type of embryo, with a distinctive red eyeball popped out! I reckon the vinegar killed off this clear unknown creature, what I call a monster within me! Thinking it was my hellish imagination, I blew the other nostril, and out popped an inch-long inhabitant, but the problem didn't end there! For weeks, it felt like an abnormal pressure or bandage was being pulled tight across my forehead! I still feel as though I've got a bad head cold, but lucky for me, I'm glad to say it hasn't happened since! I know, this weird story is unbelievable, but it's true! We visit the park and my memories of that particular afternoon linger, and one's wildest imagination can be extremely creative! I wonder, has anyone ever experienced a monster within?

Ghost of Tudor Fox

Every morning, at around six, I awake to the distinct sound of the ghost of Tudor Fox! It's as plain as that! The fact is, I know our friend has finally grown into a mature, adult fox who parades slowly up and down our splendid bedroom each day, waiting patiently for his daily walk and tasting, once again, his favourite food! That he has travelled over the majestic milky way and across the great sea of tranquillity from the angelic kingdom of heaven, through the notorious golden gates, to share himself with us! In a nutshell, that's the truth, although one cannot imagine this immense beast which now, I suggest, stands taller than an Alsatian being a fox!

Out we'd go to our car, and Tudor would spring up onto the rear seat and sit upright, like a majestic animal I'd prayed to be reunited with and my prayer was answered! The day would always begin with this ritual! I'd clamber into our car and in a couple of ticks, drive along Recreation Road or over the hill to Boscombe or Southampton common, anywhere, so long as my wife, Lorraine and of course, our lovely Tudor, wished! However, there were times our lovely fox would scratch himself until we were all tickling from head to foot! I would laugh aloud and throw a ball whilst Tudor scampered to and fro!

We went down to the beach where we would sit whilst Tudor played in the ocean, then refuse bluntly to come out! Eventually, we'd just stroll away, and he'd catch us, and that was part and parcel of his enchanting company! Daily, at twelve noon, Tudor would leave to go back to his beloved mother, brothers and sisters who passed away and now reside in middle earth! Pal, who in their right mind would believe this?

As I have no substantial evidence whatsoever to support this tale, but there is always the illogical approach, it may be true! I know, throughout this land there are many people who won't believe and are bound to think I'm a fruitcake but there are those who have experienced the paranormal! Animals that have passed away, yet family members have suggested their pet kept them awake or visited them throughout the night! Maybe a next-door neighbour said, "Your dog kept us awake all night with its constant barking!" When, in fact, the mammal passed away two days prior; now, am I barking mad?

Since Tudor passed away, old mother time has drifted by, and days turned into weeks, then months, and so on until the years mounted and Tudor decided it was time we got another animal, and since then, we've had, cats, dogs, and again, they'd pass away which, again, broke our heart but that's life! By the way, lest I forget! The evening after I brought Tudor Fox home, I returned to the cave where his mother and other puppies were! Heavy rain began to fall as I walked, carrying first his mum, as though our lord was shedding a bucket load of tears for these dearly departed!

Once again, I return to 1984, where I dreamt about this small island in celestial earth and Chew, the fox, as well as Tudor, then I'm overcome with emotion and break down in tears as one types this extremely emotional story! Occasionally, my memories of that dreadful night return, and without warning, the weather changes drastically, as I remember vividly, as the mighty storm arose and thunder snaps, crackles and pops simultaneously, a sudden flash of fork lightning, and for a moment, I am a ghostly form!

We eventually bedded down and for several hours, stayed in the cellar with only an old convector heater to keep us all warm! Outside, trees uprooted and vans, along a motorway, overturned and tiles from the roofs of houses were literally tossed a few hundred feet into the fiery air!

For some reason, our Tudor wouldn't eat, and inside, I knew something was drastically wrong! One moment, he appeared normal; next, Tudor simply drifted away into an eternal sleep! As you already know, we've had cats and dogs: Sandy, Candy and Angel, who have all travelled across to god's kingdom! Sandy was the ball girl! She'd climb a six-foot wall and retrieve a ball I'd placed, much earlier! One time, Sandy had three balls, in her mouth, which, at the time, I thought was remarkable! Now, our Candy was a runner and could she jump! We'd travel down to the beach with all our dogs, especially Angel, a Yorkshire terrier! I seldom speak about her as she was the latest to leave us, and memories, even after three years, break my heart!

Our cats were Bitsy, Pepsy, Cookie and Misty; now, we have a slender female, chiefly covered, in black with a white blaze, named Coco and a male named Sootie! The main feature of this cat is his splendid face which resembles a black mask! He's a loner but does sleep on our bed, whereas Coco likes to wander through the house and generally creates noise running up and down the stairs, which is disturbing but that's her and we love them dearly! I even think I'd be in the doghouse if I suggested caging her at night! Sootie would get off our bed and chase Coco before returning to bed! Well, that's the end! "Not quite," said, Longjohn, interrupting and my typing!

Invitation to Graceland Manor

"Sid, I believe atmospheric disturbance activates one's wildest imagination and is the key to mankind unlocking nature's dark secrets, such as the enchanting golden gates in heaven, where angels orchestrate our lives and dwarfish critters, red elves, fairies and all manner of entertaining rodents roam! Where an ogre lives in a castle and Jack climbed this beanstalk and talking mammals reside! Also, wild currents open the entrance to hellfire where Lucifer, the satanic devil, lives with some frightening beasts, ready to unleash them upon, an unsuspecting world and mischievous leprechauns are the keepers of Pandora's box! A process, once activated, generates unmanageable problems!"

"Silverhead, you're very intellectual!"

"Writer, that, I be!"

"I say," stated Harry Elves, "Gorgon is keeper of Pandora's box!"

"Ivan imp, I know what you're thinking," cried a fairy!

"What is that?"

"Not very much!"

"Our lord protector established a suitable deity as guardian of the box!"

"Yes, us fairies!"

"From this well-known container, the ills of mankind were first released!"

"After Adam met Eve and ate from the forbidden fruit!"

"So states Greek mythology!"

"God, a rabbit!"

"My word, where did she come from?"

"Thy insane imagination!"

"A while back, I had this dream!"

"Yes, in, 1984!"

"One's world was turned upside down, and life changed forever!"

"Who would believe it?"

"I hazard a guess," exclaimed rabbit!

"Warren, I'd like to retype this paragraph!"

"Why?" stated, builder!

"I'm getting rather confused, with all the various names!"

"Ok, mate!"

"Peat, Bog, unload the bags of grub for our governor!"

"And Bog, stop picking thy nose!"

"Righto, boss!"

"Munch Mellow, where's red, green, yellow and cherry pepper?"

"I do not know!"

"Moss, they're on sewerage duty!" said holy mosses!

"Basically, I love manure."

"Invitation to Graceland manor," said dung beetle!

"Fetid, flesh-eating, noxious rodent, like being the centre of attention," says inquisitive flea bag!"

"Flea, quiet down," commanded Onehunglow!

"Lame Duck, like the limelight!"

"Flea beetle, there is a vocalist with a voice of an angel!" "Lovely songstress reminds me of Shamrock singing 'The Wonder of You'."

"I say, isn't it Annie Oakley?"

"Fleabag," exclaimed sparky graham wheeler! "It's my song!"

"Swankpot, never," cried nocturnal cockroach angrily! "After this book is published, the men in black will put me in a loony bin!"

"Ain't we already?" spouts crockery pot!

"No, we are not; now, where is tea cosy?" roared kettle, curiously!

"At bedbugs ball!"

"Lollipop lady, I scream at the thought of storyteller being incarcerated in an asylum for the mentally ill!"

"Roll, over in that drawer is a handkerchief; fetch it. I'm about to cry," remarked musci!

"Moss, I'll do that!"

"Phantom of the Opera is on television!"

"Tell him to get off," stated colour vision! "And continue this fairy-tale!"

"Carrot cruncher," shouted moses, "I'm a guest in this sanctimonious nut-house but if I don't look out, they'll think I'm crazy?"

"Ain't you already?" whispered an enchanting ant, name of hill!

"That is most insulting! Give me a few details for future reference!"

"Ok, lover boy!"

"Lady ant, what's thy name?"

"I'm Miss Hill!"

"Insect folk in this lousy looney bin have a number of bolts missing!"

"Mad-dog Jagger is here!"

"Never!"

"Matter of fact, and screwballs are a bunch of wackoes!"

"Including you," exclaimed Bog!

"Roll over the road is a madhouse with nutcases," remarked tiny tics!

"Refuge is for the criminally insane!"

"Peat, isn't this holiday camp Butlins?"

"Asylum's chock-a-block with lunatics!" "Bag full of nuts?"

Graceland Manor

"That's mental!"

"Mice please!"

When I'm typing, dreams drift into one's brain, and didgeridoo, I float lazily into a prior encounter! I remember this day, being invited to play a tennis match by a stranger who lives in a huge house with a rear garden, hardcourts and a pathway leading onto a secluded dockyard! "Writer, isn't that the smugglers' joint?"

"Bog, keep quiet!" I saw something fall from this gentleman's black cloak and said, "Excuse me, squire, you've dropped an old white, five-pound note!"

"Bless you," replied this well-dressed citizen!

To which I stated, "Haven't seen one in decades!"

"We are having a game of tennis on Thursday; would you like to come along?"

"Haven't played in years!"

"You'll be just fine! Pop down to Graceland Manor! The wife and I will expect you at twelve!"

"Graceland will Elvis Presley be there?"

"Maybe not but boxers Mike Cottingham, Roger Rider, Malcolm Tottle and of course, Elvis vocalist, Colin Earley, will be!"

"That's epic!"

"See you soon, ok?"

"Most certainly!" I turned away as my wife arrived with a mug of coffee! "Lunch be long?"

"Pardon?"

"Lorraine, my dear, I must be daydreaming! I'm popping out!"

"You go, and I'll go shopping with Adele."

"Ok, my dear, but don't buy the entire shop!" Unexpectedly, light, melodic music waltzed into my mind like a beautiful Latin gypsy, gracefully serenading one's immortal soul!

Of course, I arrived, almost on the hour of noon, and entered a fragrant rose garden where I saw flamboyant guests in little groups, chattering merrily, like, an overactive fledgling, twittering excitedly. I strolled into a conservatory! Noticed this assortment of colourful flowers, embedded in peat, hung in pleasant, wrought-iron baskets, with enchanting panes of frosted glass covering a low, flat roof; suddenly, god raised an eyelid and unleashed an awesome wrath! Rain fell and lightning flashed; thunder cracked like a circus ringmaster snapping a taut leather whip! Where is that fellow I met last week? A few seconds lapsed, then I became aware of a small group of ladies, dressed in suitable tennis attire, whom I had not seen arrive! Their presence appeared somewhat artificial!

I stood there for many moments, just admiring their clothes, before deciding to visit the bathroom! I entered this stately mansion. It appeared antique in design! I'd state, interesting! Majestic paintings from a bygone Elizabethan period and a most notorious collection of water colours portraying great battles! Scenes of famous conquests, portraits from an ancestral time! An unblemished era and umpteen unusual items, appearing slightly tarnished! Actually, I reckon this home dated back to the late seventeenth, possibly eighteenth century! I looked for a maid to guide me to a washroom but this magnificent house appeared empty! I went up a flight of stairs, finally located a toilet! The room was very dim lit, with fashionable gas mantles, for an era befitting past times! Elegant wooden windows were completely covered by dusty-grey silk thread and appeared quite sinister!

A draining -board, with a grooved surface, beside a sink on which washed clothes rested! I stood there, absolutely gobsmacked and unexpectedly, I'm standing in front of a massive fire place with huge logs casting flames forth! Leaping like fish in a pond but producing no heat! "That's truly weird!" I turned, but to my utter surprise, this lounge was totally empty! Faint whispers crept slowly into my equilibrium, then a crispy crackling sound returned my attention towards the fire casting a blue-tinted flame! A creepy-crawly and little dark patches of dried blood stained a thick pile carpet! Black velvet curtains, which, had seen better days, hung loosely upon old floor tiles and statues resembling Bantu warriors stood guarding windows with timber frames! Sounds like somebody crying somewhere far in the distance, then gentle laughter! Now, I am listening for a word or two, but still, I can't understand what's being said! Is someone attempting to make contact or is this the wind in the willows, where Toadhall is situated and where badger, mole and ratty reside? Down by a river-bank!

"Don't forget tubby rabbit!" I looked up and resting his head upon my paperwork is a big thumper named Boris Burrow!

"Well, bless my soul, I haven't seen you since nineteen eighty-four!"

"Entrepreneur, why didn't ye include me in the first book?"

"I only met you for a wee time!"

"I lapsed into a coma and time passed by!"

"Well, pal, that is terrible!"

"Doctor Donald Watson said it was myxomatosis, a fatal viral disease causing swelling of the mucous membrane! I'm lucky to be alive! This disease was invented for biological warfare and to eradicate plant-eaters!" Instantly, my molecular structure altered and I was systematically transported into the master's drawing-room! Dribs and drabs lay scattered on an oak table with a drop-leaf and an enchanting engraving of the old Tudor rose inlaid! Glauber's salts! A crystalline hydrated form of sodium sulphate used as a form of laxative, dating back to 1668, was placed neatly on a marble mantelpiece and a Napoleonic painting, characteristic of Napoleon or his time, hung above!

"Hello, Sunny, whatcha doing?" I turned.

"Creeping Jesus, O'Marley, you just startled me!"

"I did, did I?"

"Crikey! I'm home, what happened?"

"What?"

"A few seconds ago, I was at Graceland Manor, the next moment, I'm back here!"

"Most likely, it was self-delusion!"

"Why?"

"Because this leprechaun has been here whilst ye was asleep!"

"Storyteller, did ye know I'm an elder with an appetite for tommyrot!"

"Have you?"

"Yes, so I have come from headache to stay with my chum!"

"Who?"

"Ye!"

"Me?"

"Daft oaf, you're our illustrious creator!

"Pardon?"

"I've crossed over from your first book to create havoc!"

"Add spice?"

"Ye never know, there may be other lesser mortals ready to take a leap!"

"Travel across?"

"We've heard ye finished our saga and about time!"

"God, O'Marley, you stink of manure!"

"Fell in a bucket of horse dung!"

"Goodness, dwarfish fellow!"

"I am, am I?"

"Yes!"

"Do ye know a good honest solicitor?"

"Yes, Keith O'Neal, why?"

"So I can sue you for definition of my diminutive size, and I say, have you seen Ivan Imp or tigress, Tiger Lily?"

"No!"

"Peekaboo, Ivan's my name, tigger taming is me game!"

"What brings you to our home?"

"Bewitching, bugaboo tiger and hobnail boots be requiring repair!"

"I'm no cobbler!"

"Leather Strap misinformed me!"

"Mark these foul words, I shall have his guts for garters!"

"Most of you self-assured sprites are very intelligent!"

"I definitely am!"

"Would you like a salmon and cucumber sandwich?"

"In homemade bread?"

"Ok!"

"I'd like three eggs on toast!"

"O'Marley, you've got good taste!"

"Never ate it but I heard Pork Chop say it's monster! Boris, like, an omelette?"

"Got a big bowl of fresh orange carrot?"

"Lorraine, could you make us breakfast and a couple of splendid roots?"

"Pardon?"

"To feed our guests?"

"Dearest, that's novel."

Karaoke entertainers, Paul and Dawn Knight, from Dorchester listened intently as I recalled an encounter of an unpleasant nature! Unexpectedly, Paul said, "You've lived an interesting life, why don't you write your memoirs?"

"Tell tales about the olden times!" Well, pal, here goes; after writing my initial book, which I appropriately named headache, I began typing my life story! I started work at Newbold's flour gang in Bradford, humping one-hundred and forty-pound bags of flour and stacking them ready for mixing! I joined the junior leaders at Strensall, near York, in 1962! I served in the regular army and in 1964, did a tour of duty in Berlin, West Germany. This was followed by active service in Aden 1965/66! I was decorated, three times, as was most of our regiment! 1967, I left the Prince of Wales and worked, for Lindley Parkinson, Arndale Centre, in Poole, using my brother's cards, then I worked, subcontract, for Conways, an Irish firm full of Paddys, what a grand bunch, and there was Christmas spirit twenty-four-seven also at the same site. But all this fun ended 586 days later on the 6th of January 1969. I went to the police station and returned to my unit, stationed in Colchester! On the 23rd of February, I was court-martialled for desertion! An act, still punishable, to this day, by death but I served a total of six months, four days in the Glasshouse at the Military Corrective Training Centre across the road. I was released on the 10th of June 1969!

August 1970, aged twenty three, I became a professional boxer under the strict guidance of boxing manager Jack Turner who fixed us up good and proper with bouts at short notice, such as the evening before a boxing venue was due to commence! Where a boxer booked to fight couldn't attend, we took his place! I should say we were the fodder mainly in London against local pugilists! Would you believe I was given less than twenty-four hours' notice against Dave Parris, where? In London!

Unbelievably, like Cassius Clay, I was too pretty to be a fighter, and the result went to their man! Well, the contests kept going in my opponents' favour; finally, distressed at the outcome and disillusioned with the unfairness of boxing, I told Mister Turner I'd finished with this rigged sport, and that's my bouts in 1970! Whilst working for W S Try at a multi-story car park at the rear of the Arndale Centre, recently renamed Dolphin Centre in Poole, Dorset, I was employed at the Neptune bars situated by Boscombe pier, Bournemouth, a nightspot notorious for trouble where, prior, four doormen were glassed by shameless skunks. Everything was hunky-dory leading up to Christmas, then, as a passenger, I was involved in a terrible car accident! I've made a few mistakes in life; firstly, getting involved in this car incident wasn't the brightest idea and certainly didn't help my ascent to riches! The collision has cost me dearly, and I'm afraid to say the other vehicle won! I went home shaken but not stirred, but that morning, I awoke, paralysed and drained of strength! I'd suffered a broken or fractured spinal cord and pelvic girdle—a cartilaginous structure in vertebrates, to which the posterior limbs are attached. I lay there for over three months, feeling sorry for myself, then one morning, after a few shed tears, I went for a walk! The desire for fame and fortune never left! Now, I'm making no excuses for my boxing record or bouts but I would like you, the reader, to judge and make up your own mind as to the validity of the results! This dramatic story is an insight into my world, full of the joys of marriage and parenthood.

On 13th December 1971, a year and four days after my previous fight and after serious deliberation—to be or not to be, that was the question—I entered in the boxing arena and guess what? I lost and once again, thought about retirement but something or someone inside me, as though our Lord was speaking, advised me to carry on boxing! How unjust this sport is, when the chosen few virtually always win! It didn't give one much heart, I assure you, to carry on, especially when you knew, in your heart, that you've won, and the referee hoists your opponent's arm! By the way, boxing reporters from the boxing news rarely venture to venues outside London but instead, relied on information from reporters acting on behalf of the chosen one! There is no mention anywhere stating the pure fact that when I boxed Graham Sines, he was floored by me; at the time the bell rang, referee Harry Gibbs led him back to his corner and Sines could not come out for the next round! Where was the boxing news reporter, possibly in the toilet? Our second match, at the Empire Pool, Wembley! Reports fail to mention the bout was reduced from eight rounds to six, why? Was this promoter afraid I'd drop the protege again, and I only found out after round six, as I rose from my seat for the seventh! I do rant and rave a bit, don't I? Well, let's get back to the nitty-gritty stuff, where those who dare tread, win! I decided to give boxing another go, and hallelujah, praise to God. the 11th of January 1972, I won, reversing my previous bout against Vic Humpfries and remained undefeated throughout that year, although devilish pain interrupted many training sessions for prolonged periods, but faith kept me sane, safe and guided me along the righteous path! I just love this garbage and have a tendency to repeat myself but don't worry, this load of absolute rubbish adds light-hearted content, variety and nonsensical humour, ok? When reading reports from the boxing news bias crusade against gladiators, especially pugilists outside London, boxers of the likes of Terry Lawless and George Francis, I assume reporters must live on another planet, watching a show at some different venue, because when I boxed McEwan at Wolverhampton, there was no mention of the mere fact, I dumped him on the canvas or pure unadulterated fact, Garfield, in the last round, ran away from me, like a chicken being plucked or devil possessed with fear until the final bell rang, and I must say, it is difficult to catch a man frightfully afraid of his own shadow! The second occasion Eddie Fenton and I met, I opened his eye with the first jab! Fact, nowhere does it mention, he didn't show up for our scheduled, close encounter of the third kind! Where was the headliner after bashing Dave Hawkes, the official number four light-heavyweight contender? Had Peter McCann won our contest, the headlines would have been splashed across centrefold of boxing news, but after I'd punched McCann's shoulder out, with such tremendous force, it was of no interest to sponsors and indeed the boxing authority under the guidance of local promoters and board of directors, etc! At the time, I received a very degrading report, and no mention of this fact, Peter McCann, no relation of southpaw Pat McCann, climbing off the canvas and the bell ringing! I say, look at natural light-heavies, Lloyd Walford, who beat number one contender Roy John from Wales three times, and Pat McCann, who whipped gypsy Johnny Frankham (twice) and Graham Sines (twice) and was robbed blind of the result against, of course, a certain Kevin Finnegan, brother of Chris and one of the chosen few, Maxie Smith and Calton Benoit. Incidentally, Eddie Fanton failed to show up for our third encounter. No wonder this brilliant boxer Pat McCann, whom I have the utmost respect for gave up, his Southern area light-heavyweight crown without defending it and retired! He may as well have become Doctor Doolittle and talked to the animals for all the boxing board of control were bothered! I ascended the British ranking list, avenging most earlier results and overtook Mick Quiqley and the rest anyway and scaled the rank and file, leaving them in my wake! Once again, back pain escalated, beyond imagination, forcing me into submission and retirement! Words in the boxing news suggested fighters had punished me in contests, which wasn't true, and I never, ever stated boxers punched themselves out on me, then I'd reap revenge like the grim reaper, and so, I returned! Even when in great discomfort, I rolled off the sofa, crawled on my hands and knees to the door, hoisted myself up, hobbled over to the car to box Garfied McEwan because I was married, and we had a child to support, and of course, there's my pride! According to the official weighing scales, the day I boxed Londoner Johnny Wall, I was overweight and had one hour to rectify the situation, so we went to a sauna bath where I skipped and shed loads, then weighed! According to the scales at the sauna bath, I was 12st 2lbs, well inside, the scheduled 12st 7lbs, light heavyweight limit but when we returned to the venue, somehow, my weight leaped like a frog and jumped up to 12st 7lb, and I say something was dodgy, don't you? Of course, who can question British Boxing Board of Control's officialdom; anybody want to upset the apple-cart? Certainly not I.

For eight years, I fought as a part-time boxer, so I didn't do too badly, did I? And the calibre of the boxers have beaten British and Commonwealth Champions, so this makes me extremely proud to have shared the ring with these remarkable athletes! I fought as a professional gladiator, up and down the country and abroad and spent six years on McCowan's old boxing booth at Poole, Bournemouth, Christchurch,

Marlborough, Southampton, Cambridge and along the coastline to Torquay, Painton, Redruth, Bude, Somercourt! Micky Keily, a booth promoter, invited me to box at Barnstable and other locations. Eventually, I ran a security business with my wife, Lorraine! Next, my mother, wife and I purchased a nightclub! I agree with an old saying, 'everybody has a book in them' but believe none of us ever truly grow up, and the storyteller inside me is rooted in the youngster we all keep stored within us! Back in 1984, I began writing a book named 'Headache'. In 1990, we purchased Valentinos nightspot in Bournemouth; then, in 1992, I let my literature work lapse but after several years, and some extremely vivid escapades relating to Headache, resumed writing. I believe in the appeal of this audacious novel which relates solely to my life having, firstly, invited family and friends to read and received an incredible response, and I never had the faintest idea I'd write a story, especially regarding myself! Now, I would like to dedicate this book to Paul Cassidy! Without his help, I could never have travelled from Poole to Bournemouth and reach the gymnasium, and then, this tale would not have been written!

Next paragraph was taken from a boxing brochure, dated 1975! In, 1935, a black-haired youngster began a professional boxing career that continued to fame, fortune and the World Light-Heavyweight Crown. Freddie Mills was his name, from Poole, and he displayed our banner across the entire globe and did us proud. Fight fans with the nostalgia bug will recall those pre-war times with pride when our town became the boxing mecca of the south. Back then, Jack and Bob Turner, both former professional boxers in their prime, steered young Freddie to the pinnacle of the British middleweight tree, defeating Eddie McQuire, Dave McCleave, Charlie Parkin, Yorkey Bentley, Butcher Gascoigne, Ginger Sadd and the infamous Jock McAvoy, to list a few. The Second World War broke up this combination, with Freddie and Bob Turner joining, the RAF and Jack going into munitions. Mills, by now a ready-made champion, went right to the top with Ted Broadribb, defeating Gus Lesnevich in 1948 to become World Light-Heavyweight Champion. Now, we've another prospect in Sid Falconer! Like Freddie, Sid has a mop of black hair, a crushing left hook and incredible toughness. Falconer, ranked 7th in line for the British

Crown, is due to fight for the Southern Area Title. For the past three years, Sid has mixed gloves with the best of fistic company in Britain, losing debatable decisions to Maxie Smith and twice, ABA Heavyweight Champion, Graham Sines, and wrecking the boxing career of brilliant prospect, Peter McCann. Last July, Sid almost destroyed the fistic hopes of the No 1 contender, Tim Wood, whose title ambitions were severely wobbled, and he was certainly a lucky man to survive two counts in a seventh-round blitz to record a victory by the smallest margin. British and European Heavyweight Champion Richard Dunn believed Falconer was robbed of the decision. Can Sid emulate his hero and make the championship grade? This contest against Guinea Roger could go a long way towards answering this question and promises to be a real belter.

This book hasn't taken long to type, unlike my first novel which took 28 years. This tale has been fun. People will probably say, this can't be true, but I assure you, every word is. Unbeknown to us, much danger lurked everywhere. We were scallywags, rascals, thieves but that was our business; finally, at long last, the truth and nothing but. I grew up in London. Our father was a professional boxer and trained alongside Johnny Williams and Freddie Mills! Their manager was Londoner Ted Broadribb; mine was obviously Jack Turner. His older brother, Bob, sold Mills' contract to Ted. Back to the script! Our elder brother was Barry, then came David and finally me! Baz was a clever youngster but may have jeopardised our safety on more than one occasion; maybe he did endanger our well-being, and of course, at the time, us children didn't see the dangerous side of life until this lad was stabbed to death at a bus stop along the road from where we lived, then no more penny for the guy mister or excursions to Battersea funfair and trips along the network of underground tunnels were finished. If drunkards had caught me, things may have been serious. A bomb-damaged site around the corner was morbid, but we liked playing there! Fights were ripe and life was worth living, then we moved from London's East End to Bradford in Yorkshire.

We lived at the top of Edward Street where workmen built a police depot for maintenance of their vehicles, then we made an effigy of Guy Fawkes! Dave was put on a bonfire which frightened the pants off him and us! Life was different, but soon, we made pals. Friends are like stars; you don't always see them, but one instantly knows they are there! I'll never forget Peter and Alan Manning or Gurden Singh from Roman Road, and they are still in my heart until this very day. In Bradford, we used to play on Hindles, haulage wagons and in Blamire's yard. This company wrecked buses and guard dogs patrolled, but we soon befriended these hounds and searched for money. It was like Dave working on the buses back in London. It was grand and coins were in every corner and crevice. Father went to work as a coalman, then I dropped this fifty-six-pound weight on my left foot. Aged 10, we moved into the Exchange pub, and Tinker, our dog, was put down, then dad started knocking customers out, and beer went stale in its barrels. I took a couple of small bottles of alcohol and cigarettes to school to sell but got caught and a nice little earner was gone up in smoke, so I challenged the lads to punch me in the stomach. I'd pay two shillings if they could wind me; if not, they'd pay me sixpence. Soon, their dash came rolling in, and I was rich once again, until this hard man, Keith Sharkey, punched my belly, and did it hurt. I got grumbling appendix, stomach pains with swelling. A terrible time which lasted five years; meanwhile, I left St James and moved to Usher Street School! I purchased a motor bike for ten pounds, then one day, the police stopped me and that was my lot until I was fifteen, but it didn't stop me driving dad's car. Once upon a time, on Thornton Road, in Bradford, I waved at a police car passing by, and dad wasn't amused as he watched from the corner of Ingleby street. Aged fifteen, I joined the army and arrived at Strensall barracks on September the 4th, 1962! What a wonderful time we had in those days, then John F Kennedy was assassinated! I remember Elvis Presley, and Berlin, in 1964.

Back at Strensall, I gave a haircut to Carver. My pal, Johnny Jagger, finished off. I'd say it resembled a bootlace tie.

I was born at 6 Portalet Road, Bethnal Green, London E2 at precisely one fifty-three am on the morning of 22/07/1947. I cannot recall any of this stuff but according to reports, mum stated, "It was like shelling peas."

Dad, according to mother, voiced, "Far as I can remember, it was like a huge humpback whale in labour."

A midwife remarked, "Bill, I see you've been here before; you've got a good pair of lungs, gonna be a boxer just like his dad." We lived in a narrow Nissen hut, a tunnel-shaped accommodation with a corrugated roof and cement floor; finally, we moved to 106 Roman Road. Dad opened a second-hand clothes' shop with the entrance situated on Roman Road! We stayed there for three years. By the tender age of two, I'd twaddle down the yard. I recall open land full of four-wheeled stalls. Folk paid rent to keep them there, and Sunday morning, they'd pick them up for market at Pettycoat Lane. Our parents loaded a stall with clothes which mum, I distinctly remember, pressed prior. Daily, dad punched a kit bag like some madman, continually banging on a big bass drum. Hours, he'd punch away like a mean machine. This bag was situated in an out-house at the rear. This building was like a work room with walls running along each side up to our house. On the left side, looking from our abode, was a set of slatted wooden gates.

Panels with gaps maybe two inches wide, enough room in between, for my small left hand to enter and pass through! One day, a child carrying an ice cream, with his mother in attendance, came along the pathway as I stood watch, and a second later, out flashed my hand and it was firmly in my grasp! He shed tears, and his mother stormed in the front entrance to complain! "How old is your child?" my father enquired.

"Six," stated the grieved parent.

"My son is only two," he said and gave her some coins to rectify this situation!

We moved along this road, opposite Bonner Street School, which I attended. Our folks purchased a house and converted it into a sweet shop, which was great news. One day, papa brought home a container full of hands of bananas! They went out that night, leaving us alone with that box of delicious bananas. Next evening, dad came in from the shed after punching the heavy bag and said to Mum, "Did you move the bananas?"

"No," came a reply.

"We've been robbed."

"No."

"Yes."

Mother changed the bedsheets, only to find the pillow cases full of banana skins. Mum, said, "Not the best hiding place." As we grew up, our Dave got the knack of climbing anything, from walls to trees, like a mountaineer. Down the road was a large humpback bridge with a canal beneath! Situated nearside was an enormous building, reaching up towards the clouds. One day, our Baz noticed this door sited at the pinnacle of a shabby-looking premise, which reminds me now of a Yorkshire mill, which, in fact, was a warehouse! He decided it was time for our brother to go up. "David, it's climbing time." By the side of this warehouse was a tree reaching skywards, brushing against a door which was ajar. "Report to me," exclaimed Barry.

"What's inside?" Jack couldn't climb a beanstalk quicker! Like a lumberjack, he clambered up that tree and in no time, he was up there! He found this room filled to the ceiling with army uniforms, and there was a rag and bone merchant inside a mile! We stood watch, a wall behind protected us from prying eyes, allowing Dave access without danger of being copped. Next, he's back, peering out, "Anyone around?"

"Nope," came governor's reply.

"Right," said our brother, chucking out clothes. "You stay here, whilst I fetch a wheel-barrow, ok?" I felt scared in the eerie darkness and was glad when David reappeared. Later, Barry returned, and soon, they were loading dust-ridden clothes onto a pram he'd managed to borrow from a little old dear living next door to Alice! Whilst I kept guard, Baz covered them with a dirty sheet, then next morning, we went to the rag shop where the boss man, I P Freely, shouted in a deep throaty tone, "Get me, more!" His voice thundered, echoing around this building and still lingers!

His brother, U P Freely, hollered, "We'll take everything, including jam jars and newspapers." But no way were we going to give him our bog roll! Over the course of a year, we visited that premise at night and stored these large army issue condoms, which, at the time, we thought were white water bomb bags, in a hole beneath a wooden shed which Tinker, our dog, had dug and inside our den, which Barry had made for us away from father's prying eyes.

One day, when I was wearing a white shirt, grey cardigan and a pair of knee-length matching trousers, with black braces attached, long woollen socks and brown sandals, and flashing my knobbly knees, as usual, I walked down the road towards Bow with my brothers and noticed this general or maybe field marshal and officials wearing army clothing and others dressed in plain black outfits! "Possibly senior officers from the constabulary," remarked Dave! "Police commission or Chief Superintendent Sherlock Holmes of Scotland Yard, Serious Crime Squad," replied Baz! These blooming creeps were looking out of the doorway, searching below, scratching their bald heads! "Organised gangs," exclaimed this rolly-polly, wearing a pin stripe suit!

"They're a long way off the mark," whispered Barry!

"Let's scarper before them old Bow Street runners nab us," said Dave! "Those robbers have stolen our livelihood," exclaimed Baz. That was the last time we went back, but soon after, our guv found a loose pole in railings at the rear of a bus depot, where buses were parked in neat rows! "David, I've a job for you," roared Baz! On three sides of the stationary buses, if my memory serves me correctly, was a green painted iron fence, reaching up towards heaven! Normal eyesight suggested this mighty barrier was impregnable but it wasn't actually, far from it! The fence consisted of wrought-iron poles, with spikes like spears thrusting upward, warning trespassers will be skewered or staked out if caught by these guards! We observed conductors from a safe distance as they put boxes full of money into lockers inside buses! "Dave, we'll keep watch whilst you fetch our dosh! Only a few coins from each box, mark my words; I'll clip your ears if you take any more," commanded Barry! David knew only too well not to argue; anyway, he just loved the fun of pinching a copper or two! "Hurry up, and don't get caught, and we'll go to Battersea funfair; now, off you go, and be quick!"

"Righto, Baz."

"We'll call you if we see anyone!" Off he went, and Barry said, "This is great fun, Sidney, are you excited?"

"I'm feeling sick."

"Don't worry, be happy; we'll be rolling in loot, shortly!" Dave eventually returned with pockets full of cash, and we went to the fairground via Bethnal Green's underground railway station!

We caught the tube train and arrived at Battersea funfair, which was frightening on the scary helter-skelter! A monster spiral slide round a tower, and we ventured on an eerie ghost train but I liked bumper cars and coconut shy! Baz looked for the gunnery range whilst I wanted a goldfish and candy-floss!

Meddlesome busybodies watched us strangely as we passed them by before hopping aboard a ride! Barry purchased sandwiches and I must say I loved my butty! The funfair was simply packed with giants! Folk brushing past me as I licked a boiled sweet on a long stick, which Baz, had bought from a little lollipop lady, and ice cream! "David, next time, get more half crowns, ok? We are running low!" A fat man stood on my foot, and it hurt!

Barry screamed at this geezer, "Watch it, tough guy, next time, I'll knock thy bloke off!" Somehow, I believed him but this sleazebag was mighty round, like a giant pumpkin!

"You don't mess with the Falconer brothers," said I, grabbing hold of my braces, before sticking my fingers into my pockets! Delving into my memoirs takes me longer to recall and print a correct account. Travelling via the tube wasn't the real deal by any means; even though I was maybe five years of age, nobody questioned us, and the police were handy if required! Barry would approach a copper and ask for directions, and they were helpful!

Mum once said, "Where did you get that goldfish? "A man gave it to him!" Thieving money from conductors went on for a long time, and nobody ever suspected us! When winter was in full swing, my brothers managed to sneak out and soon return with pockets full of coins! Sometimes, we were vastly overloaded with lolly, so Barry quietly distributed our wealth in the sweet shop till! I presume mother thought dad put a bit of change in the till and vice versa. One morning, as usual, we went to the bus station to get our cash but workmen were loading wheel-barrows and emptying concrete! Our leader asked an enormous worker, saying, "What you doing?"

"Building a wall," shouted an Irish navvy!

"Why?"

"Skedaddle," said another person standing close by.

"Be off, now," said a jackass! Meanwhile, the long red buses, for some unknown reason, had been shifted to the far side of this vast complex, leaving open land between us and our pay packets! This cash was forever gone! The mother ships carrying this precious loot were way out of reach! For a couple of weeks, we returned only to witness a towering wall, that even David couldn't breach, being erected; finally, they removed this fence!

"Those dirty rotten crooks have stolen our dash," screamed Barry! "It's back to collecting jam jars," called Dave! Our grand ringleader, entrepreneur, cracked a smile, then said, "Firework night isn't far away!" A couple of weeks drifted slowly by! In a nutshell, everything went quiet but our Baz still had a tidy nest egg—those massive water-bomb bags, white sheaths, stashed safely in our hideaways to sell, and there were plenty of men willing to pay a fortune for them whilst stocks were available, and we had a few thousands of them from that warehouse, but for the life of me, I couldn't understand why men wanted to chuck water bombs at their wives, and neither did Peter, Alec or Gurden!

"David, get our pram off Alice; Sidney, fetch Singh!" Barry dressed this Indian lad as an effigy of Guy Fawkes, then off we went to the nearest bus-shelter! "Penny for the guy, governor, governess, can you spare a bob or two?" As a young boy living in Bethnal Green, I had three pals, Alec and Peter Manning and young Gurden Singh! No greater mates have I ever had, hopefully, one day, we'll meet again! Maybe this story will reach out to them! At the sweet shop, I remember this dimly lit cellar where dad punched away at a heavy bag when he couldn't get to the gym! Since being officially discharged from the army, where on active service, he was blown up by a German land mine! Later, the king's surgeon operated on him at Whitchurch, Cardiff, Wales! The War Department awarded him a medical discharge and a small pension!

Dad made a living in a variety of jobs before applying to the local district council for a hawker's licence which they refused but eventually relented, "bravo," so he could now sell various goods from house to house and at the notorious Petticoat Lane, Brick Street, where, each Sunday, many traders would do their business selling pots and pans! Every item beneath an equatorial sun could be purchased, from dogs and cats to chickens, even an odd ferret! Somewhere in the back of my mind, I recall this chap from India playing a flute with a cobra hissing and rising into the air from a magic basket before settling back! Maybe it's my imagination playing tricks but whilst this man sat there, my father's eyes, took him back to the North West Frontier where, at night, tribesmen and women crept into the latrines whilst an unguarded soldier, unaware of their presence, sat discharging a motion! A sudden scream of fright registered in the darkness, loud and clear, as somebody grabbed his sacred crown jewels from beneath him; suddenly, a knife, and his penis and testicles were away! This was one of many nightmares he carried of men dying in the line of duty! Father, who was having his third professional fight aged thirty-four, boxed Johnny Williams, who was having his twenty-third bout. Williams hit a blood-stained canvas in round four. The ref took up the count, then stopped, walked over to poor old Johnny, hunched over, and then led him to his corner seat; then came an announcement. Williams couldn't continue; subject to this, dad wasn't disqualified but on a technical merit, the bout was awarded to Williams, who was carried out on a stretcher, and the rest is history! Folk can only judge by what they read, but I assure you, don't believe everything one reads is always true! Nowhere will you read about me planting Sines' on the canvas but it occurred at the York Hall, Bethnal Green!

Ringside, that evening, was Don Cockell; then, dad stopped undefeated prospect, Johnny Prince! Father's next opponent was Cockell but the evening before this fight, he pulled out; then the boxing fraternity put the skids under future fights. Thousands of boxers get a raw deal like the verdict set against my father. Folk might think this is humbug, sour grapes. This is not a load of nonsense but there are many boxers who can vouch for this! Outside London, pugilists are treated with unfair decisions. One such contest was Johnny Wall. According to my corner man, Peter Faye, I won eight rounds out of a ten rounder but lost this match. How? Where? London! Ref, Harry Gibbs! A debatable decision? Memories, pressed between the pages of my mind, have haunted me for years. Everybody knows Henry Cooper thrashed Joe Bugner, although there were two people who believed Bugner had won, and that most certainly wasn't referee Harry Gibbs, even though he raised Joe's arm. It was a diabolical decision, but I will say, citizens watch sport the same as I and have said who had won, only to see the referee, or maybe the ringside judges, award the contest to the other boxer. There is a lot more to be said regarding professional and amateur boxing and other issues, and I'll not for a moment mince my words! Whether names of the following promoters and managers are correct, I'm unsure, and whatsoever you think, I am not saying every referee is bent, but in my experience, I've come to the conclusion that most of them are corrupt! On a lighter note, they are like a can of worms: once the money is laid out before them, out the window goes all honesty, would you believe? Well, that's my truthful opinion! If you want to sue me, hard luck, it's all true! And I'm flat broke, again!

I don't know the personal lives of opponents but found them to be most trustworthy adversaries, wanting to win but not at any cost! When a contest is over, I've always shook my opponents' hand whatever the verdict, but when I knew, without doubt, the match had been rigged, I felt bitter towards the judge! An umpire doesn't give a hoot who won the bout; it's plain and simple, cash is what counts, not tobacco! If you disagree, that's your prerogative, but I stand by every word! Loot is the route of evil, where bribery resides and decides the fate of boxers before a punch has been thrown! Promote local boxers, because they draw gate-money! London boys invariably win in London, and their devout followers pack venues to the rafters, and currency flows into the cash registers. It's banknotes which make the world revolve, megabucks! Who's bothered about the verdict? Most, of the fighters outside London are Joe Bloggs, fodder, ignorant pumpkins but not all! It's glorious dosh, what counts. Out there are rogue promoters, matchmakers and managers like Jack Turner, who are willing to sacrifice their boxer for a few extra quid, and let me say, a mention for crooked referees and special praise for straight judges, Harry Humpfries, Billy Simpson and Mike Jacobs!

The evening I boxed Peter McCann at the Royal Albert Hall, London, on the 14/04/1973! McCann's manager, Lerry Lawless, made an error in judgement booking me to box his protege, and his fighter paid the ultimate price, being knocked into permanent retirement! I was supposed to be fodder! The sacred lamb for their god, to be slaughtered! What a joke! My cosy changing room, in this magnificent coliseum, was a putrid dungeon in the old gents' toilet and smelled of fragrant urine. An amazing insight for anybody, don't you agree? That night, Jarvis Astairs and Micky Duff spoke to my manager, Jack Turner, who, I may already have stated, managed Freddie Mills, originally from Parkstone! With elder brother, Bob, they sold Mills' valid contract to Ted Broadribb! Interestingly, two geezers came to me; by the way, Peter McCann's suite was in the plush quarter, not squalid district! The establishment had already pencilled in his next bout for the British light heavyweight championship, and they were now in talks, reference, a world title match! Fact is, these two pals of McCann visited my humble parlour, attempting to intimidate me, saying McCann was a frightening banger who had previously knocked out all his opponents! I'd already seen an article and told them this did not matter, for when the bell tolls, I will be tossing a few awesome punches, and he'll be eating leather, ha ha ha, and it's go to sleep, my baby, and it won't be me hitting the canvas; now, please leave!

Point of interest, I met ex-heavyweight contender, Roger Tighe, in Bridlington when on holiday, and I must say, what a genuine guy with a fascinating boxing record, certainly of noteworthy praise! These bouts are not in categorical order but selected at random. Back to the Royal Albert Hall! London promoter, Jarvis Astair, and matchmaker for the York Hall, Bethnal Green, Micky Duff, came to my plush quarters, where this theatrical entrepreneur, Astair, asked me a simple question! "Are you a Londoner?"

I replied, "I was born within the sound of Bow Bells, which makes me a cockney!"

This promoter said, "Go out there tonight and win, then show me your birth certificate, and I'll put your name in lights like Joe Bugner!" My word should have been good enough but it wasn't! These chaps were gods of the boxing business; who the devil was I? A mere tradesman, Jack, the lad, mister, nobody, that's who! Never did show a birth certificate, and of course, I was never topped on major billing! Looking back, one was made an offer, which maybe I should have grabbed with both arms outstretched! To possibly be a megastar but had I accepted his generous offer, I'd not have met my wonderful bride and our children, Sidney and Matthew, would never have been born! I'll cherish the day this promoter offered me the real deal! From the first round, I knew McCann was apprehensive, and my conversation earlier with his two pals had penetrated! Round one, this gladiator with the finest skill I've ever boxed came at me, cautiously probing his jab, then retreating like a fleeting shadow in the moonlight as I attempted the old crash, bang, wallop routine, and he threw everything at me except for the kitchen, according to the boxing news! What a load of baloney, for I finished this epic contest upright and without much visible damage! I knew, sooner or later, I'd catch him using my kind of tactics, and sure enough, in round four, I tagged Pete coming in with an unimaginable force and out popped his shoulder blade, followed by a swift hook, dumping him on the spot like a large bag of bones inside a body liner upon a blood-splattered canvas for a long count! The referee stood there; then, as precious time tick tocked, ushered me into a neutral corner before beginning the count! At nine, he somehow managed to stand upright, then the bell rang! My corner man, Peter Faye, shouted, "It was only two minutes into this round!" Later, in my fragrant dungeon, an elderly gent came to me stating he'd, overheard a conversation in Pete's corner, advising his team to send McCann out for this round, and Falconer would be disqualified; now, what do you think of that?

When I boxed Central Area Heavyweight Champion Peter Freeman, he weighed 15stone, 4lbs, whilst I was a mere 13st, 2lbs! Brendan Ingle, who has become Britain's greatest boxing coach, training world champions, was in my corner! After four rounds, under his strict guidance, this gigantic gladiator was bleeding profusely from eyes, nose and mouth; suddenly, out comes the head butting, and blood flowed. The crowd loved this rip-roaring action! Brendan attended to the wounds! Round eight, Freeman's eyes appeared to revolve in the opposite direction, or my mind was playing tricks on me, and I'm pretty sure heavenly birds were twittering merrily whilst fluttering around inside his brain! I stepped back gaily as his arms fell but his body remained upright, just leaning against, the old ropes! I turned to face this referee, and he just looked back, so I walked towards Pete and touched his stomach and head, then stepped backwards, looking, looking all the time towards the ref, but again, this judge did nothing; then, a fellow in this over-crowded auditorium, with a wooden eye, eyeballing me, shouted, "Bang the ref." And after I made another move, this umpire stopped this contest! After the bout, Brendan Ingle said, "Sid, you're the hardest man I've ever met!" Which was the most fantastic compliment a boxer could receive, especially from such a renowned personality! For the record, Freeman boxed Leon Spinks! Back in one's dressing room, a doctor inserted fifteen stitches into wounds, then said, "Don't spar for six weeks."

Unfortunately, Danny Mahoney had already signed contracts to fight Denton Ruddock for the Heavyweight Championship of the Southern Area!

Five weeks after that blood-curdling match, I was sitting in the changing room when somebody remarked, "Denton is outside, running up and down, getting ready to rumble!" Our bout was scheduled for 9:15 pm. Just after 8:10 pm, my coach, Peter Faye, said, "Two bouts have just been cancelled, and the initial fight has ended, and the main event is next!" At 8:25 pm, I entered the ring without any warming up! This is how I see it, no disrespect, to Denton Ruddock! Casting doubtful shadows over this contest, clouding one's view maybe and good judgement possibly, and I'll say I wasn't pleased with the referee's decision! Why was this southern area champion outside at 7 pm, preparing for our titanic clash scheduled at 9:15 pm? The matchmaker, Con Mount Bassie's ex-manager, was Londoner Danny Peacock, Ruddock's manager! "It must be codswallop, there ain't no such thing as a rigged result," shouted a fellow in the changing room the night of this venue!

"What?" replied Paul Cassidy.

"It appears highly unlikely," remarked a journalist!

Peter Faye piped in! "Very suspicious, don't you agree, hey, what?" "I say, it smells a bit like haddock, wouldn't you?"

"Dead fishy," roared old Captain Smellit, sitting in the corner, reading the daily echo!

"Was the ruddy umpire up from London?" enquired Rodney Rickeard!

"Purely coincidental, I would say," hollered our drama queen, Ann Puzey, looking eagerly over my shoulder whilst simultaneously reading this passage!

Outside our house in Chatsworth road, Upper Parkstone, my new manager Harry Legge hooted his car horn, signalling he'd arrived and awaited my company, so I rolled off the old settee and crawled over to the door, groped the handle and hoisted myself upright! The date was the 10/03/1976! And I was due to travel to the Civic Hall, Wolverhampton, in the West Midlands! In December 1970, aged 23, as you already know, I was involved in an accident which left me paralysed, luckily, for me, only temporarily, because when I was moved, it freed me from the paralysis but left me in great pain, weak and constantly sleeping!

Every day, I'd wake up, shed a few tears, then walk umpteen steps from room to room and then fall asleep! After three months and more, I decided, enough, and began walking along the Ashley road in Parkstone, Poole Dorset and down Constitution Hill to Bassle Hurrack, a friend I'd worked alongside and his wife, Joan! A couple of months passed, and before too long, I was back in the gymnasium, training, shadow boxing, sparring and approaching Christmas time, I was ready for battle!

A match with Garfield McEwan was duly arranged, and we were travelling up to Wolverhampton for that bout! Unbeknown to me at the time of my accident, I'd suffered a broken or fractured back and pelvic girdle! Agony was hell but somehow, thanks to God, I managed to get fit! Look up my boxing record, and you'll notice bouts recorded 10/12/1970! Next tournament, in black and white, was in 13/12/1971! Inactive for just over one year! I'm a firm believer in faith healing! Now, back to Wolverhampton venue! By this time, I'd got married, and my wife, Lorraine, presented me with a baby boy which we duly named Sidney after my father! My back was very painful but I was booked to box and laid down in the back of Harry's old car until we reached Wolverhampton, then weighed in! Harry and I went to a cinema to watch a rock musical, a film called Tommy but it was awful noisy and extremely cold inside this picture house, and so, after suffering this infernal racket for an hour, left then found a smart cafe where we dined on steak and eggs; finally, we arrived back at the venue and eventually rested! I was suffering but the fight was fixed, and I had to box because I'd responsibility and a family to feed!

I was stiff as a board but once this fight was three rounds in, I sprang into action, like many times in the gym but at this precise moment, I felt grumpy, and as the ringmaster called us together, wished I wasn't there! For three and possibly a half rounds, reminiscent of my training sessions, I've moved stiffly then I'm back, normal and relaxed, my reflexes extremely virile and bobbed and weaved and enjoyed this bout, and Garfield felt my power and didn't like it one bit, especially when I laughed! Next, he paid heavily for his mistake of underestimating his adversary! I switched from head to body then back, and this crowd screamed for more! Round seven, I was not comfortable and felt this round maybe in jeopardy, so I upped the ante; suddenly, I launched myself from a satisfactory platform, connected with his jaw and over went McEwan! I literally poleaxed him! The referee took ages before beginning a count! After fourteen seconds, by Harry's calculation, a tired looking Garfield somehow managed to beat the count of nine but now, this ref wanted to wipe my gloves before allowing this excellent contest, which was now clearly one sided, to proceed; finally, a damn bell rang! Ding-dong! After a good minute's rest, round eight commenced! McEwan, who'd been dropped, moved around this arena, avoiding me like the dreaded plague, continually shifting, constantly running, absolutely terrified and to his sheer relief, the sound of the final bell tolled! Everybody in this hall knew I'd won, including the referee! Now, let me point to this actual fact, I knocked McEwan down for possibly fifteen seconds and lost once again to a local boxer, do you think I'm a wee bit paranoid?

"I'd be skeptical who you box, from now," exclaimed Lorraine when I arrived home, feeling quite low and somewhat down trodden with pains, would you believe? I agree with her statement but one cannot tell officials that you won't fight a local boy in London! Now, this 10-round contest at the York Hall, Bethnal Green, against Londoner and two times amateur Heavyweight Champion, Graham Sines! I must state, what a spineless freak to deliberately head butt me before round one began, and of course, who was the referee, Harry Gibbs, would you believe? He turned a blind eye and the audience turned away from their man! The judge stopped the bout, checked my eye, which. had a swelling then ordered box on, instead of disqualifying the punk! In round four, I planted this manger on the deck where he belonged. For some unbeknown reason, Gibbs stopped the count before leading Sines back to his corner, naturally, I took this as a result! A signal that this contest was over, with me as the victor! Wrong! Gibbs came across, took a squint at a cut less than a quarter of an inch, "Boom-boom, remember wounds in Rocky Marciano's fights on both his eyebrows." Next, old Harry stopped the contest, awarding this farcical fight to a skunk! A creature in my mind of the lowest grade! What a terrible decision, so I spoke to the fat, ugly, bent judge, suggesting this blodger was out on his seat and was still in a bad way, and I'd knock him out in the next round and invited this scumbag to carry on and show his gore but this gutless pig-face just sat there, ignoring my invitation! How can a judge award a bout to a man incapable of getting off his stool, with me standing ready for battle; it stinks to high hell, I shouted at Gibbs, "Give me another round, and I'll knock this unprofessional ogre out!" This downright bent umpire wasn't entertaining any of it! Geoff Shaw was a casualty of a diabolical decision against Sines at the Albert Hall; incidentally, I'd just like to say, Alan 'Boom Boom' Minter, what a marvellous young person and future world middleweight champion was on the under card and supporting bouts included Gerald Gooding, Johnny Wall and Peter Freeman!

Bjorn Rudi! A Norwegian powder puncher weighed in around 18st 4lb whereas I weighed 13 st, 4lbs, if my memory serves me correctly! Next, with his distinct weight advantage, he grabbed me, then put my head in a half-nelson; is that boxing? The judge looked but did nothing then this low life, seemingly, with this umpire's authority, stuck a leather thumb, part of his glove, in my eye! If this is the only way a person can win, with the obvious consent of a ref, then I'm retiring after this contest which I duly did, because I was disillusioned with the sport and didn't want to be associated with absolute toerags! I boxed because I had no money and honestly believed if one was ahead on points at the end of the final round, then they got the verdict, but how wrong was I and how naive like most people, I would imagine! Rudi, with the approval of German referee, turned me into the ropes and punched me in the kidneys! At the end of round six, I waited to return for the seventh when I was informed by their corner man standing inside this arena that this bout was over! He stated, "This venue was booked until midnight, and seeing our bout had overrun that time period, the bout was reduced in the ring to six rounds!" This Norwegian was awarded this fight; surely, it was a no contest and should therefore be void of any result! I say Bjorn Rudi was a disgrace not only to himself but his lovely wife and Norway! "Sid, that statement appears a bit harsh," remarked local historian Winston Churchill.

"There are millions of honest boxers out there but a minority, I believe, should be banned for they are not warriors in our sport but outlaws! This is my opinion which I honestly believe is true, and I make no bones about it, because being robbed by these authorised shysters and bent referees is no joke and still leaves a bad taste in one's mouth!" Now, Guinea Roger was a brilliant professional and very astute! Sid Paddock, a friendlier guy one could not possibly meet, and Ralph Green appeared what I'd certainly call a true gent, like gentleman Jim Corbert! I also admire Maxie Smith, a smart athlete with swift hands, and Tim Wood merit gladiator status such as Eddie Fenton, Dave Hawkes and Dave Parris, Terry Jones, and in particular, Lloyd Walford, Terry Armstrong, Mick Quigley, managed by Johnny Williams, the former heavyweight champion of Great Britain, who incidentally boxed our dad, aged thirty-four! I'd like to point out our dad was only having his second contest whereas Johnny was having his twenty-third bout! Fact is, at Smethwick, our father dumped Williams on his rectum in round four! The Referee led number one contender aged twenty-one back to his corner! This umpire didn't disqualify dad but on a technical merit, awarded the contest to Williams! Would you agree, another debatable decision?

Later, Johnny Williams was carried out on a stretcher; eventually, it came to light, he'd sustained bruised ribs! On this occasion, at ringside, was Don Cockell! Papa dispatched undefeated light-heavy Johnny Prince in four rounds! The night prior to a scheduled contest, dated 8/04/1948, between Falconer senior and Don Cockell, from Battersea, Cockell withdrew! Before I go any further, I'm going to say I've said things which will possibly upset my opponents but I am writing the truth as I honestly feel! On reflection, I should not have made such allegations and therefore retract unproven assertions in my previous statements! Fact is, no fighter is a coward! On the contrary, quite the opposite! Every boxer is a gladiator but an odd few, on arriving where a path divides, either take the righteous pathway which leads up the straight and narrow or choose to stride along another track which drawn these guys into aggressive acts of ill repute, most unbecoming in my code of conduct which does include intentional head butting but who am I, just a boxer and certainly not a judge, referee or umpire! I was simply an honest fighter who wanted to win by my own merit natural ability but not at any cost! Yes, I may have stated a few things about boxers but it isn't too late to admit possible mistakes and sincerely apologise if they are incorrect?

After the Cockell incident, dad couldn't get fights, now, Broadribb wanted a sparring partner for the illustrious Freddie Mills! Notorious for lacing his boxing associates but when he's attempted to belt my late father, he came unstuck; suddenly, blood spattered from Freddie's eyelid, next second, a right hook laid him horizontal, out cold like a plucked turkey! The great AI Phillips was at ringside and witnessed the entire shebang! Later, Ted Broadribb called my Dad, weighing 14st 7lbs, after training to his office where he said, "Mills required a sparring partner!" Without much cash coming in and being registered disabled from the British Army, my father accepted. In the war, Dad was in Burma when he landed on a German SIS Mine! On impact with the hard ground, he tensed then automatically rolled and it exploded, leaving deep cuts full of shrapnel, totally covering his body but unexplainably missed his face, luckily for papa, the kings surgeon operated on him at Whitchurch in Cardiff, Wales! I must point out, Freddie didn't attempt any more monkey business after that initial incident; Mills became a tad less aggressive? l wonder why? At this time, Dad was paid around eighty pounds for sparring with the light-heavyweight champion. I understand the national wage was in the region of four pounds per week!

I boxed my heart out against Smith, only for this referee to raise his arm aloft! What injustice I have witnessed in amateur contests and professional! Soon, as our match ended, Maxie lofted my right arm and the audience agreed but Roland Dakin lifted his arm, and everyone knew it was rigged prior! In a return match, with Smith! Let me first say, when Danny McAiinden fought Jack Bodell for the British Heavyweight Crown, he removed his boots and socks because the canvas was a new type! In my match against Maxie, I did not and slid all over the canvas! The evening prior to the first contest with Smith, I was working at the Badger bars in Glenfern road, Bournemouth when Glyn Thomas informed me that my opponent had been changed and my new adversary was Smith. This bout was originally myself against Lloyd, who'd beaten Roy

John from Wales three times! According to my manager, Walford suffered appendicitis then he'd been involved in a car accident subsequently, Max was a late substitute. What a load of bullshit. I was never fighting Lloyd Walford. It was a scam. A fix from start to finish with my manager Jack Turner involved for the money, as usual. Another complete carve up, which I've come to realise is very common. The date of this bout was the 9/04/1973 and the venue was the Winter Gardens, in Bournemouth! On the 7/05/1975, I boxed the reigning Central Area Champion Lloyd Walford in Bradford. At the Yorkshire Executive Suite, Norfolk Gardens Hotel and knocked Walford, formally ranked number two in Great Britian, down in round seven and won on points. It must have given the judge a headache to award me the verdict but what else could he do? Lloyd told me he knew nothing about our contest and never suffered appendicitis or been involved in a car incident!

The match against Maxie was a carve up! I must say Walford was an exceptional gladiator, as was Gerald Gooding, Vic Humphreys, Peter McCann, Ade Ajasco, Barry Clough and Terry Armstrong.

On 18/08/1972, at the Free Trade Hall in Manchester, Armstrong's home town venue, Terry was bleeding profusely from both eyelids, nose, and mouth, yet he received a draw? At the Royal Hall in Harrogate, Barry Clough was next in line to fight me and certainly paid the price. What a boxer. We stood toe to toe for seven rounds but eventually, he succumbed to my non-stop pressure and was KOed. Barry recorded victories against Terry Armstrong, Alan Butters, Billy Baggott, Gerald Gooding, Vic Humphreys, Mick Quigley, Dave Parris and drew with young Randolph Turpin Jr on the undercard of my bout against Maxie Smith before losing to John L Gardner, where? The Royal Albert Hall, London! Denton Ruddock was an exceptional boxer who beat Neville Meade, Danny McAiinden and boxed the likes of Heavyweight Champion of South Africa Kallie Knoetze who incidentally beat Richard Dunn, Neville Meade and fought Gerrie Coetzee! Maxie Smith fought in the company of Bunny Johnson beating ogre Graham Sines, Pat McCann, Roy John and boxed Steve Aczel of Australia for the commonwealth championship! I may not have aspired to greatness but the calibre I was privileged to box were the premier league, thus awarding me outstanding credibility!

Johnny Wall of London, well, only two folks thought he'd won, would you believe his father and some goon named Steve what's-his-surname? Harry Gibbs raised his hand, but he knew

I'd won eight rounds out of ten rounds and lost? I beat him silly, now let's go to Henry Cooper verses Joe Bugner! Bug, by name and nature in my book! I've never witnessed a more bent one-sided contest in my life! Why wouldn't the bookies, not mentioning any names, allow this contest to proceed until they had Harry Gibbs in their pocket? The answer is the £20 million they would lose. No way did Joe win but Gibbs lofted his hand. Our Henry vowed never to speak to him again and we all know why, don't we? The Boxing Board of Control should have held an inquiry but no, why? What an epitaph for our great champion Sir Henry Cooper, who in his heyday was leading on points against Muhammad Ali at Earls Court when stopped by cuts, which could happen to anybody, finally, beaten by a nomad, a giant bug. This saddens me, period, and makes me angry. Henry was an icon and loved by folks everywhere except by those motivated by greed, critters ruled by money! I know officials won't like the truth but I firmly believe I never lost a contest but quite a number of results went against me. I boxed Parris in London for my first contest, which, to my utter disbelief, was awarded to him, then he got the verdict on the second occasion in London but on our third meeting, I didn't lose a single round, so however did he manage to win twice in London? Never, absolute rubbish, but of course the referee, would you believe, Harry Gibbs? I say, to all upper coming boxers from rural districts, avoid London venues like the dreadful plague, need I say any more? And get a top-class manager who picks fights to suit you.

Danny Mahoney stated, "I've fixed you up."

"And that, my love, is exactly what happened with a bout abroad in Copenhagen against heavyweight, Flemin Yensen," said Lorraine. Yes, I went on my Jack Jones up to London and eventually arrived at Heathrow airport where I met George Francis who informed me that I was booked on a flight with his lads to Oslo in Norway! We arrived at the venue and we parted company! A chap asked me to wait in the main lobby but instead, I went into the weighing room and was informed my opponent wasn't Flemin Yensen but Rudi Bjorn! Apparently, they pronounce their surname first! I'd never heard of him, then a fellow pointed this giant out as he weighed in. His weight registered 18 stones and 4 lbs! I was 13 stones 2 pounds, but this never bothered me. Now, I was boxing the champion of Norway for peanuts! Is there a Flemin Yensen? Should I refuse, they pointed out there was no return ticket available, so I'd have to pay for my flight home! Now, this gigantic oak tree would feel my wrath, and I intended to fell this enormous blubber mountain! Rudi was a total scumbag just like Mike Tyson, and I don't mince words! Not skilful but deliberate head butters who should have been barred for eternity, but they were allowed inside a boxing ring by officials seeking money. Why the hell were these thugs ever allowed to box? What a disgrace, don't you agree, boxers like Tyson were to the traditional noble art of boxing were a disgrace and should have been slung out and the infamous Queensbury rules, where did they go? Gentlemen, please, let's call time for this type of guy because these evil vagabonds cannot be credited as gladiators in our sport unlike our great legends of the heavyweight division such as Lennox Lewis, David Hayes, and of course, needless to say, myself, need I say more? And most of my courageous opponents!

According to Bjorn Rudi's corner men, I possibly scraped every round, leading up to the seventh even when this ginormous goon grabbed me followed by a rabbit punch before holding me in a headlock and sticking his thumb into one's eye right in front of this German. umpire! What did the referee do? Answer, absolutely nothing, nowt; finally, a small cut from his constant nutting opened! Had I returned his dirty compliment, this judge would have disqualified me, no doubt in my mind whatsoever! I stood up for round seven, only to be told this match, a ten rounder, was now over!

Apparently, the venue was booked until twelve midnight and had overrun. And he was awarded this contest, bull, it was because I was hammering home some heavy artillery, which did not suit their promoter, so when I returned home, I got in touch with the boxing board of control because this bout should've been a non-contest, and they did, would you believe, nowt? Thanks a bunch, correct! Guess where our British board of control is? Fact, in Cardiff, Wales, and what did they do for Michael Watson? Answer, zero, sweet Fanny Adams! I'd like to point out undeniable facts! According to the boxing records, I've been KOed by a pillock powder-puncher named Bjorn Rudi! This is rubbish, seeing I've never been floored by anyone in or outside a ring, although there are some yellow dogs who have made claims behind my back, which are untrue! I've been attacked by citizens from the rear like back stabbers, the lot! These gutless freaks aren't worthy of another mention. The evening I boxed Tim Wood, the Heavyweight Champion Of Great Britain, Bunny Johnson was at ringside and the European Heavyweight Champion Richard Dunn was also in the audience and this theatre was chock-a-block. Incidentally, Richard Dunn, who later boxed the great Muhammad Ali, came to my dressing room with his son and said, "I want to shake your hand," which was magic, truly fantastic, then he stated, "I've beaten Wood, and you've been robbed by a crooked referee!" Or words to that effect! What a wonderful gesture, don't you agree? The reigning champion of Europe came into my changing room to speak to me, a Joe Bloggs! I'll never forget that evening.

"God bless you, Richard Dunn, for that amazing gesture which I sincerely appreciate and so rightly deserved, Richard, just joking."

"Crash, bang, wallop, Del boy."

"What? Rodney."

"Sid dumped Tim Wood in the seventh then walked into the wrong blood-stained corner, would you believe?"

Crunch "No."

"Yes."

"Unbelievably, Sir Sugar Ray Robinson did this on a prior occasion."

"Referee John Coyle looked at Wood's corner men before commencing his official count then stopped, ushered boyo into the other corner before continuing the count from where previously he'd finished but by this time, precious seconds had elapsed."

"According to this umpire, Rodney Wood raised at nine but he'd been definitely floored for a lot longer, maybe fourteen seconds? Then Sid poleaxed him again."

"Del, blood splattered this canvas finally, the bell rang out."

"Yes and the last round, he ran away like a caged rat, constantly avoiding Falconer, reminiscent of a small mouse being chase by a cat, Tom and Jerry springs to mind then the final ding dong registered!"

"A bent Coyle, sorry, Johnny," cried Derek Trotter, sitting ringside as the referee hoisted the arm of top contender for the light-heavyweight championship of great Britain aloft!"

"I bet a lot of folks in the audience reckon Umpire John Coyle should have gone to SPECSAVERS."

"Rodney, you plonker, I'm in agreement!" Next, I'd like to point out ABA Champions like Peter McCann, Graham Sines, John Conteh and Garfied McEwan were poached by the top brass professional fraternity and groomed for stardom at the Royal Albert Hall in London! Conteh climbed down from the heavyweights to light heavy and became the number four contender, taking my official ranking!

This meant I was not eligible for the British title eliminators! My manager contacted Conteh's management and stated Falconer wanted a match in order to rectify this situation but they refused so Jack Turner contacted Finnegan's management and offered them the entire purse! I had nothing to lose and everything to gain; should I lose, then I'd lost to a former Olympic and reigning British champion but if I won, the next fight would possible be against Bob Foster for the world title but Chris Finnegan turned my offer down! Maybe he thought I was a lunatic, instead, boxed Conteh, and I'll state now, as I was an undercard that evening at the Empire Pool, Wembley, I was blatantly robbed of the decision against Sines! That occasion, Chris won by a mile but the umpire awarded Conteh the bout! Only my opinion but I'd state Sid Nathan, Roland Dakin and Harry Gibbs were in the palm of the bookies. Fixies are real common in every sport, possibly even including championship darts but who would ever believe that? "Hey, Barry Hearns, what do you reckon?"

"Ask the B.D.O," cried a rodent!

Heavyweight Eddie Fenton and I touched gloves and stood toe to toe matching blow for blow, which I won then our second meeting took place in Birmingham, West Midlands, United Kingdom, according to the record books but I firmly believe it was in London! The return fixture was duly organised then a week prior to the bout, I was informed Eddie wanted to box me at light-heavy, which I accepted. I was heavy and to oblige him had to reduce my weight so my wife and I went to Cardiff, where her cousin, Roy Agland a former Olympic and professional boxer, resided. At the WMCA training facility, sweat rolled off me, and I've shed weight! The first evening, I weighed in at 13 stone 2lbs! The air felt hot and by the end of the training session, I weighed out at 11 stone 12 lb. Every night, I drank plenty of liquid and ate quite heartedly, not realising too much weight loss in such a short period would weaken my metabolic! I weighed in for the Fenton fight a week later at just over 12st 6lbs and inside the statuary light-heavyweight limit! Eddie was not at the weigh in but later, his official weight was recorded at 12 st 13 1b which I refute! Who witnessed this weigh in? I don't believe for one minute Fenton was under fourteen stone but never mind. A straight left jab connected solidly, opening an horrendous gash above his eye within seconds of the opening round, and this corner man said, "an early evening just attack that cut." I wanted to beat him fairly because I certainly could, and anyone can sustain a wound! No way was I going to attack his misfortune but round seven, I became lethargic and by round eight was extremely tired, which was not normal for me. Usually, I'd get stronger but this night, something was obviously wrong! Eddie finished badly mauled, and I was well aware from corner men that I'd done more than my share to be awarded this fight especially as I could have blasted that cut but the contest was awarded to Fenton! Rex Hurley said after the bout that he'd expected at least a draw! Six weeks later, my Manager, Danny Mahoney, saw Eddie Fenton and spoke to his Dad, enquiring as to the condition of Eddies face! "Who had Ed fought since Sid?" "Nobody," came a reply! "This is the result of boxing that gladiator!" My manager asked for another contest saying, "Sid wants a third fight against Big Ed as he wasn't happy with their last meeting and has stated he'd fight Eddie at any weight!" His father replied, "My son will box Sid on the very last show of the year because it takes six months to get over boxing him!" What a wonderful compliment? A bout was arranged just before Christmas and I turned up but Eddie did not! Nothing was heard from the Fenton camp, and I want no excuses from them! I suppose Fenton didn't relish the thought of six month in plaster! To fill this venues boxing menu, I offered to fight two light-heavies simultaneously but they refused! On reflection, I wouldn't box me anyway, as I'm an ugly beast at the best of times.

The Southern Area Light-Heavyweight Championship, at the World Sporting Club, Grosvenor House, Mayfair, 17//1975! Against Johnny Wall was obviously staged in London, and of course, the referee was honest as a second is long, would you believe, old Harry Gibbs? According to my corner man and coach, Peter Fay, I won at least eight rounds out of ten but Gibbs awarded Wall this contest! I immediately refuted his verdict, saying, "I won that bout by a wide margin," he just turned away! What a shitehouse! I'd beaten Johnny easily and at no time felt in any danger or doubt of the outcome so one could imagine how I felt at the outcome, and Wall never had the guts for a return match, and it was me, not him, who climbed the British ranking! Apparently, only two people in the crowd thought Wall had won. His father and Steve, what's his name? I say, ring-siders are better judges than Harry Gibbs, the most bent umpire in history, according to yours truly, and they said I'd won, and as far as I'm concerned, they'll do for me, amen. Anyway, for a man who'd suffered two broken feet, a fractured back and broken pelvic girdle, I didn't do too bad, did I? A few years later, circumstances changed, altering my perspective; now disillusioned with boxing, I retired at the age of thirty-two! I was organising door security at night-clubs, pubs in Poole, Bournemouth, Christchurch, Southampton and Lymington! Now, this brings me back to my boxing days and Mick Cottingham! A Trojan warrior is how I would describe him—a gladiator with immense physical durability and quality. He'd stand there, displaying his hardware, then like the phantom of the opera, unexpectedly, he'd slip a punch then counter, with a powerful jab, then moved away, intelligently! We installed bouncers but as I like to say, pleasant gentle giants, in umpteen establishments, who would say, "Hello, good evening, and welcome!" That's what I liked, not mouthy idiots, like Stevenson and Co, who were just thugs in my opinion! Now, changing the subject, let me assure you, not all councillors are crooks but I think maybe, at least, ninety-nine percent, I reckon, are. Later, I'll tell you a whimsical little story! Boxing gave me an excellent name, and citizens trust me!

Our police force are indeed exceptional except for one particular licencing officer, Inspector Malcolm Roberts! A nasty piece of workmanship just like W02 Dennis, from Strensall, and Staff-Sergeant Moose Rielly, whom I knew in Berlin!

"Titter, titter," remarked Frankie Howard.

"Oh flipping 'ek, Your Majesty, another one bit the dust," said Tommy Cannon.

"Would you believe it?" replied Liz Frazer.

"Yes, I believe," exclaimed Johnny Jagger. In complete contrast to Sergeant John Matthews of the Poole branch, this fellow was a marvellous chap, as were Ian Swarbrick and Inspector Roger Pierce!

"And you can take that from the horse's mouth," exclaimed Roger!

I'm heading back in time to days when working for Unigate Dairies at Fleetsbridge, delivering milk and goods. My round began at Springdale road in Broadstone, Poole, Dorset. Let me state I was in full training, so I ran along each driveway to the rear of properties and deposited a pint or two, however, there was one particular house where this lady would leave a message, "No milk today but would you please leave half a dozen eggs?" I'd place milk down and next morning, leave eggs in order that she learn how to treat a milkman. It never worked, but I must say, that Christmas, she left me a wonderful card, with more money than any of my other customers, and I will also say I had a fantastic clientele. I eventually left the milk company after a bust up with John, the manager! The staff at Unigate were absolute mustard, jolly jesters, the bunch, and I'll never ever forget the day they took a case of milk off my loaded electric cart! Towards the end of my road, I ran out of fresh milk, would one believe? And I couldn't, for the life of me, think why.

Back at base, a person said, "Sid, did you forget this?" pointing towards a crate full of milk.

"Yes, by the way, are these your set of keys to that jaguar?"

"They are," he replied.

"Cheers, I'll deliver my milk, thanks." Funny, it only happened once. A day after leaving Unigate, out of the blue, nightclub door manager, Bob Shepherd, offered me an evening job attending the door at Raffles, in Bournemouth! We resided at Chatsworth road in Parkstone, Poole, Dorset! On a more serious note, next door to us lived the Onion family, who were a fabulous bunch. John, their marvellous father, died in a car park which was tragic, and I'll never forget the day that such a wonderful man passed away. We were gutted, and as memory lingers, I recall our neighbour's children playing merrily with Sidney on our stationary speed boat out front and cheerfully knocking a football around and reading my comic books, and I also remember, their happy nature. What a wonderful period of my life; sadly, there are occasions of sadness mingling with joy. Daily, I'd spend time practicing my golf swing in the rear garden, for six hours, before attending a golf course, but sometimes, early in the morning, I'd travel to Queens or Merrick Park with my official caddy, Francis Payne, who I'd taught to box, and indeed, he became extremely good. Fought as an amateur, winning the lot, then abruptly retired; now, let us take a trip down memory lane and those double wooden gates in our rear garden with slits between each strip of wood of approximately two inches, just enough room for me to slip my hand through. I was two years of age. This day, an older lad passed eating an ice cream; out went my hand with speed of lightning, and that cornet was mine! He yelled! His mum went to the main entrance at the front to report a theft! This was hilarious, a real scream; father could see the funny side but this woman couldn't.

Dad said, "My God, your son must be at least six whereas my son is two!" He paid for their ice cream. Next occasion, I went into my parents' bedroom and found a stash of notes in a hidden drawer! A pile of white things, printed, crisp paper but unbeknown to me, they were new five-pound notes! I was four by then, so I went to my pals who distributed them amongst the community! Father, finding the cash missing, went to the Mannings' house, searching for his dosh! Found some in black dustbins, but by then, all the ladies in Bethnal Green had gone shopping! Mister Mannings went to the dog track! Years later, my dad told me there were a thousand pounds in that compartment! Those days, dad was paid £80 a week, sparring cash! Folk paid for storage of stalls and lots of cash came from sale of second-hand clothes! One didn't put money in banks! I expect he didn't want the taxman prying around, hence the secret location!

After leaving Unigate, as I've stated previously, Bob Shepherd offered me the head doorman job, paying £80 per week! I said I wouldn't get out of bed for that sort of money! One knew this nightclub was having trouble with a few unsavoury customers! He upped the ante to £150 to which I said,

"Make it £180, and I'll let you know." We shook hands! I started work, watching the customers but doing nothing! Working on the till was either Johnny Fuller, a former Mister Universe bodybuilder who was also an ex-professional boxer, indeed, from Jack Turner's boxing stable which included myself, or one of the bosses. Every night, people would say, I'm a pal of Johnny Fuller, then walk past them as though they were infantile! After a week, I attended the door.

When those weasels knocked, I opened to words of, "I am a friend of John," to which I remarked, "I run this show, not Johnny! Should one like to come in, I'm Sid Falconer, and manners must improve or you'll not come in this establishment again! Do you understand? Now, enter!" I said, "Fuller, if you ever raise your hands to me, I'll take your head off, do you understand?" When I knock clientele out, it's because they were getting out of order, and I wouldn't tolerate this type of nonsense! After a time, I said to one of the owners that I couldn't work with an urchin who did nothing when trouble was in store! He was frightened of Fuller, so when Johnny came into work one evening, I told him I'd sacked him and to leave! He did so without any fuss! Everything was running smoothly, shipshape, hunky-dory, and I was running the door, along with two special associates, Paul Layton and Nigel Drew, and I also knew my back was well guarded! One could trust them with your life! At times, this was monster. The third doorman, Roger Rider! An outstanding, professional boxer who fought Tony Sibson and Errol Graham left the club because I let riff-raff in the nightclub! This was true, but I could control them when I was around! This gave me leverage! Nobody but me was in charge, and that's the way I liked it!

Bob Shepherd was Paymaster General, our bread and butter. Next door to this nightclub was the owner's restaurant, managed by Sean, who looked after us like lords of the manor! He supplied me with cooked meat for our dog! Wednesday, sandwiches were arranged for members! I took a supply home for my mother and wife! Nightly, people would invite me to have a beer. I replied, "Tell the barman! He'll give you a chit. I'll collect the drink later, if that's ok?" I took a case of ale every couple of days. Each week, there was a raffle draw which I won. Every week, one of us went next door with our wives for a meal and a bottle of wine;

eventually, one of the owners said doormen are not allowed to win the raffle. I won the draw and sold it. Bob Shepherd got a job at Oscars, Royal Exeter, and invited us to join him with the understanding that my wage increased and that I ran the door! He agreed! Bob was sheer mustard, caviar! Got in a pickle on more than one occasion but I, like a knight in shining armour, came to his rescue as he'd done for me! Bobby supplied smart black dress suits paid for by our boss, John Church. One night, at Raffles, I overheard Paul Layton say, "Let's get Sid drunk!" At the time, I was standing at the entrance, speaking to a bunch of ruffians!

Earlier, I went down the stairs to the lower section of this nightclub, returning shortly after. At the desk was a queue reaching outside, gathering three abreast. Two Irish navvies were about to pay when I noticed their genitals were on the loose! I rushed over, grabbed them in their privates and marched them through the door! One of the owners said, "Are you, insane?"

"No," said I, "they were privates, not sergeants!" What a hoot! Now, back to Paul's conversation with Nigel. It was time to teach them a lesson which they'd never forget, knowing they'd already downed a pint. This was my chance! Let the battle commence! "Lads, do you fancy a beer?" I was falling into their trap, or was I?

"I'll get it," exclaimed Paul. I drank the first pint slowly, then Nigel placed a second before me!

"Thanks, gentlemen! Shall we toast Her Majesty? God save the Queen!" And quite slowly drank from my first pint, then it was my round and so on, until time was right, then four gulps and this glass was empty! Next beer went down a treat. Before long, I'd overtaken them and I could see they were struggling to cope with this quantity! By the end of this evening, they were drunk as skunks and walked like two drunken sailors, and I drove home, sober as a judge! No way, I caught a taxi, and that was the end of that particular saga! On the grapevine came word of establishments having terrible problems with difficult customers! I approached the owners, inviting them to Oscars! To show how control could be and that I would supply them with staff to manage their doors, if that's what they wanted! I would supervise their door personally with their guide lines! Black dress suits became my code of practise! Along the southern coast, Falconer Security became trustworthy door staff! Owners flocked to my doorstep! Soon, my security was situated everywhere in Bournemouth! Pubs, clubs, wine bars, then I expanded to the outer regions: Poole and Bascombe Christchurch, Lymington Southampton. I purchased walkie-talkie radios for each premises under my control! In cars, units and masts were positioned at our house, another on top of our night-club which we purchased in 1984! I had radio link-up in establishments, and I'd talk to my wife, Lorraine, from anywhere!

If anytime, day or night, staff called for assistance, back up was duly sent! We had cars, mobile units with six beefy men, ready to attend any situation! Roger Ryder, Paul Layton and Tony Brooker are my friends and indeed, perfect managers, Paul being our funny man! They delivered wages and collected money from the proprietors! One evening, this rainstorm swept in. A little elderly lady, down on her luck, asked me for a pound for a cuppa. I gave her £5; next, Layton handed over a £20! We were flabbergasted by an obvious generosity! I said, "Bravo pal, one takes one's hat off to you!"

He said, "Why?"

I said, "That is really a touching thing that you did."

"Why?" We were amazed by his generosity towards this lady, then he said, "It's your dough!" What a joker? He never failed to bring out his good intentions with other folks' cash! That's our Paul. We loved him to bits! One couldn't have picked better than these three mates! Each new day came little and large incidents! Does that ring a bell? Tony Carpenter joined us and Peter Robinson, Ted Siddall from Liverpool! By this time, the Branksome Arms at Bournemouth Triangle was like our headquarters where men could be contacted. We took up residence at the Gander on the green. We took security to the Pinecliffe, Southbourne! One Sunday night, Peter Launder rang, saying there was some heavy trouble in store! Could we send a mobile patrol? Instead, I went. Tony Carpenter accompanied me for back up. Inside, two people, one approximately six-feet eight-inches tall and built like a brick wall. His arms were reminiscent of a big, giant, oak tree. I sat at the bar. These characters put their pints on the counter, then turned away! I signalled to a girl behind the bar to remove the drinks and tip them down the sink. She did, without wasting a moment. Next, they got loud.

I said, "If you are looking for trouble, you've come to the right place! Let's walk outside and sort this out!" Outside, they walked away, then punched a window. I said, "That is silly!"

One remarked, "Come on, let's have a punch-up!"

"Let's go back in the hall, and sort it out!" In the hallway, I tickled Patrick O'Finn with a well-timed fist. Six teeth popped out, and blood poured profusely!

"In future, keep your mouth shut, not open." And another gobshot bites the dust!

"You hit, Pat!" He came at me but a crashed blow from my huge left hand sent an Irish Navy to the promised land! "Drag him out," said I to the other man.

Peter said, "Why didn't you knock the other prat out?"

I replied, "Who is gonna drag this ogre out? Not you or I, now, wasn't that good fun?" I don't like knocking folk out, but if you are going to hit somebody, one might as well enjoy! Know what I mean? Ha-ha-ha. My hands are me good luck charms!

We moved from London a day before my ninth birthday up to Bradford; mum wanted to be near our grandmother, who lived in Haworth outside Keithley, Yorkshire. I went to school and met cock of the school, Keith Sharkey, a hard chap which certainly became fact! This fellow said, "Let's see what you're made of!" He punched me in the midriff; well, blow me down, he could deliver and I knew what it felt like, being hit with a jackhammer, but I took his punch, knowing he's gonna be my mate, and until this day, I'll never ever forget, it really hurt! I met Audrey Dilger, a pretty girl, then served in the army with her brother, Albert! At school, a dozen children smoked and wanted whisky! And so, I supplied it! (Nice little earner).

The Principal contacted my folks and invited them for a chat! I got it in the neck, because Audrey grassed on me by telling the headmaster that I was supplying cigarettes to them, which I was, for a price! Nice little earner until then! From the age of eight, I suffered grumbling appendix—a wee outgrowth of tissue forming this tube-shaped sac attached to the lower end of the intestine! It seemed to worsen after exercise or at night-time. At the age of fifteen, I joined the band. 1st Prince of Wales own Junior Leaders. Stationed at Strensall, five miles from York! We underwent training on an obstacle course, in weaponry and unarmed combat. The assault area consisted of a variety of equipment. Pieces ranging from the death slide to scaling rope ladders, before creeping under wired sections. Later, everybody attended education and band practise. Bandmaster Mister Green, a brilliant fellow. Warrant Officer Dennis was a real nasty little pig and one horrid son of a goat! The best people were Corporal Gee and education officers Major Bachelor and Captain Cave.

In our troop was Barry Flood who attended Usher Street school in Bradford; I attended the same school. There was rivalry between us: who was best at maths? At Usher street, Barry recorded a higher mark than me and finished top of the class! Now, revenge! When the final score was published in our exams at Strensall, I avenged the defeat with a victorious perfect score. What a triumph! My mum remarried and was now Jean Lovell. Her first husband was killed, hit by a German Sniper, then she married my dad, finally, came John, her third husband! He was magic! What a singer, sounded like Dean Martin, Bing Crosby, and Mario Lanza all rolled into one! Never in my life have I heard anyone match that. He died aged fifty; I was gutted. Met Johnny Jagger. He's in my other book named Headache, about elves, pirates and rodents, one named Musci Moss; he's the boss and has a couple of devout followers, Peat and Bog. If you get a chance, I suggest you read it! You may find it's just your cuppa! Johnny was, I'd say, slightly schizophrenic, hence I named him mad-dog Jagger. Picking the different tales is enjoyable!

Roger Ryder springs to mind. On this occasion, we were outside a wine bar in Christchurch road, Bournemouth, having been requested by the owner to attend. When we arrived, there was a confrontation at the door with Steve, his business associate. Three fellows were arguing saying they were going into this establishment or they'll cause a fracas, even said they'd bash Steve! That was out of order, far as I'm concerned, they're noisy and causing a disturbance! Argumentative and quarrelsome! Now, we approached them, then a punch sailed through the air towards Steve; I blocked it. A moment later, Roger said words like, "That's it, leave before you get hurt!"

Paul remarked, "Easy, Rider." One moved behind me threateningly; Layton swung into action! "This guy has a blade!" Fearing for my safety, he moved in front of me! Should this knife implant, it was my mate who'd take it, not me! Layton counter-attacked, sending this villain back; Paul head butted the assailant. "That was a close shave!" An encounter we don't need! Roger danced around floating like a butterfly, next second, stung like a bee; well, this ogre lay prostrate, and I said, "Jolly Roger, another one bit the dust!"

Everything appeared quite bizarre, most surreal, not even the rustle of leaves, just a deadly hush! Moments passed, then an elder spokesman said, "I can't feel a pulse!" Ryder was gone with the wind! Clark Gable couldn't hold a candle to our comrade! That's fact! We eventually located him, propping up the bar at Enters nightspot!

Paul said, "Roger, it was self-defence! What other option was there?" A couple of men gave statements, but nothing became of this incident! I can't recall what happened to the dagger but, I say, this hostile clash may have resulted in a fatality! There were a number of fracas at Spats but frankly, they were against gutless, back stabbers, nonentities not worthy of a mention, except for one particular occasion! A contract was issued, put on me!

It was about ten pm Sunday evening. Five men, including Jake Lovell, who sat in a getaway car outside Spats. Four duly entered. I was working as the duty doorman, had phoned in prior. Looking back now, he knew a fracas was due. He'd been warned as he was an ex-employee of this club security. In those days, apparently, I was treading on Dave Smith's toes! This, I say, but a year later, we became the best of pals! One day, Lorraine and I were ordered to attended his funeral by his direct command, just joking! Dave was a character. I miss him, believe me. Four tall, roughly dressed gents I'd never before seen entered Spats! Two men, resembling gangsters, came around this bar and approached me! One henchman was Alan Spurlock, the other, Peter Hannon, who resembled an orangutan. My reputation proceeded me. Apparently, they were wearing protectors and mouth guards! Spats was full! Pete said, "There's trouble at the door!" I'd an idea these goons had come for me as, earlier, I'd been informed trouble was on the way. My wife was sitting at the bar, speaking to Denise, Wim Vanderburg's wife; he was one of the owners. I certainly did not want her involved!

The only option I had was to say, "Gents, I'm aware you've come for me! Let's go outside, and we can continue this discussion." They agreed to my request so, I went between these thugs, knowing they'd attack me from behind like cowards, then this monumental blow to the back of my head! I turned, saying in a dull-witted tone, "I'm slow!" My hands raised to protect myself as umpteen blows from a truncheon rained in! Another assailant hit me from the rear! I turned into this darkness and couldn't see anybody. Turned out to be Bebby, a coloured gentleman. This fourth person named Nigel Young was recognised and decided to stay out of this unprovoked attack! Fearing this situation was now getting out of control, Pete rushed me, and I fell between a table and a partition onto a wooden seat. This table was laden with many empty glasses and bottles! All this time, Peter hammered me with a long lead pipe! Alan Spurlock picked up this green bottle, which appeared red, as I swept this table of glassware! I knocked the bottle out of Spurlock's hand. Next, two pretty ladies hopped on his back! Hannon kept banging away with the pipe, then I landed on a concrete floor with Alan calling, "Have you had enough?"

I casually remarked, "Pal, give me a break," and got up, suggesting I haven't started yet, then I punched him in his stomach as Wim shouted, "Take them outside!" It was a moonlit night and the air felt cool.

Peter said, "Stick his head through this glass window!" Fully conscious and aware of their intention, I struck Hannon in his flabby midriff; instantly, I knew he was now indisposed; finally, I could turn my fullest attention to a despicable badger. This was going to be a sincere pleasure and now, the time is nigh, and so, they face the final curtain!

I'd suffered but now, it's your turn! Spurlock stepped back bewildered; I was still standing! My clenched hands flew into action in double quick time; one, two, three! Both sides of the ribs, then into his face! His eyes glazed. "Yes, it is my time! The end is near! It's playtime! Come to daddy!" Next instant, the police rushed me. I yelled, "I give up!"

Two females, seeing the constables take hold of me, said, "It was those attacking him!" Now, Pete punched a copper! They moved away, leaving me unattended. I turned towards an officer,

"Plod, answer me, have I the authority to act on your behalf! without prejudice?"

"Yes," came his reply. I punched Hannon, and he bent over like a large toad! My word, didn't I enjoy this moment! Four police officers carried Hannon to a Black Maria. A police vehicle and Alan went to hospital. I went to Madera road station where I made a statement, then home. A cop said he would let me know when I could attend Poole hospital. The time now was after midnight.

The incident occurred around ten pm. At four am, I decided it was time I went to hospital where they stuck me in a cubicle; finally, a surgeon came to me, very apologetic! "I am sorry to have kept you waiting but I've been busy operating in the theatre since ten forty, rebuilding a person's nose; unfortunately, I removed several broken teeth and repaired three broken ribs."

I replied, "It was me! I did that to those putrid plonkers outside Spats wine bar!" The police retrieved two gum-shields and foul proof cups, also a truncheon. Hannon was rushed to hospital, suffering internal bleeding. Apparently, he nearly died! After the court case, where their brief stated how well I appeared and that his clientele had suffered so much, Alan Spurlock applied for a job with our security, which I granted, provided he said hello, good evening and welcome! I never got any complaints; then he went to London! I gave him a good reference, and he got the job. A few years passed, then he died. This hurt! Nigel Young also worked for us and Jake Lovell. After that, Dave's business nose-dived and he too worked for us but as a genuine friend. His sister, Sylvia, became a barmaid at Valentino's Nightclub. Steve, their younger brother, came to help me with great effect. I've no regrets meeting them Smith clan. It was one hell of an occasion, mark my words; I'll not forget Dave, that is for certain! For this chapter, I dedicate to an amazing character who built an empire.

Once again, I travel back in time. Father used to take me into the basement where the light was dim and this rugged bag hung like a gigantic green monster, swaying to and fro, squeaking like a little rodent caught in a mousetrap. This gave me the creeps; eventually, I punched the bag. Tap, tap. That was me back then. Now, it's crash, bang, wallop! Next, I'm travelling forward from those very early times, not to this present day but to a time when

I ran the door at the Halfway House on Bournemouth Road which has now been renamed Grasshopper. It was after midnight when Tony Carpenter and I were going back to my place where he'd left his car then as usual drive home. He lived with his dad, John, and mum, Lorna. On this occasion, he said, "I've a funny notion there is trouble in store!" Next second, the car phone rang!

"Hello Lorraine!"

"Sid, where are you?"

"We're coming home."

"There's a fracas at the Halfway!"

"Be there in a minute!" Outside the pub was a large crowd.

The door attendant, Peter Launder, approached me saying, "This fellow was causing trouble," and pointed to a maggot. "Earlier, he withdrew a blade and threatened us, and he's got mates so I called for assistance, ok?"

We were standing in a car park, an area for maybe forty cars, like a cattle pen. It was dark but light from a doorway gave us a clear view of everyone. Tony Brooker had already arrived from Corkers wine bar and restaurant in Poole and was organising security. Earlier, he'd been informed that we were now on route and advised not to entertain these rough diamonds. Mister Brooker approached a man who'd caused a disturbance suggesting he should stop creating problems and leave before he gets hurt. This culprit said, "I am not going until I'm good and ready! I want my knife and jacket!" Next instant, he called out, "I'm gonna take those bouncers out!" I advised him against this course of action and told him that I, in fact, was their boss and could call the constabulary who'd possibly arrest him. He became most aggressive and threatened my life!

I replied, "I'm Sid Falconer, an ex-professional boxer, so refrain from using such uncouth behaviour."

He said, "So what! I'll take you!" Plus, talk which I can't repeat!

Another gent came over, stating, "This beefy lad is my nephew, and if anyone wants to fight my brother's son, they'll deal with me, do you understand?"

"We want no trouble but he's quarrelsome and causing a disturbance and wants to fight everybody!" This chap repeated his former statement!

"Ok," said I, "now pack up or pick up ya dukes!" A punch a piece and both were sleeping quite peacefully. I looked down at the uncle. His head was in a bed of roses which looked undisturbed like Jesus Christ wearing his crown of thorns! My God, I've never witnessed such a sight! We went inside the Halfway; later, when we left, these two characters were walking with arms around each other's shoulders.

I shouted to them, suggesting they come across. The uncle murmured, "What do you want?"

I replied, "Come here!"

"Why?"

"I want to tell you something!" Next minute, over they came. I said, "Do you know what happened earlier?"

"I don't remember," exclaimed the uncle. "Well, I'll tell you, your nephew went to punch a chap in the face but missed, instead hit you!"

"Did you?"

"I can't recall," said the lad; next, Uncle Charlie was chasing his nephew down Bournemouth Road! What a wonderful night!

Friday evening, I, Roger, Paul, Tony Brooker and Tony Carpenter went to the Halfway to inspect our troops. When a person approached me with an invitation to box Tiny, his pal, I said, "Don't be stupid?" He went back to report my reply. After a few moments, I decided enough was enough! I went over to them. Tiny was in the region of six-feet six-inches tall, maybe even more and wide as an oak tree! I said, "Would you like to fight me?" Now, his attitude altered. "No, I saw you box Guinea Roger at Rockley Sands, Pavilion!" This faggot was showing off in front of his mates at my expense, then go around West Howe in Kinson, a notorious area for villains bragging that Sid Falconer refused an invitation. I wasn't going to have any of his shenanigans; his offer was duly accepted. He refused!

I remarked, "In the back of my vehicle is a pair of 16-ounce boxing gloves and bag protectors which you could use! We can box; I won't land a punch on you but move around you until you're tired!"

"You won't hit me?" he exclaimed. What a gutless plonker! We went into the car park. At the bottom end was an open space, so we marched over. Gloves were removed from the rear of my car. We boxed for two minutes without me laying a glove on him. How useless this prat was! He remarked enough or words to that effect. His friend suggested boxing, "Same rules apply?" It's like the ok corral, and I accepted.

This gladiator asked a fellow watching this charade to hold his watch. This rogue was better superior than first punk but after a while, decided he'd had plenty. Shook my hand, saying I was an amazing boxer and thanked me for this exhibition; finally, he turned then said, "Where's that boyo who was holding my watch? He had done a runner!

Another person in his mid-twenties, I'd say, asked if he could box. "Ok," came my instant reply. "I do kick boxing! I'll remove my plimsolls!"

A rubber-soled canvas sports shoe. The ground was covered in lose shale. He removed them and placed a watch for safe keeping inside, then this car came around the car park before running over his plimsolls. My goodness, a distinct sound of crunching rang out and the last occasion I saw this young man was running up the road after the car, screaming, "I'll kill you!"

Now, this buffoon called Tiny said he'd like another crack at me, same rules apply? I stated they were. Next, this bigot struck a foul blow, middle stump! Goosegogs, genitals and knew instantly he'd tagged a big fish, hook, line and sinker. Now, he came in for the kill but his plan wasn't going to work! Punk had urinated against the wrong tree! To sum up this situation, he'd made a bad calculation, an error in judgement. Adding up was tipsy-turvy! Let me say, it was time for me to terminate our agreement. Hasta la vista, partnership! I grabbed him as ferocious physical pain, without warning, escalated upward, then it subsided. What a cowardly act, don't you agree? Now, it was my turn! Over the top came a right hand into his face. He went back as blood spurted from his nose. "Prat, how dare you punch me in my rugby tackle?" His eyes glazed. "You git, you're lucky I don't thump the daylights out of you! Go before I thrash you! Is there anyone else? Punks make my day!"

His gang of thugs declined my offer. Lot of self-assertive, conceited bumpkins, inept morons left us with their tails firmly between their legs; know what I mean? A couple of weeks passed, then I saw him. A plaster covered the bridge of his nose. I remarked saying, "What's wrong with your nose?"

"It's broken," he replied.

"Ain't you the lucky one?"

"Sorry, Sid!"

"If I ever see you in this neck of the woods again, I'll extract your old teeth, woe betide the cost!" And I've never seen him since. Wise man! I was walking to Spats when I heard a noise coming from this alleyway so yours truly investigated. "What's going on?" Three men rushed me; suddenly, my natural instincts came into effect. It was dark and pretty eerie; then I'd hooked one and down he's gone! The other two ran into Christchurch Road. I turned back. Light from street lamps shone like a torch and I could see a black coat. Underneath this garment was a man, and he was very afraid. "I've been mugged!" I took him to Spats, then I went home; sleep beckoned. Later, the telephone rang; we were in bed. Lorraine answered.

"Spats calling for assistance!" It was around twelve fifteen pm.

"Tony Carpenter has been punched in the face, and there's three men threatening to slaughter him! He's cut and bleeding profusely!"

I remarked, "I'm on my way!" The wine bar is approximately five miles away. I dressed, hopped in the car! Six minutes later, I opened driver's door at Spats; the main door was closed. Three chaps were talking to security within. I assumed it was Tony, then it opened. Yes, my assumption was correct! He said, "I've already told you before, you can't come in!" pointing to an urchin. "You've already punched me in the eye!" Blood ebbed down his face.

This fellow replied, "I'm gonna deck you!" He continued, "Who's the hardman in there? Send him out!" What a dickhead! We'll mash his head in!" I walked over and touched him. He turned, "Who are you, the ruddy manager?"

"No," I replied.

"Who the heck are you?"

"I'm the tough guy, and there are only four of you! Now, pick up ya dukes!"

"Your Highness, he's at it again."

"Put him in the tower," commanded Elizabeth contentedly. Next words I can't repeat, but I did say, "I am your worst nightmare," then stepped forward and extracted his teeth as his mates legged it. Later, one returned.

Tony enquired, saying, "What are you doing?"

This oaf stated, "I'm searching for my pal's missing gold tooth!" Well, we laughed!

Longs wine bar in Old Christchurch Road—there are two sections to this establishment; lower is a wine parlour and upper a beer bar. Peter Launder was head of security, stationed at the main entrance when four thugs with girls entered the top bar! Throughout the evening, this group teased the door staff, mimicking them, suggesting they're in fancy dress, monkey suits! Taunting, intending to cause trouble. After a while, two suddenly attacked Peter Launder, breaking his teeth. These girls laughed! The manager, John Bloomfield, called for assistance. Within three minutes, we arrived, informed of the situation by the management who said, "No fracas, just get rid of them!" In front of the proprietor, I asked them to leave. Instead, they gave me verbal diarrhoea! I informed them saying, "I'm an ex-heavyweight professional boxer, and I am requesting all of you to leave this building!"

One replied, "If anybody is leaving, it ain't us!"

"If that is the way you lot want it, pick up ya dukes!" They came, but I conquered! The police attended. A sergeant took some statements as follows:

"Did you see Mister Falconer slap him?"

"Yes!"

"Did your boyfriend knockout this doorman's tooth?"

"Yes, in self-defence!" I went to court and produced witnesses to verify everything I'd done and response I'd received. Only when attacked did I defend myself using minimal force; unfortunately, when four people try to assault me, attempting to cause physical harm, that's when my gloves come off and I hit these louts blooming hard. Four against one! Not very good odds for them, but I am human. The judge advised these holiday makers to stay away from wine bars. Ladies, thank you for stating I gave them a slap not a punch. These girls should have been awarded a George medal for lying!

As I travel down memory lane back to Bethnal Green, I'm acutely aware of nights spent outside the forester public house, fifty yards from our sweet shop! Barry was eight, David, seven and me, four years of age! Baz, as we called him, would say to a drunk, "Give us some cash, and we'll take you home!" This man would reach into his heavy pocket and out came a handful of coins, plus on one occasion an old white five-pound note which I took. Barry said, "Sid, put it back!" David took it. After that, we'd leg it! My next memory is Victoria Park. This is a blast from the past! In a playground, Dave passed a swing-boat which looked like a gondola, light flat-bottomed boat.

Next second, this apparatus caught him in his stomach, lifting him into the air and over a fence! A woman called an ambulance which took him to hospital. X-rays revealed he'd damaged his intestines. An emergency operation was performed to replaced part with a type of plastic. David was in a coma! Doctor said he didn't think he'd live. Of course, we knew this was wrong. Dave, no way! He's strong as a lion! In the school assembly, all the children prayed.

Dad and Mum stayed by his side all day and night, then he woke blind as a bat. First words, "Dad, are you there?" We were staying with relations. Eventually, he regained his sight!

Our headmaster informed the children saying, "It gives me the greatest pleasure to announce David John Falconer is awake!" Dave had a swelling covering the left side of his face. The doc said it was a malignant tumour. These were the early stages of pioneering days.

"If he is going to live, we must operate!" Father asked for their honest opinion. "Not much hope, I'm afraid!" He was strapped down upon a bed or bench; I wasn't there so I'm unsure, but I do know they placed radium seeds on his face to kill the growth! Later, a nurse left him for several minutes! When she returned, he had broken free of the restraining gear and wiped these radioactive metallic element off his face!

They apologised for this very unfortunate incident but they were not able to repeat the procedure; apparently, the financial cost was ten thousand pounds! A time passed then surgeons removed the remains of a growth from inner layers. This operation was a success! An era passed, then Dave went back into hospital and underwent surgery to remove further tissue. Thankfully, they managed it without any complication! The first operation being successful, he returned to school. Eventually, we left London, which was absolutely terrible, completely devastating! We moved up to Bradford where we built a huge stack of timber for bonfire night but they disappeared so we went down to this place where a heap of timber, chests and skeps, large wicker containers, several settees were stacked! It was raining heavily, and there were no sentries on guard duty! Lovely, easy-peasy, simply take the trove, but Dave somehow got caught! They put him inside a mill skip, then hoisted it to the pinnacle and told him they were going to light it; later, they left! We returned soon after the storm gathered. Heavy thunder and lightning raged; then after maybe an hour, we heard a voice say, "I'm up here!" My word, God is speaking to me!

"Lord, where's our brother?"

"Sidney, up here, get me down!"

"Thank you, Lord, for giving us our brother back!"

"We'll be in church on Sunday without fail," stated Barry, and we were! At nine years of age, I was religious but never acknowledged this fact. Why? I don't know except Bradford was full of empty-headed, teddy boys with long razor-blades, flick-knifes and motor bike chains beneath their lapels!

Back from the fifties, into the eighties! Longs wine bar! The manager called for assistance! Some Liverpudlians were using threatening behaviour towards doorman Colin Hayes. Tony Carpenter and I attended the upper lounge where Monkey Joe, leader of this wild bunch, was sitting down, observing the situation. I stated, "Want a pint?" I got him a beer. "Where are Roger and Paul?"

"Joe, they're around!"

"Lads, quiet down!" His words were effective. I went to see the landlord.

A short period elapsed before I returned; well, Monkey was gone as were his funny baboons. Fearing our managers were about to arrive with recruits, they'd legged it. Later, we came across two ugly apes from longs at Spats, drinking Grolsch. This bar closes at twelve pm but there is an official half hour drinking up time. At twelve twenty, the bar attendant said, "Gentlemen please, ten minutes drinking time!" I noticed these Liverpudlians did not attempt to drink any alcohol!

"Bottle of Beer!" I just love mimicking parrots! I asked Paul Lody to advise these idiots of legality involved.

After which Ron Patterson, the bar's official glass collector and odd job man, approached these two horrid thugs. "Gentlemen, it's time."

Tony Carpenter talked to them for five minutes, all this time drink remained untouched. He returned, then Paul Layton, all to no avail. Now, it's my turn! "Brother, I'll tell you a little story! Firstly, this barman shouted ten minutes drinking up time, then Ronald Patterson came across and asked you politely to drink up! You swore at him! My colleague walked over and spent time, explaining the law! By allowing you both to drink after time, we were, in fact, committing an offence, and you haven't the slightest intention of drinking up so I now suggest you stand up and take your beer and place them on the counter then leave!" The guy nearest stood up with a bottle.

"Gopher, take it!"

"Thank you, I will," then I hooked him, simultaneously catching this bottle on his way down!

I turned towards his pal "Drag this foolish nutter out of this fine establishment and don't ever let me catch either of you in Bournemouth!"

"Sorry, boss, it wasn't me!" Paul Lody escorted him to the main entrance whilst his mate was obviously sleeping like a log. I do hope the daft oaf was taught an honest lesson! You don't mix business with pleasure! Imagine, I'm paid for dishing out this type of service! Well, I say, if you've got it, why not flaunt it? Really, I'm a big softy with a heart of purest gold! Would you believe it? "What a load of codswallop," stated Lorraine. This writing lark appears to bring out my good nature. I twitter on like this saying, birds of a feather flock together, singing sweet melody! This brings me back to a time at the Guildhall in Southampton. An incident occurred a few weeks earlier. The management asked if we could manage security at the Solent Suite. Paul Layton and I were attending this lower level bar when our doorman approached! Accompanying him was a chap who said he'd been attacked two weeks prior and these men were inside this building just waiting to pounce! He pointed to nine blokes, "That is them!"

I said, "Sit down where we can keep an eye on you!" He sat a short distance from where we stood. At the end of this evening, he came to me, asking could he use the toilet. I said, "Yes, why not?"

"They are in the gents!"

"I will check the ablutions!" It was empty. Outside were six beefy fellows plus their girlfriends. The three of us escorted him to his car. Our doorman returned to tend to his duty inside, leaving just the two of us to face this mob. Next, one of the louts directed his attention to this short stout fellow saying "We're gonna have you here or up road and give you a kicking!" A girl screamed, "Murder the punk."

I said to the lad, "If they stop your car, we can't protect you! It's outside our jurisdiction!"

He replied, "Can you call the police?"

I said, "Paul, dial 999 and ask for the police!"

A tall sucker remarked, "Who the hell are you?" This situation was getting out of hand!

"I am your worst nightmare, Sid Falconer, head of security and an ex-heavyweight professional boxer!"

He came forward, raising both arms, "Come on, shite face, I can take you!" He did not conquer although I cannot remember; I must've caught him clean as a whistle! I can't for the life of me recall what happened as it was over in a flash, with him stretched out.

Paul said, "Fight happened quickly!" After the initial fracas, someone behind me leaped forth, striking me with a truncheon! Layton said he sorted the scumbag. My head seemed somewhat weird! This chap apparently thanked us, but I can't remember! I presume we didn't go back inside the Solent Suite but instead went to our vehicle. Shortly after, Paul drove my car. I wonder why people keep banging me with fancy gadgets? Maybe in a dozen years I will think about all the punch ups and get out of this class of rat race!

At last, break time, Lorraine has brought me egg, bacon and beans on toast! "Lovely cuppa would be much appreciated!" I went to the horse and groom wine bar in Christchurch where security officers Malcolm Tottle and old pugilist, Bob Roberts, two former professional boxers, looked after the welfare of customers whilst inside or out this fine establishment. Bob Shepherd had left Oscars night spot. Now, he was managing this nightspot. He approached me, stating two thugs notorious blodgers were outside, one of which was Johnny Rivers, a well-known wrestler. "I don't want them in!" I arrived at the entrance! Boxer Tottle was keeping them at bay.

"Hello, Sid," said a gent; I acknowledged him. The other, what a doe-nut! I didn't like the look of him! He watched me with evil intent.

"Are you Sid Falconer the boxer?"

I replied, "That I am!"

"If you wanna fight!" What a plonk! "Come outside?"

Now, the last thing he expected was my reply! "Why should I come out there when you'll only stand a minute at the most?" He was rattled and taken completely by surprise; finally, he repeated his previous statement! I stepped out onto the main walkway. He removed a donkey jacket and wore bovver boots! I looked along the road. A police constable was a hundred yards away. I said, "Shall we go into a car park across this road where we won't be disturbed?"

He replied, "I don't give a tuppence about coppers!" River moved to attack! Out flashed my hands, catching him in the midriff!

"Did you like that?" Next, I prodded him in the face followed by a hook; suddenly he's on the ground! What an absolute mug, I was angry and enjoyed this!

"And another one bites the dust," said Lorraine.

All this time, across the road directly opposite us, was a black police car with four officers emerging! They'd witnessed the whole shebang unfold. Fidel, the owner of Spats wine bar, came across saying, "Sid, that was most impressive!"

This police sergeant touched my shoulder and remarked, "Sunshine!" I turned to face him. "Fourteen years I've worked here, and I've never seen that son of a bitch decked! You've made my day."

I replied, "In that case, can you inform that dickhead coming towards us to leave well alone as he's a complete moron?"

"I will do that," exclaimed this officer, patting me on the back.

"Well, I'm off inside, if that's ok with you?"

"Keep up the good work!" They turned away then walked towards this constable. I know from past experience there are always a few officers with common sense, and it's magic to meet one in Christchurch! Who would believe it? Back in 1984, we purchased a nightclub in the town of Christchurch which had been in the hands of a councillor name of Robin Green! For twenty-seven years, he operated this club illegally, but I never found out this fact until later! Of course, it is legal for a councillor but not for outsiders! Licence application was in the palm of the magistrates, then the situation changed. The council took the mantel. They had the power to refuse applicants! They were at the helm! The chief fire officer visited our club and informed me everything was illegal! We must strip the tiled ceiling. "A fire hazard, replace lighting throughout the building! Remove the bar!" It was now in way of the emergency exit. "Put a metal barrier outside to prevent fire attacking clientele leaving this way! "Install a new fire door, and make sure extinguishers are tested." Funny thing was these premises had been checked by the same fire officer prior to our purchase. Do you agree this all sounds quite strange? What a carve up and by the chief fire officer of Christchurch! I complied to his command. The fire department inspected and eventually passed our club. I repeat this fact.

For twenty-seven years, this splendid nightclub opened seven nights a week! We were raided one Sunday evening and were fined three thousand pounds! This is British justice for anyone who isn't a councillor or MP but just an honest worker. Ten months later, the chief traffic warden visited our establishment and stated, "I'm afraid you can't have a delivery of ale at the front or rear entrance anymore! You've caused a complaint!"

"Who are they?" He refused to divulge any information. I said, "How can I get a delivery?"

He said, "Get a helicopter!" That was the end of our nightclub. What sons of bitches, then I was told by a councillor that Robin Green only sold us the club to finance an election campaign for re-election and that he intended to run me out of town then purchase our club from the building proprietor at a bargain price. Robbing bastard! Well, I smashed up the club. Left everything, bar, seating and disco, which I had built with my own hands, in a neat little bundle in the centre. Funny thing was nobody purchased that nightclub!

There is a saying, once bitten, twice shy. A few years later, I acquired another nightclub, Valentines nightspot, which made me a small fortune. It was situated near Madera Road, police station. Quite handy, actually. On the corner of Stafford and Old

Christchurch Road. Looking back, my pal, Larry Allen, who I must state is a remarkable person and indeed, one of the best, was the previous proprietor. I took over the mantel and did pretty well at first and really can't complain, thanks to Allen!

Hats off to Larry! Actually, I am indebted to him. At this point, I'd like to recommend Valentines restaurant owned by Joe Flacky. They serve magical pizza. Our club, once again, became the most successful nightspot along the south coast but then, up popped Richard Carr! Never a nice oaf or a self-made man but a liar. I'm not bitter, at all, in fact, because he unintentionally did me a very good turn! He lifted a heavy load off my shoulders. It was a Sunday night in 1992 when I slung a set of keys into a black letterbox at Valentines then walked away carrying, what? Never mind, one day, I may reveal its content, but until then, I'll say no more! I've lived an amazing life, writing about things that go bump in the night and eerie occasions when visitors creep about and weird little leprechauns from over the sea visit me but I'll say no more in case I incriminate myself. Read all about it in my other book called Headache, the true story! I know much more about Richard Carr than meets an eye, but he isn't worth my time or energy! Now, I am off into those mediocre memoirs. Folk probably think I'm making this account up but I'm not. Dad and Mum went out a few times, leaving Baz, then aged eight, in charge. Barry had a mind of his own. He was a bit of a rascal and decided he wanted to go and watch a film at our local picture house we called the flea-pit! A dingy, run-down cinema but they couldn't go without taking me, so along the road, we'd go to the back-door of the roman flea-pit! They were double doors with a gap in the centre!

Barry placed a wire with a loop at one end like a lasso, then he'd catch a retaining bar and presto! The doors opened! This time, the film was the creature from the Black Lagoon. We peered through the centre of a pair of red velvet curtains, looking for an usher. She was at the far side.

This was our chance! We crept into a long row of bucket seats. Sat down, then from our rear came a loud voice. "Barry, David and Sidney, go home!" Father and Mother were sitting three rows back! In a flash, we legged it!

July, 1962, I went to Westgate, Recruiting Office in Bradford, Yorkshire. To enlist and so, I joined the army aged fifteen, along with Johnny Jagger. He was mustard and took the Queens Shilling before me, hence, his number, 23935469, mine, of course, is 23935470! Johnny was a madcap!

Wildly impulsive! Sometimes when on a route march, he'd hide under a bridge or in a ditch then as we returned, he'd re-join us without drawing attention! There were times when we were called for physical training, and he would chance his luck and hide beneath a bed, but he certainly had the golden touch with a trumpet. The bandmaster would stand at the head of the band, next, Johnny would march out to the front of the band and drums, then play music ranging from military marches to modern classics, and sometimes we'd go to the Odeon picture house in York to watch a film but he couldn't sit still for more than a few minutes.

Every time we visited a cinema, I'd wait patiently just watching him count the number of females in there, then he'd say, "Sid, I'm fed up! Let's see who can kiss the most girls?" I'll never know why but in this picture house, there was always young lasses in pairs, and we were the only single men in there! We had a field day! John was off and running over the seating like a young gazelle, he would go, and I followed. He never messed around! Straight for their jugular. "I'm Johnny, give me a kiss and cuddle?" If a reply wasn't to his liking, he'd ask me to swap partners then off he would go in search of another conquest but I, on the other hand, formally introduced myself, spent a few minutes getting to know these beautiful ladies. Johnny made me laugh! Never did see the film! Back at Queen Elizabeth barracks, Strensall, he was the joker in the pack, and we were his subjects! At the weekend, after church parade, we'd thumb a lift to Bradford via Leeds to meet friends and see our relations, then later, we'd catch the 9 pm train from Foster Square station and change at Leeds central, then take the 9:40 pm to York! Catch a bus back to camp but one occasion, I was with our Dave travelling from Leeds to York when a regular soldier, standing six-four, gave me grief. We arranged a fight to settle the issue. He was a big guy. Outside the train depot, we walked along a pathway until coming to this disused cobbled road; suddenly, he came but did not conquer! Not quite fast enough! My jabs flashed onto his large nose, and blood spurted! Lubbly jubbly! I felled the giant oak tree with a combination of, I'd say, umpteen fast, solid blows at speed of lightning followed by this one hook. Out clean as a whistle! My brother was pleased as punch. On the way back to base camp, another regular said, "I'm gonna take him apart!"

At this time, David said, "Who?"

"Him, seated at the front!"

"I wouldn't go there, if I was you!" "Why not?"

"One, he's my brother, and two, he just KOed an ogre at the train station!"

"That doesn't matter!"

"Ok, nobody else gets off this bus until it's sorted!" I went down the stairs, next, someone lashed out from behind with his boot! I got off the bus at the Silver Oyster, public house!

Dave followed this creep down the steps then said, "Ok nobody gets off this bus, and let it be a fair fight!" He turned back in my direction and was utterly surprised to see this soldier was sleeping it off! "My word, Sid, I thought it may have been a good match but it's quite obvious, I was mistaken!" Proudly, we both marched back to barracks! News of this fight spread like wild fire and I was made up with all the attention! Apparently, he was a good puncher. I'll never know because by the time he raised his hands, he was asleep.

Next, I was approached by Sergeant Garrigan, regimental boxing instructor! "Falconer, I've heard you're useful with those fists! I'd like you to box inter-company championship!" I accepted; unfortunately, the final went against me because I was toying with this opponent instead of scoring but later, Garrigan invited me to represent our regiment! Yes, those days in Colchester were grand and I enjoyed every minute but RSM Ben Campey changed everything, and circumstances altered!

One moonlit evening, after returning from town, I placed my clothes covered in beer, blood, and sick from an earlier fracas into a bath! Next morning, Lance Corporal, Mick Langthorne, who I first met at Strensall and had previously stated he'd bashed my brother, shouted out, "Whose are these clothes in this bath?" Prior to this occasion, in Berlin, I was sent to B Company 7 Platoon with Langthorne but that's another era which I will talk about in a latter part of the book but now, I'll continue this story! Mick said he punched our David. This was most unfair as my brother had part of a plastic intestine and therefore couldn't take a blow! He'd done the wrong thing, telling me, but that time wasn't right for me to exact revenge but now, it was!

"Mickey Mouse, they are mine!"

A couple of moments later, he replied, "I'm gonna put them in the garbage!" I heard this watery noise as my clothes coming out of this bath and must say this was magic! The day I'd been waiting for!

"Michael, you son of a goat," said I, walking into the bathroom. "Pick up ya dukes, pal, I'm sending you halfway to paradise," then he slid on the tiles like a stretcher case along a red polished surface, coming to a halt beneath a sink. "Good night, sweetheart!" Behind me, someone grabbed my arm. I turned and automatically slapped him! It was an acting sergeant. I can't recall his name but I was formally charged with striking two Non-Commissioned Officers, Mick Langthorne and this acting sergeant! The Commanding Officer, Lieutenant-Colonel Todd, awarded me four days detention! As a bandsman, I joined the regiment stationed in Berlin! My tutor was the Solo Cornetist for the Berlin Symphonic Orchestra! Now, everything was good until a night! Prior, I'd caught a common cold which meant I couldn't play at a venue so Band Staff-Sergeant, Reilly, known among his fellow non-commissioned officers as Moose, obviously because of his size and stature, informed me that I will be attending this concert to keep the band's instrument cases safe. Tony Morrison! A Lance-Corporal in the band said, "Purchase six cases of beer!" I went to a pub, asked a bar attendant for "Ine beir, bitter!" That's German for one beer, please! Later, I returned to the musical performance with a case which I put inside a one-tonne transporter. I went back and forth until several cases were safely stored in this army lorry. This evening was extremely dark. Shortly, after ten pm, someone was in the vehicle with the beer. I said, "Get out! What are you doing? I'm responsible for this drink!"

Somebody said, "What's up?" His voice seemed quite familiar in this darkness. I thought it was a corporal in the band named Dan Tempest, but I was mistaken!

I said, "It's ok, Corporal, I'm sorting it!" Now, walking away was Reilly! "Sorry, Staff, I didn't realise it was you!" The moose was an athlete! A big man, former rugby player.

He walked back, then said, "If you ever call me Corporal again, I'll knock the living daylights out of you!"

I'd drunk enough beers by this stage to loosen my tongue and replied, "You great lummox, pick up ya dukes!"

"God, this kid is a troubled youth," cried Windsor Davies. I jabbed him, followed instantly by a hook, and another one bit the dust, but I was arrested! On the way back to camp, I asked the Bandmaster if I could take a leak. They let me off this coach then left me barely seventeen and miles away from our base and alone in Berlin, so I visited boozers until eventually arrived at Montgomery Barracks, Claddow. I'd drank a few beers, accompanied down with Penrod and coke! Finally, reached my grand bed. Slept like a log but on awakening, required water. And became intoxicated again. Every time I've awoken, it was the same, an urgent need for liquid. Early one morning, I was awoken by two NCO's. "You are required to report to the guardroom. Commanding Officer's orders!"

"Why?"

"At ten o'clock!"

Outside the CO's office, the RSM knocked on the door, stood me at attention and off we went. "Quick march! Left, right." I entered. "Right wheel, soldier, halt!" Colonel Beckett sat behind this mahogany desk, a devious-looking man I wouldn't trust with my cat, let alone a battalion!

Sunshine softly shone through a window that morning and behind Beckett stood rat-features Reilly with, I must say, a pretty blue shiner! Massive actually, and I was most impressed! Yes, I recall this stupid blodger offering me out! A big mistake but now I'm going to suffer the consequences, that's for sure! I can't remember exactly what was said! Words went like, "Charged with an unprovoked attack!" Not true! "Whacking a Neolithic ape, more like!" True, but I only punched a toe rag! "Guilty!"

Scumbag did not tell the truth, the whole truth, and nothing but the truth! "Regimental Sergeant Major, take him away! Assigned to B company now, march him out!" "About turn, quick march!" Under guard, I was marched back to my billet! My clothes were packed; two bandsmen carried my belongings down to B Company and a corporal assigned a room, bed and locker! "Get unpacked, I'll return in one hour!" He left, closing the door! Next moment, this door opened and in came another corporal. At the time, I didn't have a clue who he was.

"I'm Rosenquest!" He could have been Adolf Hitler! "I've done your brother, now, I'm gonna do you!" This was an inopportune time to exact revenge but I'll not forget. "I don't want any trouble!" I'd just left the commanding officer's office! "Let us wrestle!" I allowed him to pin me down with his heavy legs on my shoulders then, I said, "You've won, ok?" Next second, he punched me straight in the face. I arched my back and raised my arms and over the top he went, and I stood up. Now, I was ready and willing to put this urchin in the nut house. I was trained and fully loaded, a powerful young man, ready for the kill! "Corporal, your invitation is accepted!" Next instant, this door opened once again, and in marched four NCO's!

"You are under arrest for striking Rosenquest." I calmed down but looking back now, I should have dropped them all and left their blood and guts spread across this room! I'd just come out of jail, only to face B Company commander, Major Robinson. "Stand at ease," said this sergeant. "When I knock on this door, our commander will bid you enter. I will bring you to attention, open the door, say quick march, left wheel, private, halt, do you understand?"

"Yes, Staff!" I stood there for five minutes, finally, he knocked on the door!

"Come in!"

"Attention!" He opened the door. "Quick march, left, right, left wheel, private, halt, salute, and remove your hat!"

"Soldier, you've been charged with assaulting one of my junior ranks, how do you plea?"

"Sir, not guilty!"

"Tell me what happened?"

"Sir, it all began in church! I had no Bible so I removed a deck of cards from my uniform and knelt down, then I placed an ace! On a bench! This card, Sir, reminds me that there is only one god! Lord in heaven!"

"Holy Moses," cried Major Robinson. "What are you saying?"

"I don't know but sir, Wink Martindale got away with it, so why not me?" Folks, this story is true; I know, I was that soldier!

"Falconer, think before you speak!"

"Yes, sir, I am!"

"Private this is a very serious offence!"

"Sir, Rosenquest, I believe, came from D Company looking for trouble! I've come from clink and the commanding officer with references. I need this like a pain in the neck!"

"Is that correct?"

"Yes, sir!"

"Fetch Corporal Rosenquest."

"Sir!"

"This case is admonished, march him out!"

"Sir."

"Dismissed!"

"Salute, Company Commander, about turn, quick march, right wheel, left, right!" Now, let me return to a day when two strange-looking guys arrived at Curtis Road! I looked out the window and saw these men who could've been louts, vagabonds, thieves standing by our car! Let us face it, how would you feel? What would you say or do if someone came onto your private property without introducing themselves? I went outside and asked what they were doing on our forecourt with an iron bar. They could have attacked me with that large burglar's crowbar. I said, "Who are you? What are you doing?"

They replied, "We are police officers!"

I stated, "in plain clothes?" Now, the pavement is a dozen feet from our front door! On our private forecourt stands my pride and joy, a 4 point 2 Jaguar car!

I couldn't believe this! Two people claiming to be the constabulary, who never once produced any identity card, stood by my car with a jemmy, ready to force entry and damage our car without first consulting us! "What the devil are you doing with that iron tool?"

"Falconer, we've been information from an informer that your tax disc is fake, and we are acting on this information!" I'm unsure of their exact words. "We want that tax disc!"

"What?"

"We believe it's a forgery!"

"What the devil are you talking about?" I was totally confused! Still, no identification! "What are you gonna do with that jemmy?"

They looked at each other, then stated, "We're going to open the jaguar door!"

"With that crowbar?

"Yes!"

"Where's your authority?"

"We're police officers!"

"Why couldn't you knock on my door and simply ask to see the tax disc?"

"We don't need your authorisation! Now, I was hopping mad! Let's face it! Chief Constable, Prince William or any reader, what would you say or do if the police came to your house and planned to jemmy your car and remove your tax disc without showing their badges or any identification whatsoever? And one isn't allowed or supposed to say anything! Could this be right?

I said, "I want police officers in uniform here!"

They replied, "We're going to report you for obstructing the law!" I said, you'd better leave before I leave you both in a pool of blood!

They left saying, "We'll fix you!" I received a notice to attend the magistrates court charged with using a false road tax! I went to court but it was obvious they were for the police, and I wasn't going to get a fair trial, so I decided to go to crown court. I couldn't afford legal aid, so I was forced to represent myself in court, I produced several documents from Swansea verifying I had a current tax disc for this period in question, so why would I have a fraudulent tax disc when I have a current one; it doesn't make sense! A letter from a criminal residing in Dorchester Prison was handed to the judge, which I believe he should not have accepted and the jury shouldn't accept this kind of information, but this judge is the law! The fellow stated, in writing, that he had never met me but forged a tax disc for my-plate number.

This criminal did not appear to give his testimony! The law court found me guilty! The judge said if I'd pleaded guilty, the fine would've been £100, but because I pleaded not guilty, the fine is £1000! I said to the jury! "Because they're police, you believed their fairy-tale! I'm not guilty of this charge and common sense tells you but instead, you have found an innocent man guilty!

"How do you want to pay?" I replied, "Ten bob a week!"

The judge said, "You will pay twenty pounds per week!"

I shouted, "Beam me up, Scottie!" This judge was not amused! "Any more of that and I'll charge you with contempt of court!"

"In that case, I'll pay," and produced a thick wad of notes! Approximately £2,000 pounds or more! What a show off! A massive crowd in gallery cheered, and I laughed. What disgusting British Justice! This judge wasn't amused, far from it. "Mister Falconer, go upstairs, and pay the fine!"

"Ok, your honour, don't get your knickers twisted, have a great day!" A few years passed, then I went for petrol on Ashley Road, in Parkstone, and behind a counter was this rogue constable! I was outside, standing by a fuel pump and shouted, "Hey, punk, come out and fill up my new jag?"

This ex-copper replied over a mike, "It's self-service!"

I replied, "Pig, get your body out here and fill my tanks before I fill your tank with my fists!"

Yellow dog came out and literally cried, "It wasn't me who fixed you up but my mate! Because you said you'd leave us in a pool of blood if we didn't get off your forecourt!" Well, that was correct! I did say it but at the time, they were going to force entry into my precious jaguar. Now, there is an old saying, he who laughs last, laughs the longest, and all that, well, I must say, I'm still laughing, although one thousand pound was a lot of dosh! Luckily, for me, I did have wads of cash! Loads of dough! It was like a drop in an ocean! I'd coins coming out of my ears! All that luscious loot but it's only money!

Health is what matters! No amount of guineas can purchase that. I maintain my innocence but this jury was handpicked. I would still like to know why a millionaire gets legal aid yet I wasn't entitled? Well, that's justice, and I'll let you, the reader, decide if the action I took was correct or wrong. Yes, the verdict went for the crown but does that suggest I am guilty? Truth! I was without a council! Should you ever attend court, always engage a solicitor.

Here I go, ducking and diving back to 1984 and the New Regency nightclub situated on the second floor. I had a camera installed at the main entrance with a monitor behind the bar. Late one evening, the doorbell rang. I observed three men in casual attire; naturally, I allowed them in! They asked for a pint and a barmaid served these somewhat unfriendly types. It was a rather quiet night with Dave Partridge, the residential DJ, playing dance music. Several customers were frolicking about. One of these gents said, "Are you Sid Falconer?"

I replied, "That I am!" "I could beat you in a fight!"

"I suppose you could in your sleep!"

"Want a wager?"

"Nope!"

"I could stand a round with you anytime!"

"Nope, you couldn't," came my reply.

"Chicken!"

"No, I don't need your money!"

"I'll put fifty bucks on the counter!"

"Nope, it ain't right taking candy from a baby!" Folks were dancing and music was playing.

"I'll bet a thousand pounds!"

"Give fifty pounds to the barmaid, and I'll match it! Louise, get dough out of our till!" He handed his cash over to the bar attendant, and I remarked, "Come on over to my boxing arena!" This buffoon walked slowly over to the dancing area, then changed his tune. Away from his pals, he didn't want to fight! "Ladies and gentlemen, could you leave the floor? This man wants to box me!" I knew then, if I accepted a cop-out, this goon would return, suggesting I opted out! This wasn't gonna happen! He'd invited me and I'd accepted. "Punk, pick up ya dukes!" Instantly, this chap is horizontal, and the next song Dave played was 'It's Over' by Roy Orbison, and another one bit the dust! His colleagues rushed across and one was about to give him mouth-to-mouth resuscitation but declined! Later, they took him home. A week passed, then the phone rang.

"Sid, I'm the man from West Howe, the fellow you knocked-out!"

I replied, "Actually, I do have a distinctive recollection of an incident now you come to mention it!"

"What about the fifty pounds?"

"Pal, you placed a bet then lost!"

"I did!"

"I am entitled to keep the dosh but I gave your mates the money!"

"Ok, thanks."

"Buddy, you're welcome, anytime, hasta la vista!"

One night, the screen on the upstairs monitor operated. Outside the Regency was a scuffle, some sort of an affray, so I went to investigate like Sherlock Holmes and the music played. At least five people were involved, then I noticed one being a copper, so I intervened, brushing off a couple with a swift hook or two then pulled the rest away! They legged it! The constable was lucky, only a few minor bruises! Not much to write home about but he never said thanks, kiss my sweet fanny adams, but went on his weary way! Why did I ever get involved? Back to the fracas with Johnny Rivers outside the Horse and Groom! The officer in question was standing along the road until I'd sorted it! Years passed, then one sunny day, I bumped into him! He recalled this particular occasion when I'd possibly saved his life and thanked me!

Another incident, I was coming around Bournemouth Square. Now, this reminds me of a time in London! I'll tell you about it then I'll return to this tale! David purchased a car in Colchester! He hadn't a licence at this time, seeing he'd never taken a test. Looking back, it was daft to drive without a licence but in those days, we were very foolish! At this time, we were stationed in Roman barracks! One weekend, he decided we'd visit Dorset to see Mum and Jack! We left Colchester, heading towards Poole via London! We got to a roundabout, then the car failed. Dave attempted to restart it, instead, flooded the carburettor. A dozen police were stopping a crowd of people; it must have been someone important for them to keep folk at bay. I got out. "Officers, can you assist us? The carb has flooded!" There's my brother in a stationary car without a licence. Officers came over and pushed and off we went! Whosoever said long arm of the law were right, for pedalling push bikes, just joking! It was much appreciated, thank you, London Constabulary, back in 1966!

Now, back to the day of the student riots in Bournemouth. I was driving around a roundabout in the square when a policeman's helmet came sailing across my path, causing me to stop then I noticed a constable being kicked left, right and centre. I got out of my car then ran across this road and somehow, managed to fight my way through an ugly crowd to protect him against this ferocious onslaught! I punched and shouted words like, "Get off, you stupid morons!"

Next, reinforcements arrived. "Thank the Lord you're here!" They grabbed me; now, luckily, this policeman shouted telling them that I had, in fact, helped him! An inspector told me to go! His exact language was impolite. A thank you would have been welcome! Now, I hope this constable reads this book and knows that day it was me who came to his rescue.

The aggressive officer was swearing! Is that the normal way you speak to someone aiding one of his constables? Well, I legged it without any further advice. Nice, when one's appreciated! There were, and probably still are, many truly admirable policemen, believe me, and the Poole police force are the best, in my opinion, across this country, possibly the world, but there's always a bad egg in every basket! Let's face it, there's never a cop around when you need one! Yes, I'm joking, and no, that is not funny! What is next? Heavy rain tumbled against window panes directly in front of where I am sitting! Lorraine came into our bedroom, carrying a cupful of piping hot cocoa as the sound outside diminished! In two ticks, I'll drive away the ghosts of past and present. "Drink and the devil be done for the rest, yo-ho-ho, and a bottle of rum! Away with my silvery tongue, there's work to be done!" For a few moments, I flipped through several pages, checking for mistakes! Now, I'm returning to the army days and the chapter of Mick Langthorne and that acting sergeant incident! I sent a guard to tell Mick should he carry this matter any further, whatever the outcome, I'd exact my revenge! His complaint was withdrew. Betting, apparently, was rife amongst troops how long would I serve in MCTC, Military Corrective Training Centre, for striking this NCO. One, maybe two years or longer! Maximum penalty awarded was three years' detention! My word, I received four infernal days! "Would you believe this? Somebody up there likes me!" Back in 1967, in Colchester, Colonel Todd was our commanding officer! And I was the ration clerk responsible for the battalion's provisions! On Sunday morning, whilst preparing food for privates, sergeants and officers mess, our Colonel walked his dog! "Good morning, Sir. I've a bone for the dog!" Funny, it was covered in meat! Now, back to the four days in the guardroom. "A bit harsh, don't you agree?" Provo-Sergeant

Simpson said, "Falconer, tomorrow there is ten-tonne coal for you to move!"

I replied, "I have, have I?" I remember this thick set thug as a corporal, a training instructor and a bootlicker! Army bully! "Staff, I think I'll be boxing training!" Maybe it's no surprise I served plenty of clink, because I did not have much respect for many rank and file!

My regret is, I didn't hammer more! Sure enough, the following morning, regimental policeman, Phil Pratt, an overzealous boxer, arrived. "Staff-Sergeant Falconer to report for boxing, back for lunch!" That's all I did except this adjutants' parade! RSM Benjamin Campey, a real mean ogre, accompanied the adjutant! "Falconer, these boots are magnificent; why haven't you bullied the tongue or sole?" This was downright degrading as my ammunition boots truthfully sparkled!

"Sir, I don't bull boots!"

He looked at me for a moment then enquired, "Who does them?"

"Sir, I have many batmen who sparkle my footwear!"

"Pardon?" remarked the Officer with Campey, close by, peering with his beady eyes!

"One doesn't have a dog and bark oneself!" I could see jealousy expiring from our RSM and knew he paid for his shoes cleaned.

"Soldier, I asked you a question."

"This lousy lot of scallywags, these jailbirds, spit and polish my boots," pointing to two rows of friendly prisoners, standing to attention. "They're the dogs' buttocks at clean and shine, and in here, I'm the top doggie!"

"Private Falconer, maybe that is true but I am watching you!"

"Sir, Falconer sincerely apologises." Next, the regimental sergeant-major stepped forward, but the adjutant saw the funny side!

"Sir, Robinson over there is seeking early release!" Early on the last morning, I'm released!

"Training as usual, get ready to rumble," exclaimed Philip Pratt. Don't get me wrong when I talk about my brother, Dave! He's maybe a little careful, trying to avoid a wee confrontation but he's no coward, and let me say on his behalf, far from it! I recall an evening, we were playing cards with the Brook brothers, and if I distinctly remember this correctly, tough guy Dick Ledgeway played opposite David! Something happened, and Dick went limp, kind of dippy, accusing everybody of cheating; well, I calmed the storm but in the tremulous air Dick, brewed! He was losing heavily; eventually, he began threatening! Ledgeway had a mean streak, violent temper and a reputation to match! Dave lost his rag, "Let's sort this out!"

Dick was hard like a rod of steel, according to reports! "Come on, you've been asking for this for quite a long time! Always using uncouth behaviour but this time, you have gone too far, you're unforgivable!" Well, the fun and games commenced! My brother knocked two bags of manure out of this oaf! Magic, I never realised he kept a tiger in his tank! Later, we went to the Naafi to celebrate. Somehow, the news of this event preceded us. Dave Falconer had bashed Dick Ledgeway! Word passed through our battalion; now, soldiers stepped to one side as David and I walked in the Naafi! "My God, news travelled fast in this neck of the woods," exclaimed Billy Brooks with a wide smile on his face, and I was proud as punch!

In 1966, our battalion moved to Aden. One day, I was standing on the first story landing, quietly observing the new intake, men recently arrived from England. This corporal, who was a powerfully built fellow by the name of Pete, was giving these troopers a lesson, instructing them in the use of the Carl Gustof—a shoulder-held rocket launcher! "This is how to strip the weapon," remarked the corporal, and for a moment, I could see he'd forgotten one had to cock the launcher before dismantle!

I said, "Cock it!" He turned, looked up in my direction, went red in the face then quickly, marched inside and up the stairs! I was facing him when he arrived. In my eyes, I'd done nothing wrong. He started threatening me and everyone below heard his idle threats; unfortunately, I did not take kindly to this type of approach! "Pete, you are very aggressive!"

"Corporal to you!" A bad attitude! "Next time, I'll sort you out!"

"You insult me, for God's sake! I'm a battalion heavyweight boxer! Punk, pick up your dukes!" Next moment, he's unconscious and I am arrested, would you believe? I spent a night in a calaboose and said to a guard, "Don't lock my cell, I suffer from a phobia, and should you attempt to lock it, I've nothing to lose, so another one will bite the dust!

"You live," he remarked, "in cloud-cuckoo-land and give me the collywobbles!" Klonk went every cell door except yours truly's, which stayed ajar! Next day, I went before the company commander. "Quick march," shouted this sarge. Major Johnson said affirmatively, "Private Falconer, go across to HQ company rations department and apply for the position of clerk! They are interviewing at this moment. I'm fed up with you knocking out my NCO's! Falconer, have you got anything to say against this extremely violent charge of assault?"

"He drew first blood!"

"Sir, 7 platoon are going up country, back to the Yemen border!"

"Staff, march him out!" A few weeks later, our platoon came under fire. This corporal, who replaced me, was shot in the arm but continued to return fire! My mate, Mad Mitchell, called out and he replied, "Mitchell, I am ok!"

Next instant, a Russian rocket struck him in the stomach, killing him instantly! Mitchell called to him but no reply returned. He reached over to his compatriot, and his hand went into a huge hole, sending him crazy. He picked up a GPMG, general purpose machine gun, full of ammunition! Next, he turned it towards the enemy before cutting loose like a devil, killing many! An officer unloaded two grenades! Later, he was awarded a medal! Corporal Jeff Hawker received a military medal!

And Mitchell, a real-life hero, what heroic films are made of, I'll state for service beyond the call of duty, received nothing! Imagine what he must've gone through! Hearing that explosion and his comrade, dead? I won't say what happened to him but later, he was subjected to a military court martial! Jim Cadden was shot in the arm and Phillip Webb and Jack Howarth were in the middle of this ugly battle! My eyes fill up whenever I think of that soldier. It could have been me! God was my saviour! I walked across to HQ company for an interview. When I arrived, there was a queue. A staff-sergeant eventually shouted, "Falconer," finally, I marched inside!

Captain Heyward said, "Are you any good at mathematics?"

"Sir, it's my best subject, apart from music!"

"What is thirteen times thirteen minus thirty-nine?"

"Sir, one hundred and thirty!"

"You've got the position of store man!"

"Sir!"

"Work begins in six weeks until then, you are the swimming pool lifeguard!"

"Yes, sir!" While serving in the army, I don't think I'd received a full weeks' pay, would you believe, for bludgeoning a few NCO's! RSM, Ben Campey, and a motor ordinance, staff-sergeant were mean pilchard but there was several even worse blodgers around and they all wore stripes! Many years later, in Poole, I saw Captain Heyward and memories flooded back. In Aden we guarded this place on a hill they called the fort where special forces interrogate prisoners. If one wanted to observe, they would look through an eyehole situated in a door. Hearsay was, after interrogation, special branch took prisoners out to sea, cut their hands and tossed them overboard! Back at Colchester, military police came to Roman barracks and questioned us regarding what we had witnessed! I was advised to keep my mouth shut but I can now state, I never saw anything because it wasn't any of my business, so I kept my nose out where it wasn't wanted! I say, there were people in seven platoon certainly worthy of a mention in this book, like Philip Webb and Cyril Vunnie-Valoo Jack Howath. Excellent bunch of men, and I am truly honoured to have served with them also, Mad Mitchell, who served out his sentence in Colchester's MCTC! It's about time somebody wrote this story! I'm absolutely disgusted and gutted this war hero was treated this way! I request something is done and they get to the truth of this matter which I've written, and what about my medals which I've never received or can't the army afford it?

Now, let's pop over to East of Eden! This particular evening, weirdly innocent Roger, Paul and I were at the main bar, talking to the owner, a hustler, with a fabulous sense of humour, when a small incident in the pool room occurred which we attended. A young man was out for the count on the floor! Another person with his hand across both nose and mouth! Dark red blood oozed profusely from between narrow fingers! Point of interest, one of our employees, David Cobb, at the age of sixteen, trained as a bodybuilder at Trinidad Boys Club and was coached by Jed

Gifford! He broke a Dorset County record for power lifting, bench, squat and dead lift! Now, back to the action! My attention was drawn to a strapping goliath! I soon got the gist of what had transpired; apparently, two pals were playing pool when this big blodger came to their table, seeking a match! The one spread-eagled was still out cold when his pal said, "This guy asked for a game, and my friend said after we've finish our game, I'll play you but this tall, blond bombshell decided it wasn't the answer he wanted to hear and dropped an innocent victim with a left hook sending him spiralling into unconsciousness then this man with a clenched hand exploded a punch in my face, possibly breaking my nose and damaging teeth!" By this time, I'd heard enough to warrant my wrath! I informed this man that he was out of order and there were only two courses of action available: either leave or put up ya dukes? Stupid, idiotic punk raised clenched fists; now, what can I say? Faster than a speeding bullet, I attacked, sending him twirling like a gigantic spinning top, and rock-a-bye-baby, another one bit the dust!

I went to Churchill's Nightclub; Tony Carpenter was with two girls when I entered! One of the owners, a conjuror with exceptional skill, presented me with a fascinating fountain pen with magic ink which I'd seen him previously use. A pretty lady wearing a white dress and accompanied by, presumably, her handsome husband also wearing a white shirt came, passed! I said, "This fountain pen isn't working," and flicked it! The ink sprayed onto this woman's dress; instantly, a blue stain appeared across her entire gown!

"What the devil are you doing?" stated the chap.

As though I hadn't heard him, I said, "It's not working!" Next instant, I propelled the fluid onto his shirt!

"What are you doing?"

I looked up, "Sorry, old bean, what's up?" If looks could kill, I'd be dead!

"What's up, look what you've done?"

"What? Where?" He turned to his companion but the mark had, in fact, vanished! He looked at his shirt then laughed! Later, I ordered two steak sandwiches, one for me, the other for Tony then we went back to the East of Eden! Roger was outside, talking to the chap I knocked out earlier! Tony climbed out from the car as Roger informed this man mountain that I was the one who'd knocked him sparko! Mistakenly, he turned towards Carpenter with red eyes blazing like a raging bull. "You knocked me out?" Tony looked at me then laughed.

"Sorry, friend, wrong person, it was him!"

"Punk it was me!"

Now, this fellow's mate arrived in the nick of time! "I've never been knocked out!"

"There is always a first time!" He moved forward towards me menacingly, threateningly! I said, "Pick up ya dukes, good night, cope this!" He hovered like a fly for a moment in mid-air as though suspended in time! My hand went around the back of his body and I supported him to the ground, totally unconscious, and another one bites the dust! A few coins splashed onto the road!

"Pennies from heaven," exclaimed Roger! "Who's purchasing the first round?" remarked Tony, collecting the money and bought the next beers. Paul and the owner were playing pool when we entered, totally unaware of the fracas outside! Although we operated the door at Eden, John, the owner, a stout Irishman, retained one head of security which didn't bother me one bit! This doorman was an Arab, and as I'd done a tour of duty in Aden, I'd got to know them pretty well! He did a fine job but kept constantly moaning. One night, our doorman said to him, "You've got a big chip on ya shoulders!" Well, I think he'd purchased the fish-shop. I got fed up with his snide remarks directed at me and invited him outside where he raised his hands, but this time, I decided to take my time and danced, then tapped him in the belly, and he turned then ran and I chased him! He stopped then turned and I knocked him down then tripped and sat in a puddle of water! Next, I've bitten him out of sheer temper, and he screamed, then legged it, and that was the last time he worked on the door but I did see him again but only for a fleeting moment as he'd disappear out the door!

One of the security officers, John Lilley, came to our house dressed in his best black suit, white shirt and bow-tie! Whilst Lorraine was speaking with John, I shook this magic pen towards him and ink ejected onto his new shirt! His face was a picture! He looked but didn't say a word! A minute later, this train of ink disappeared, and I casually murmured, "It's a magic fountain-pen!"

He replied, "I didn't like to say!" We laughed before going to the club, Enter! Inside, it was full to the rafters! The owner, an Arab, supplied us with pints then we went downstairs to the lower level where music played and folk were dancing. Lubbly jubbly! Things couldn't get much better, or so I thought! The night was still young and so, I decided it was time to depart! I'd get some food from the Godfather pizza joint in Poole road and give our children, Sidney and Matthew, a feast! They just loved spare ribs, burgers, etc, with all the trimmings! Paul had gone upstairs to the main bar to check everything was working smoothly as he'd finished his pint but came back quickly. "At the bar," exclaimed Layton, "there's a group of pigs who gave me grief!" Both of us, with Roger lurking in the wings, went upstairs then stood alongside these louts! Paul was situated between me and them, so I shoved him into this pack of ugly hooligans; suddenly, they're sprawling across a wooden floor like massive ten pins and resembling drunken sailors! They got up and walked back to the bar and finished their drinks, watching me all the time, then left! We went down the stairs and Paul seemed much happier now! Those punks attempted to intimidate one of us but incurred our wrath. A good lesson for them! Never pick on one because we are the A Team!

We never invite trouble but it always appeared, now, going back to an afternoon when I was the main attraction on a fairground! What can one say about that? Nothing much but it was good money for old rope! The venue was in Sommer Court, Cornwall! Several country yokels came to the boxing booth looking for a fight, not for themselves but for the village idiot! They were farmyard attendants, labourers, carrying massive jugs of scrumpy, searching the fair for a scrap and I was in the right place! They were all built like giant haystacks. An awesome wrestler, back in my youth, weighing, I'd say, twenty-five stone or more! This absolute giant clambered through the ropes into the ring! This arena almost collapsed under the heavy burden! Ringmaster Jack Turner climbed slowly, carefully, under the worn ropes into the boxing enclosure! A local lad acted as timekeeper while referee Dudley Garwood, from Jamaica, also entered the ring! Cornerman, ex pro, Peter Fay stood with an ancient time piece. No, not Ann Puzey or Alan Baines but a pocket watch in his hand! "Ladies and Gentlemen!" said the master of ceremony as my opponent was handed a jug of rough cider. He was wearing this grey woollen vest and a pair of dirty trousers of the same material. Overall, looked a West Country bumpkin! Jack continued, "This contest consists of three rounds, each round being three minutes with a minute interval between rounds!" This titanic ogre drank liquid reminiscent of a mighty ocean liner in the final seconds before plunging beneath an awesome wave and scrumpy cascaded until exploding onto the canvas!

Turner stepped from this ring as the corner man rang a bell, signalling commencement of the first round! I stepped into the centre intending to give this audience a grand exhibition and waited for my challenger to hand over the large jug! He turned in my direction, with evil intent in his dark blue eyes, and clambered across towards me! What happened next was accidental on my behalf because I'm in the ring to award the crowd entertainment, but I still cherish what occurred for the rest of my natural life. Inside this colosseum, people gathered closer to ringside as this large amphitheatre filled with over four hundred folks eager to watch their neighbour perform! Shouts of encouragement sounded loud and clear as their colossus gladiator moved within striking range! I stepped in close with raised gloves clenched in a ball, then in a swinging motion, swung a punch, high and above, suddenly connecting flush on his jaw, followed through and back came my arm, completing a perfect movement! For a brief period, he appeared suspended in mid-air before crashing upon the floor! His legs raised off the canvas slightly, then stiffened. Suddenly, the front door bell rang, turning my attention from this tale! "Hello," said Pete Hardy, a sky engineer and karaoke singer. "I'm here to fix the satellite disc!"

"Ok!" Now, back to our saga! His body shook as the referee stepped closer and began counting. One, two, etc and signalled the bout was over! His elder brother, quite larger in stature, climbed into the ring! Now, their combined weight and my own plus the referee caused this floor to creak! I stood still, as moans and groans from old wood under duress and waited to hear timber cracking but the ring held fast! This monstrosity rolled his brother to the apron then tipped him over, sending a gallant crusader plunging down upon the green grass! This was like taking money for old rope!

One night, I was on the McGowan's Boxing Booth run by Bernard, Stuart and Barry whilst their mother was cashier. On the outside apron, Master of Ceremony, Jack Turner, entertained an audience while observing us performing with a punch bag and a speed ball! An unlucky punter said, "I'll fight him!" pointing in my direction! This chap was what we term a straight. There are two types of boxers on the fairground! First is agee or friend where we stage a boxing show! The second is a genuine contestant from the crowd! Could be this man is a professional or maybe a former, amateur boxing champion! Who knows?

The match was arranged and a packed house waited for the entertainment to commence! We climbed into the ring as the announcer entered! Jack delivered his speech then introduced both boxers. "This contest is three rounds." We came to the centre as this referee explained the rules! This afternoon was almost over! Next second, we travelled to respective corners! The bell rang, sounding commencement! I danced around the ring like Lennox Lewis, picking the challenger off. Ducking and diving for three minutes, literally acting, performing the last rites before carrying it out! A jab and a double then move, swing to left then right! I could see the public, and they wanted blood! I jabbed a powerful straight left onto his face, and his nose exploded! Next, came a combination, a flurry of punches, constantly switching direction, connecting with midriff and head, then a hammer blow sent him crashing upon the canvas, "And another one bites the dust!"

His brother quickly responded, "I want to fight him."

Jack replied, "You are on the next show!'' I stepped out and returned to my dressing room. "Good work," remarked Barry. Later, I went and stood upon the front stage before rest-bite! Between five pm and six, when the evening show was due to commence, this local, with his brother, seemed exceptionally eager, swearing abuse.

I punched a bag whilst sporting gesture continued. The crowd grew larger and probably greater than those earlier shows combined! A full house was certainly guaranteed.

The total number of folk attending a house ranges from three hundred and fifty to four hundred. This show exceeded five and

I was definitely going to entertain, perform magic! There were young ladies present, and I certainly like giving the girls an exhibition. "Value for money," cried Turner. "Citizens, we bring you a festival of the highest calibre!" These fair maidens were laughing and smiled when I stepped into this boxing arena. Jack paused, knowing he'd caught their attention!

"In the right corner," pointing over, "is our gallant opponent!" Turner could make his public address last longer than a boxing match! He would've made a fine actor until he fell down a manhole! "And in the far-left corner is Sid Falconer! The official number two contender for the Light Heavyweight Championship of Great Britain!" I winked at this girl! Later, I went back, and she was waiting! Her name, Edwina Rowbotham.

The referee called us together and explained the regulations, then we returned to our respective corners; suddenly, a bell rang, signalling commencement. He came like the raging bull but did not conquer. I moved into a quickstep then fast foxtrot, prancing around this ring, covering plenty of coarse canvas! Instead of punishing the guy, I laid off, simply enjoying this contest. In hindsight, he'd over estimated his ability but there wasn't any point carving this courageous crusader. His bullying tactics weren't working! He went about the arena, constantly hitting thin air; eventually, he became totally exhausted; now, realising his mistake, he attempted to jump and dive out of this ring, only to get entangled between the ropes, screaming! I said, "Bon voyage!" I'll give him credit. He showed bags of guts and enthralled everyone, including yours truly. I worked for two years from 1974 at the Badger bars in Fir Vale Road, Bournemouth! While working there, I was employed to work at La-Maxine, an English equivalent of an American speakeasy, an illicit liquor diner! A drinking establishment during prohibition, this restaurant was licenced to midnight but we sold alcoholic beverage until four or maybe five am. I worked with Mike as coequal managers; in the kitchen was Giovanni! A lovelier man one couldn't meet, and although he constantly moaned and groaned, we all liked him. This waitress, name of Gee, gave the place an air of glamour and the taste of refinement and respectability. She had a natural flair and delighted local customers with her charming personality! Four self-assured Chinese gentlemen, Makki, Tauro, Toshi and Kim, were employed as waiters, but their manners towards me were disrespectful. They regarded me as an infidel! One Sunday evening, I arrived but before I could say Jack Spratt, Mike shouted, "Sid, there's a fracas in the passageway!" I duly attended. Well, they were truly in dire straits! This small area was not sufficient for them to perform, and they were in a quagmire! A real pickle, taking kicks; in fact, they needed me! They were getting beaten to a pulp by several rather large men from Libya. In the nick of time, I waddled in up to my neck in blood, guts and bullets! Now, I'm really exaggerating! In two ticks, I'd taken their load upon myself, chopping down two like felling ginormous oak trees. Took another as they attempted to flee! I walked into Old Christchurch; three assailants charged me. Next moment, an uppercut lifted one off his feet! He landed on the curb, and another one bites the dust! Not bad for a Joe Muggins; soon after this episode, my surname changed to Mighty Mugwump! After this minor incident, these Chinese gentlemen called me the boss man, even chief. I liked it, and we eventually became friends. They trusted me and I, them, but time came for me to move along; then I became the manager of Texas Beef further up Old Christchurch road, approximately three-hundred metres from the Lansdowne! My friend, Mister Garry Heyward, has just turned up for a game of darts! Everyone calls him Mr Pickles! I wonder why? Well, I'm back after thrashing him. "Philip Taylor, watch this space! Ha-ha-ha." One evening at Texas Beef, two couples from Ireland had eaten their meal and polished off two bottles of red wine and a third, except for a tiny portion, then complained about the food, then said the drink was absolutely rubbish and refused to pay! I spoke with them, but they were adamant and were having none of it; finally, they left the restaurant.

I followed them outside then stated, "It's an offence to leave an establishment without paying for the meal and I am entitled to call the police!"

One of the girls shouted, "My husband belongs to the Irish republican army! In Ireland, he'd kill you!" Now, her fellow was heavily built and the other, a fair portion, obviously, typical bullies!

Along Old Christchurch Road came a patrol car! I waved him down and explained the situation. What this copper said as he stood by the far side of the driver's door didn't go down very well; next, this man went behind the lawman then choked him! Unfortunately for this policeman, I wasn't in much of a hurry to assist because this officer was in serious trouble and without me, he was off to the happy hunting lodge! I only hope this constable reads this statement! I was now in charge and wanted cooperation, full authority. I plodded around and placed a Chinese strangle hold; hey, presto! The man went rock-a-bye-baby and the officer recovered. The other person cried, "I'll pay the bill!" One of the restaurant business partners, Saleem, had only just arrived to witness this fracas. He was quick to state, "That's 25 pounds," which was honestly way over the top in those days but he paid without any fuss and his lass who'd told me he was IRA made a theatrical scene by collapsing in the centre of the main road! The patrol officer let those blodgers go. I don't mess with politics or religion, but I say, if this foolish woman reads this, madame, I don't think Gerry Adams and the official IRA would recruit lunatics like thy husband from their not worthy society!

Now, let us travel back in time to the days of my childhood when London was recovering from the Second World War. We used to play on bomb-damaged land, still vacant and covered in rubble where folk dumped rubbish from Bow! Along to Mile End the walkway was newly laid with large flat slabs. Dad purchased three pair of rubber-wheel skates, and daily, we raced along the pathway back and forth, then we allowed our pals the chance to experience this fantastic thrill but after a while, we got bored, then looked for more adventurous entertainment! I can't remember much more and I've told you about the Roman fleapit and rags, bus station etc, that's it, episode over, short and sweet, and that's the way I like it! There is plenty more yet to come, and I'll sit back and let it flow! Where? God only knows! We used to go round houses, asking for their old jam-jars, old newspaper and any rags or scrap which made us another nice little earner!

Back in the army, Dave and I, went along to the yeoman border on a non-commissioned-officer's cadre! The chaps were cheating left right and centre but beefy Sergeant Brian Swales appeared to condone cheats! Everybody, including my brother, was promoted except yours truly; well, since that period, life, in comparison, has been like a bed of roses! As a private, I became ration clerk for the Prince of Wales's own regiment, taking over the position from a corporal. It may not appear a prestigious post but as the only store man working in the stores, I was literally my own boss! Daily, I collected the battalion's provisions from various depots, then put them in storage. Soon after returning to Colchester, Frank Walker took over the reign of our ration department! Steve Kennedy became ration sarge and life was grand! Steve would issue an official quota, and I'd supply the privates, sergeants and officer's mess with their entitlement! Each soldier, including officers, had a fixed allowance. It was a magical time! Back in Aden, Captain Heyward was solely in charge and one couldn't have wished for a finer officer! Staff-Sergeant Anderson was a person of the highest quality and like a father figure! Today, my brother told me he'd died. This brought great sadness. Daily, I'd pick up a self-loading rifle from the armoury! Anderson issued a docket, containing a list of fresh supplies and dry rations to be collected from an RAF warehouse in Steamer Point. What lovely memories come flooding back! We passed along the Mala Strait, happily named the murder mile, into Steamer Point to collect the regiment's quota. On this voucher or docket was a container account! The corporal in charge of our stores prior to me should have returned the boxes but was either too lazy to pick up the empty containers or didn't get a chit signed by a clerk, thus, it was in the red! £200; I enquired as to what this was for? Anderson said, "Outstanding container account such as banana boxes haven't been returned!" The RAF compound was surrounded by a wall with rolls of barbed wire bearing sharp pointed spikes, close together! Next time we went to this depot for our supplies, I noticed, as we drove through the warehouse delivering what few boxes we had, an area of open space with literally hundreds of containers stacked a mile high! "Stop, driver, and reverse back!" We piled at least twenty boxes aboard then drove over for our fresh supplies!

One day, this rat staff-sergeant approached me, "Hey, got any coffee?"

"Staff, what did you say?"

"If you get me a large tin of coffee, in exchange, I'll give you a couple of hind-quarts of beef!" In two ticks, a message registered! "What if I get you two?" came my reply. My brain was working overtime, lordy longhorns, that's half a cow! My God, was this my lucky day!

"What about some eggs?"

"That would be nice!" "I'll throw in 1800."

"Staff, I'll give you a box for that and say, you're a gift from heaven!" How in hell did I ever manage to get away with taking the camp's coffee and exchanging it for all this wonderful treasure; well, I don't exactly know but nobody asked me or referred to coffee! From then on, I ran the entire operation with this driver! We'd deliver food to our store! Lance-Corporal Slim Savoury was our butcher! My list of punching non-commissioned officers must have preceded my arrival at the ration department, for Slim kept a stilled tongue and instinctively knew not to pull rank or boss me! Actual fact, I was in charge of the stores which included the butcher's shop. All the staff got on, really well, and Savoury made me laugh just by looking at him! He had this natural-charm, and I, by Jove, was happy, and this job was very grand!

Daily, we fetched the troops' supplies and issued the offices and mess with coffee, supplied privates' mess with twelve hundred eggs over official allowance! Nobody complained, then the sergeants' mess with three hundred extra and finally, the officers' mess with three hundred. I gave Slim three hind-quarters and said, "Give part of one to privates' mess, half apiece to the sergeants' and officers' mess." Slim was a petty tea leaf when it came to meat, and I was the piggy in the middle but in Aden, Savoury was a good man. Unfortunately, when we returned to the UK, Slim would take meat without telling or consulting me; now this was extremely different from Aden where I organised stuff with the rat. These were several complete strangers. I'd travel into the town of Colchester to the depot! Eventually, I made a few contacts, so we were, once again, back in the trade, and business was blooming.

Captain Heyward retired and lieutenant Frank Walker became our ration officer! Luckily for me, he was absolutely magic! Back in those days, head chef was a quartermaster sergeant-major. Daily, he'd walk in the ration stores and take whatever he wanted, but this never bothered me until, for whatever reason, he charged me with not having a shave, which I'm still baffled as to why? Another NCO also charged me with not having a haircut! Meanwhile, our regiment had moved up to Stanford PTA on manoeuvres, an official training area, sixty miles away. Daily, I picked up the food from Colchester before returning to camp, put the rations in the stores at Roman barracks which remained with a skeleton staff! I made up supplies for privates', sergeants' and officers' mess! Later, delivered them then returned back to the main stores! Time was now kicking on so I put up all the rations for Stanford PTA, then we took these fresh supplies there! By early evening, we arrived, and I put the rations into the storage depot, and once again, I put up supplies, loaded the lorry, then delivered to three messes!

My brother was at Stanford on duty. Nightly, between ten and midnight, whilst he was on duty, I'd occupy his bed, then set off each day for Colchester at 4 am. This was repeated, then one evening, I arrived at Stanford! This warrant officer, would you believe, stopped me and I was charged for not shaving! This was eleven o'clock at night, then I'm charged, me, with not having a haircut or maybe it was vice versa. Next, I'm rostered for weekend guard duty at Stanford! I asked a warrant officer if I could be taken off guard duty because I was working from 4 am to pm each day! My request was denied, so when I arrived at Colchester, I decided it was time to leave the battalion; it wasn't the regiment but those characters who'd charged me were of high rank and I was a mere private! Who could I turn to, aged 20, and alone? If only I'd turned to Lieutenant Frank Walker but instead, I caught a bus, then a train, yes, homeward bound! After a year, these two policemen, a Sergeant Katthews, the other, a constable, arrived at my family abode! Asked me if I'm Sid Falconer from the Prince of Wales? Obviously, I replied, "No!" They suggested I show them my arms! I did so, without question.

The sergeant said, "You're Sid, and that tattoo proves it!" I replied, "Let me stay here until Christmas is over, then I'll hand myself in!" I was ready, willing and able to face the punishment.

"Ok," said Matthews. 6th of January 1969, I handed myself in at Poole Police Station! A couple of regimental police arrived to accompany me to Colchester. "Firstly, let's go to my home, where my mother will cook us a meal!" Later, we went for a beer, then caught the train back to the barracks! On the way, I chatted to a young female officer cadet and she wrote to me until ordered to discontinue writing to a soldier awaiting trial by a senior officer, and that was the end of a possible relationship!

Back, at camp, an overzealous guard commander gave me the third degree; now, I was fighting fit, quite mad, and casually said, "Can you remove your teeth when addressing me?"

"They ain't false!" came his reply, so I stated, "Anymore lip, punk, and they will be, understand?"

My reputation as a scallywag always preceded me, and pal, that was the last word out of that silly beggar! Later, a regimental policeman came to lock my cell door but I warned him off, stating, "I've an awful phobia and turn nasty when someone attempts to shut my cell door, so if I were you, I'd leave it ajar, ok? Thank you, kindly!" This soldier understood, because he looked around, then left, without, a word being spoken, then I slipped into dreamland!

In 1967, prior to my absconding, the Tori Canyon, a craft, ran aground in Cornwall! Our regiment was appointed to clean up this disaster consisting of oil polluting the sea and covering beaches. I don't know much of the details, because I only delivered rations, but I did hear mention, one of our lads, while moving a drum full of oil, whether aboard ship, I do not know, but his fingers were either sliced off or badly mangled! At the time, I was billeted in New Guay! When morning duly arrived, I got out of my flea-bag! After this, corporal made my breakfast— a mighty T-bone steak in beans. It wasn't often I got treatment like this, but I'm not complaining! I've always looked after the cooks, and our chefs were a magnificent bunch, and although the soldier outranked me, this wise guy knew better than to breach my tolerance level! Well, I've travelled around from coast to coast and fought in Calais, France and Oslo, Norway! Been stationed in Berlin, Germany and Aden, etc, and boxed six years, on fairgrounds from Cambridge to Redruth in Cornwall! Proprietor of Falconer security and a couple of nightclubs, the New Regency, in Christchurch, and Valentines, in Bournemouth!

Now, I'm writing my second book! The first was Headache, the true story! And I've pencilled in two more books, ready to go when this is, hopefully, published!

Back in 1984, I had a dream which seemed very interesting, as though I was transported to a small island where pirates roam and little people gather! Like Gulliver's Travels, before venturing along to this uninhabited peninsula they call Sacrifice, now, I spend my time writing this book or twiddling, upgrading Headache and singing on our karaoke machine! Life couldn't get any better or could it? I like to yodel, and we actually host a few parties. Although, back awhile, I was at Tony's public house in Pulham, when a moron came, looking for a fight! Heard that I was an ex-professional pugilist! Along came Billy the Kid, local village idiot, gunslinger! "Hey, old man!"

I turned, "What a plonker, Rodney."

"I'm gonna knock, your head off!" Now, could this be one's final curtain? I turned from him.

"I'm talking to you," he remarked.

I replied, "If you were speaking to someone else, you'd be in a quagmire, but I'm taking no notice." Then I turned away; suddenly, he tried to head butt me, but I slipped my head to one side and put my foot on the top of his, then pulled his arm and felled him like a log! I could see I'd hurt his pride. He got up, and I delivered a neat blow upon his conk! Again, he went down. "And Rodney, another one bit the dust!"

"Not quite, Del Boy, seeing they were inside at the bar!" On this occasion, he decided to stay put!

"Indeed, Sid, sensible!"

"Only fools and horses would rise on this occasion, Grand Dad!"

When Sidney, our first son, was six, one of the staff from Sylvan Road, Primary School, rang us, suggesting Sidney wasn't feeling well, and could we pick him up, which we duly did. Driving down a road, we noticed he couldn't hear, so we went to Poole General Hospital and took him to a clinic where this nasty woman clerk refused to place him on their register to be attended by a doctor! Her attitude was absolutely terrible! She didn't even refer us to the A & E department but said, "Go to your GP!" Sidney started playing tennis aged 9. Graham Holden was his coach, then Rob and Mike Booth, finally Sidney went to Nick Bolletter's Tennis Academy in Florida, USA! Me and a buddy, Lee Beeston, accompanied him.

The first night out, Lee and I went to a pub and at the bar, waited our turn to be served a drink, then this barman came across and said, "Who's next?"

A person, who'd come into this public house after us, said, "A Budweiser!" I was taken by surprised and just looked at him! He spoke, "Are you waiting?"

I replied, "I'm not here for the goodness of my health!"

"Ok, my friend, what's your beverage?"

"Pal, same as you!"

"Landlord, make that three."

"Cheers!" He told us that he'd come into this pub four weeks prior, and some chaps attacked him! Now, standing beside me were two tall, well-set fellows! Obvious to everybody, they were listening to our conversation, then our drinks arrived. This man was loud and everyone in the saloon could hear every word he uttered. "I've a colt forty-five in my pick up, should anybody give me grief." Lee and I looked at each other. This man turned towards folks playing pool whilst others looked up from a seated area! "Tonight," said the fellow, "I'll blast them to kingdom come!" There came a deadly hush as he continued, "I don't mind a fight, but there were three of them!"

Lee remarked, "Think you can fight, let me tell you, shipmate, Sid here is a professional boxer and knocked out Northern Area Champion, Peter Freeman from Great Britain!" Next, these two fellows behind me finished their drinks then left!

The bar attendant said, "Thank Christ you two popped in, those rednecks were looking for trouble but recognised they were out of their league and this wasn't the right time or place and departed!" He said we were welcome anytime! In this saloon were two pool tables and a dartboard for plastic darts or magnetic also a basket ring with a net for practicing basketball throws! Lobbing balls into a net, and we were absolutely amazed as I have never seen anything like it!

A chap playing pool looked the spitting image of a man in Bournemouth! After he'd finished a game, he came over and said, "Fancy a match?"

"I wouldn't mind!"

"Ok, not here, let's go, I'll take you to a pool hall where one can play all night long!"

I replied, "What are we waiting for, millennium?"

Lee said, "Thanks for the beers," then we left the pub! This pool room was astronomic! I have never seen anything like it, literally speaking; there were rows of tables! Each table was allocated crisps etc. It was an unforgettable experience! Later, that being between 2 am and 4 am, we left the hall and he was taking us back to the tennis centre when he was pulled over by a patrol officer! "God, I'm in for it now! I've no tax nor insurance!" "Jesus Christ," he got out then this patrolman said, "Go, I've something major to attend!" This patrol officer got into his vehicle and drove away. A few hundred yards further along this stretch of flat road, this patrolman turned right. Florida was truly most amazingly straight and flat as a pancake. Our driver returned to his car. "That was very close." Along the road, where a couple of minutes prior this officer had turned, we noticed this petrol station, of course, out there, it's called gas+ol+ene or gasoline! Every two hundred yards, there are traffic signals, now, further along, let's say, before the next set of bright control lights was a filling-station, and this establishment was being held up, and who would believe this? But it's true! We passed at least four dozen young ladies wearing short mini-skirts! Our new friend remarked, "Fancy a prostitute?"

"I don't think my wife would agree." Before leaving America, this local newspaper headline read, "Prostitutes in Florida are butchering men!"

All this excitement occurred the first evening we went out. The next morning, I noticed my son was in a group with young children, so I went searching this campus for the owner, Nick Bolleterri! Next moment, a ginormous, tough-looking geezer, like Arnold Schwarzenegger, with bulging muscles sprouting out of his shirt, called to me saying, "Excuse me, what are you doing? Where are you going?"

I replied, "I'm looking for Mister Bolleterri!"

He said, "He's in the indoor court, coaching!"

I said, "Thank you," then proceeded to walk towards the centre when this man remarked, "Excuse me, you can't go in there, can I help?"

"I hope so, my son, Sidney Falconer, is fifteen years old and we paid £20,000 pounds for him to attend this infamous tennis academy, not for him to play children between the age of twelve and fourteen! My son has come to America to progress, not to be used as fodder for Nick Bolleterri's elite squad!" I wanted answers, and this beefy guy could probably help me. His attitude was authoritative but his manner, not so welcoming! Of course, he didn't know me or what I was doing there but he appeared intimidating, almost threatening. "Someone has put him in the bottom group!"

"Yes, but they are the best in the world! Tommy Haas from Germany and the American number one!"

"Maybe, but this has cost me and my family a lot of money to send him here, and I want him to play the older lads!"

"That's the group he's in, and I'm afraid there's nothing more Bolleterri can do!" In other words, that's my lot! My blood began to boil and I maybe became partially aggressive. If this stupid goon thought I was taking this load of cobblers, he was badly mistaken! Now, I was, one could say, most angry and Mister Universe was now in line for my wrath! "Boss, let me simply explain, in layman's terms, I'm Sid Falconer from England, a heavyweight professional boxer and indeed contender for the British Title! Now, I am not bragging, just stating fact! You are a marvellous specimen, I would say. Now, imagine how long with all your muscles would you last if you fought me, probably one hundred thousandth of a second? That is like putting my son with children, whomsoever it may be, do you understand?" I don't exactly know why, but I wanted to hook this son of a goatherder! Say something and make my day!

"Mister Falconer, would it be ok if tomorrow morning you attended the group training session, then we'll take it from there?"

"That's fine with me!" That evening, I spoke to Sidney, saying, "You are fifteen! I know you like being friends with everyone, but if you want to play young children for the near future, don't bother playing, but should you want to get into another group with older lads, go out in the morning and show them what! you can do, ok?" The following morning, on the dot, Lee and I arrived at the courts to be faced by, at least, eight beefeaters! It tickled me pink! He wasn't taking any chances. Sidney was on the court, ready to commence. His opponent was German number one, Thomas Haas!

"Good morning, Mister Falconer," cried the Schwarzenegger lookalike! "I'll see how this match turns out then we'll take it from there, is that fine with you?"

Haas served, Sidney returned, down the line! Love-fifteen, then Haas moved over and served across court to Sid's backhand! This ball returned sailing down the line! Love-thirty, then once again, Thomas changed side and served down the line but the return came across to the right corner! "Love-forty!" For the fourth time, he served the ball across court, towards his backhand but this ball returned down the line! "Game, Falconer!" I was totally gobsmacked! They did not change ends!

Sidney served an ace! "Fifteen-love!" Well, one could have knocked me over with a feather! Every ball was either an ace or clear winner, and Haas looked a novice? The next serve was the same and returns until eventually, this one-sided match was finally over!

(3/07/1991) Thomas Haas, German number one, never got a single point, also, never returned a ball! That's one of the most remarkable games I've ever witnessed! The very next day, Sidney went into group six. I'm not taking anything away from Thomas. as he was thirteen and has become a formidable opponent for anyone including Andy Murray, Novak Djokovic, Roger Federer and Rafael Nadal!

Before I left Florida, they matched him against Jeff Lowre from group two! One and two represent the academy! Sidney beat him, 7/5 7/5, but nothing changed. Within weeks, Sidney reached group three! There he stayed until returning to England! By the time he returned home, another £5000 or more had been spent on his welfare, training expenses, restrings were eighty dollars a time and extra training sessions, 100 dollars, each lesson. Trainers, tennis racquets, plus some pocket money! Sid was the only junior from Great Britain to qualify for the illustrious orange bowl World Tennis Championship but unfortunately, because he was deaf, we couldn't get sponsorship. This is true fact; I sent this letter to Richard Branson but nothing matured! I tried everybody, including the deaf association, but they didn't want to know! Later, his photo appeared in The Times! (If you cannot beat them, join them! By Peter Robinson, formally from the Echo in Bournemouth.) But still nothing! One day, while training on wet grass, he slipped, destroying any chance of winning nationals, only days away! I took him along for laser treatment which lasted a complete year; meanwhile, he played at the nationals and of course, lost! Nobody knew how he felt but soon after, had a couple of matches at West Hants but lost, still suffering pain, which nobody but family knew about, left the tennis scene and got drunk with drinking buddies!

Before one knew it, ten years had passed, then one day, he was invited to participate in a tournament in Nottingham! In all those years, he'd hardly touched a racquet but decided to enter. His weight soared but after the tournament, he took up coaching! Roger Jones! One of the finest coaches in this country, possibly I'd state, along with Rob and Mike Booth and Graham Holden, the world was employed by the deaf tennis association. In terms of experience, this person was god but instead of giving him the reins, they capped his command! He wasn't allowed to help any youngsters with funding except those in the organisation such as folk working for the deaf! Sue Peglar was the first tutor for the deaf but the LTA got rid of her. Some small-minded folk in the association with influence didn't like Roger Jones' attitude. They formed this vigilante group and only gave god the boot; now, everything's gone to pot! Sidney is coaching at Clevedon Tennis Centre near Bristol. His pal, James Bassett, is a leading member and a man with charisma, certainly good taste, and shows natural fibre, and hopefully, between these two, they'll produce a few youngsters for national training! They are a very small club yet qualified along with the elite West Hants tennis club to play in the top league! What an achievement! Acknowledgement from the LTA has come, which is great. Our youngest, Matthew, began tennis, age five years! I was very harsh, indeed, on our children but at the time, I didn't realise. I wonder why? I'd turned into a blodger like ones I've knocked out for much less! Luckily, those days are far behind me! Now, it's, Dad, got a pound? Can I borrow the jaguar? I love it.

The most memorable tennis match I can recall was Matthew playing at Bristol but firstly, I drove Sidney and Matthew to a tournament! I was full up with heavy cold! This lady's son was playing Sid. She said, could I give them a lift to an outside court! "Yes," came my reply! The weather was cold, showery, and the car heater wasn't working. The window steamed up. At that time, I wiped the windscreen with my handkerchief. A dreadful mistake! Mucus was everywhere! At the time, what an embarrassment. Now back to Matthews match! He was aged nine, playing in this fourteen and under tournament in Bristol! His opponent was possibly a foot, maybe, taller and five years older! The score was one set, plus five love in favour of this lad, serving for the match, when his mother said, "It's all over, bar the shouting!"

I was a bit gutted, to state the least, because, even though Matthew was a few years younger, I knew his capability and exclaimed, "It's not over until the fat lady sings!" Lorraine walked away, knowing what I am like. I remarked, "This game has just begun!" Well, I couldn't believe it! This lad had match point six times then I turned to my wife, signalling, Matt had one game under his belt then two until a set went to him!

Now, the score was level. The last set! Matthew won. The umpire shouted, "Game, set and match, 0/6 7/5 6/3." And I was a happy chappie, and this lad's mother was in total shock! What splendid memories and the joy I'm getting, finally writing my memoirs!

One night, I was enjoying the company of Bob Shepherd, at the Horse and Groom in Christchurch. At times, Bobby was real funny; suddenly, my attention was drawn to the front door! Outside, Bob Roberts was talking to Malcolm Tottle, then they moved inside! "What's going on?" I walked over and said, "What is wrong?"

"A fellow who caused trouble last night is heading this way, and if we get any grievance, I'll drop him in the gutter," said Mal. Believe me, Malcolm is much more than capable, so I stepped out onto the pathway! Along the road, bold as brass, came Pete Townsend, a notorious thug like his brothers! Real tough guys! He was accompanied by a few young, smartly dressed ladies wearing flamboyant clothing, I'd say, and a bunch of devoted disciples!

Well, I said, "Mal, it's my party."

They approached, and Malcolm said, "I'm sorry, ladies and gentlemen, but I've been instructed by the management! To inform you for causing a fracas prior you've been barred!"

"Who's gonna stop us coming in?"

"I am the enforcer," cried Mal, grinning like the Cheshire cat who has just caught a rodent in a mousetrap!

I couldn't allow Mister Tottle to have all the fun so I said, "Excuse me but a taxi driver informed management of your intention to cause an epic altercation tonight!"

"I don't know what you're talking about? I never caught a taxi last week!"

"That's what you are saying but I said there was!"

"What are you suggesting?"

"Let us face it, our doorman wants you and your pals to leave or he'll squash your face in, but tonight, this is my pleasure!"

"Who are you?"

"I'm their boss, and if you want trouble, you've come to the right place. Wanna pop over the road to that car park and sort it?"

This evening was peacefully serene, extremely tranquil. He came quickly, without warning, but not quick enough; suddenly he's on the tail end of my fist, dangling like a battered fish. My hands popped around his neck for support, and I gently laid him out and yes, another one bit the dust. Malcolm wanted to do it, but I'm the big chief! After an incubation period, he awoke, "Now, pet, I will be much obliged if you could totter off with thy followers, there's a good man!"

Next, a tall police officer said, "Any problem?"

"Nope," came my instantaneous reply.

"Ok!" Malcolm wasn't amused but he gets plenty of heavy practise in our gym! Let me say, he's a real gent, is our Tottle!

Every time he knocks me down, always says, "Sorry, just joking!" He's my pal.

One evening, Tony Carpenter and I arrived at Spats wine bar! Outside, a queue was forming and I wanted to have a word with a doorman! Apparently, the night prior, this particular officer refused folk entry and said, "I run this door, not Falconer!"

I said, "Tony, go inside, I've a bone to pick with one of my staff!" Minutes passed whilst I observed this doorman attend to this large queue, increasing every second! Tony reappeared, dragging a person by the scruff of his collar! "According to an eyewitness, this funny character has been touching up young ladies!"

"Ok, pal, go back and I'll be in shortly!" A few moments passed, then Tony emerged.

"I say another one!"

"Great!" Moments later, he was back with yet another. That was the third and final occasion! Tony came out carrying a fellow and dumped him in a gutter!

"Sid, I'm getting fed up!" "Four out four in!" said my doorman. Later, I sorted this situation regarding who ran the door, and it was me! Inside Spats, if one said it was real packed like a can of sardines, you'd be correct!

Apparently, when Tony initially entered this wine bar, he was approached by a chap who said, "Excuse me, are you security in here?"

"I am," replied Mister Carpenter. This youngster claimed he'd seen three punks touching up young ladies, then pointed to one. Tony asked him to leave! When he refused, a fracas developed with this prat sustaining a broken nose before being chucked out! Next came the second and third; finally, Tony arrived at the bar and ordered a round of drinks. Roger and Paul were due! The person who'd initiated the whole affair was now discussing this incident with friends.

This is roughly that conversation, "Those rats who gave me grief down at Longs wine bar earlier have been sorted! I said to security staff those thugs were touching up the ladies, and he's broken three noses and evicted them ha-ha-ha, serves them right!"

His mates replied, "Wasn't it you who caused the scene in the first place?"

"Yes and those pigs won 't mess with me again, now I've got security protection!" Tony had been set up and couldn't believe his ears! He walked over, told him he wanted to talk to him outside, but he refused. That's how the fourth received a suspected broken nose! Roger and Paul arrived. They must have sniffed a free drink, because they entered as Tony paid a barman for a round and another friend, Ted Siddall, was with them and it's not usual for them to turn up as beers are being ordered.

It's quite amazing, looking back, and remembering the past! One night, Lorraine rang, informing us of a disturbance developing at the star of India on Holdenhurst road, Bournemouth! Roger, Paul and I attended. The governor, seeing us, went to this couple sitting at a table, saying, "You've eaten my food, drank a bottle of finest wine; now, you refuse to pay, why? You over developed pig."

This fat honker replied, "We didn't enjoy the food or wine, and we're not paying, understand?"

This thick-skinned punk was treating the owner with contempt like the dirt beneath his feet, and his ogress was expressing sympathy with everything he said! Next, the proprietor stepped back, and I stepped in. "Sir, excuse me!"

"Who are you?" came his reply. "You great big lummox, that doesn't really matter!"

"What did you say?"

"I said your table manners are atrocious, now pay up, or we'll make a citizen's arrest." A few minutes later, he stood up, towering above me, but his bottle was shot, and so we took them to our police station situated in Madera road where he eventually paid! On route, this extremely tough-looking bruiser with squint eyes argued and made a rude gesture; suddenly, he was lying prostrate, so we hung around for approximately ten minutes until he was fully conscious, and our Paul grinned like a Cheshire cat! Hallelujah, I think that wally certainly made one stupid mistake! don't you agree?

At the Gander, on the Green, on Holdenhurst road, these roadworthy bike riders were languishing it up! Prior at the Halfway House, on Bournemouth road, Parkstone, I barred them, then a few years later came an occasion when I've acquired the door security at the Pine Cliff public house in Southbourne where again these motor cyclist were evicted! The next time we met was at the Gander On the Green but on this occasion, the manager, John Bloomsfield, said the bikers were welcome providing everything drifted along without a hitch, and one must state these bearded marauders were a good bunch of drifters along with their wives, girlfriends and families! Now, Friday and Saturday evening, I had a pool table booked at the gander; however, one Saturday night, when the ambulance crews were on strike and the British army were conveying the sick, Tony and I arrived as usual for a game and I set the balls on our table whilst Carpenter made a bolt for the bar. "Tony, I am going to the gents!"

When I returned, two men were playing pool and using my balls! "Excuse me, friends, that's our table and they are my balls you're playing with! These lunatics were Liverpudlians and obviously looking for an argument and I said, "Pals, if you're looking for trouble, you've come to the right place!" And unbeknown, they'd picked the wrong joint! "Sorry, amigo, but that's our pool table!"

"Who said?" came an instant reply. I rolled the black ball into a pocket!

"Chaps, your game is over!" Now, these stupid mugs didn't take kindly to my jest!

"Now, it's ours."

"Here is two pounds! When we've finished, you can have our table, is that clear?" One of these illiterate goons standing behind me smashed his cue across the back of my head and this rod snapped, would you believe? I turned to face him and said, "Was that a kind of gesture?" An audience gathered, watched, waiting patiently for my reaction! I cried, "Excuse me, bikers, am I allowed to defend myself?"

"Rock and roll," came angry voices.

"Shaken but not stirred," said Bond.

I turned and said. "I like it, put up your dukes!" They appeared stunned by my reaction; suddenly, holy smokes, a couple of punches flowed, and two more bit the dust! Later, army ambulance drivers arrived and carted them down a narrow flight of stairs just as jolly Roger and headbutted Paul turned up! "I see Sid has been at work," exclaimed Layton.

I've just remembered the Jolly Sailor pub in Poole! The date, early seventies! I was speaking with Chris Long, the head bartender, when a man came to me saying I wasn't very tough and that he wanted to take me outside! I explained that in fact, I'd said nothing and that his so-called pals were winding him up, stoking the fire, but he wasn't having any of this! Eventually, I approached him saying, "I've had just about enough of this silly tomfoolery!"

He said, "Outside!"

I replied, "Ok!" He stepped into an alleyway and I followed, then I stepped back inside!

His mates shouted, "Sid, ye chickened it!"

I cried, "Any more offers?"

"Why?"

"Well, I suggest you take a peek outside?"

They went to the doorway! Outside, this chap awoke with blood oozing profusely! And one more bit the dust, ok? "Anyone fancy inviting me out?" Nobody uttered a word, just silence, music to my ears! What a gutless bunch of morons, then the band played on.

Another occasion, I was standing at the main bar, drinking coke, when Terry Barry went to the gent's toilet. We were in the company of friends, Fats and Spicy Ginger! Next to me was a lady who spoke quite regal. She said, "I wouldn't care to meet Terry in a secluded alleyway!"

"Why?" said I.

"Just look at him!"

"How do you mean?"

"Terry is naturally very strong with that broken nose and rugged looks!"

"Madame, it's not him you don't want to meet but the one who gave him that ugly mug dogged features that'll frighten the pants off a scarecrow!"

"My word, you're correct, I wonder who gave him that face?"

"Me."

"You, who do you think you are?"

"I gave him that face!"

"I don't believe it."

"Lady, I'm the one who gave him the nose job; I should have been a plastic surgeon!" Barry was on his way back. "My friend," said I, "whom was it awarded you that broken nose?" Now, this man was handsome beyond one's wildest imagination.

"You did, Sid," and I replied, "thank you," and I turned back to the bar. One day, my pal, Richard Cobb, an acquaintance, went passed the registrar's office situated on Parkstone Road! My mother, Jean Lovell, a registrar, was standing outside with newly-weds as Cobb strolled by! "Richard," said Mum, "have you got stitches on your face?"

"Yes, Sid did it!"

"No."

"Down at the old Jolly Sailor on Sunday!" This was novel! I came out of the pub to go home. Cobb started mucking around, throwing punches in my direction! Several different occasions, I asked him to stop, but he kept foolishly messing around, then I unintentionally poked my hand out, catching him on the eyebrow; fifteen stitches later, what could I say? I was just sitting here when I suddenly remembered our Dave climbing the tree into that warehouse and finding army surplus condoms. We thought they were water bombs and loaded our pram until it was full up! On several occasions, we travelled back and forth until we literally had maybe five thousand and hid them in the cellar, also, under the shed, and lined our den in the garage far away from prying eyes! That night, our mum and dad went out drinking! Barry got the rubber sheath, then loaded them with water before tying knots.

Outside our bedroom was a bus stop a throwing distance away! We peeped out the window. Ladies were standing under a bus shelter, waiting for a bus! Our window was wide open, since it was summertime! Out went a bomb, sailing through the airway and a second later came a horrendous scream! It went deadly quiet and we could feel their eyes searching our house, but we never moved! Too frightened, and I knew those ladies would skin us alive, maybe, we'd land in hot water, possibly the jail or hung at Execution Dock! I was shaking, "Never again, Lord, please forgive us!"

Barry asked people leaving the pub if they wanted any and sold them to complete strangers!

Made an absolute packet! Every day, we went back, again and again but I couldn't understand it, why would adults want to make water bombs? Baz did say the men of Bethnal Green said, "Get more," as their old ladies and girlfriends loved them! This was most intriguing! The officials in the warehouse not only robbed us of our precious rags but Bethnal Green lost their water bomb bags! Sad day for our community but never mind, we'd hid a stash for a bit of fun and forgot all about them. A year later, when I was in secondary school, this teacher had a white bomb just dangling from his overcoat, then this light bulb went on, and I remembered a hole Tinker our dog had dug, and it was full with water bomb bags, so I rushed home and informed Barry, but he knew! He said, get a shovel, and bring me a box! I began unearthing our treasure and dad came out just as I was pulling the sack out.

"Sidney, what are you doing?" Well, blow me down, dad's caught me red handed! He took the sack and opened it! His face radiated like a sun, why? "Get the rest," he commanded. Later, he disappeared, and I informed our Baz, who wasn't too pleased with me.

"Never mind, we've got plenty more," and I never saw those water bombs explode over screaming women again. Barry saw to that and I must say, at the time, them women were worse than the creature from the black lagoon!

Now, back into the mid-eighties, when I operated the door at the Badger Bars, mind you only at the weekend! On Fern Road, manager Lee Thomas, who was a great friend, had long before left this pub. It was Thursday evening, and I was doing my rounds! The badger bar was staging a hen party with a male stripper etc. One of my security men had volunteered to assist the DJ, so I called in; apparently, the advertisement hadn't worked as the girls hadn't bothered to show up! The pub's manager cancelled the entertainment and opened the doors to the general public!

The door staff were not advised to stop charging entrance fee, so continued. At this time, the place was almost empty, and those that paid never complained! It so happened a coach from Frome in Somerset was passing and saw a sign outside. They came in and were charged two pounds each, total of fifty pounds. They were informed the evening's entertainment had been cancelled but all they wanted was a heavy drinking session and disco! These fellows went down the stairs to the lower bars. Most of them paid for their alcohol but four chaps quizzed the price!

I'd arrived but didn't know they'd been charged entrance fee, which was totally out of order by the management, and the price of beer was still well over normal! A chap asked why they'd hiked the beer price. The barman said, "That's the price," which they didn't agree!

This person said, "The price on the pump says one thing and you tell us another!"

"That's the price!" The barman, in my opinion, should've reported to the boss and asked if the prices could be reduced back to the normal, but he wasn't a bit bothered.

They said, "We'll pay that pump price!" Which is, in my eyes, totally correct, seeing how this evening hadn't worked as planned! The price of beer should automatically be reduced to normal pub prices. This barman refused, next, this ogre punched him in the face! Yes, he'd got his reward for being an argumentative prat but what happened next was out of order! Well, I was flabbergasted! This inept looking lad was passing them by when this much taller person of athletic build headbutted him. This youngster fell upon the pub's old cobbled floor! This lad had done nothing but walk past! Now, I swung into action!

"You stupid twat, why did you do that? He was an innocent bystander!"

These four fellows turned in my direction! "What's it to do with you?"

"I agree with you punching the idiot behind the bar! He deserved everything, but you, twerp, struck this man who had nothing to do with your argument so that makes it my business!"

"Who are you?"

"I'm nobody, but pick up ya dukes!" In a thundering flash, he was unconscious upon hard floor! I hadn't been informed of a coach party. They'd paid two pounds each, a total of fifty pounds! Twenty-five strapping bumpkins, and I'd taken one out! Not good odds for them, seeing as Neil Chalton, one of my security, was behind the DJ console giving us an unfair advantage! Two against twenty-four! My word, one's mind boggles, at least one unconscious and before the night draws to a close, there'll be a few more, and I hazard a guess this lot came extremely fast, driving me backward as their numbers rapidly increased! I unfortunately fell over a wooden bench, landing on the cobbles! Next! this lad kicked me in the throat, and my mouth opened, and my tongue popped out! I scrambled to my feet and headed over to a wall close to the stairs doors! I turned, they were upon me, throwing punches!

I stood my ground! "Ok, punks, I'll wait this out!" My armour was intact; when I've a free hand, watch it now, here comes a blunderbuss! Out came a clenched fist, striking one clean blow for mankind! "And one broken nose for sale!" Next one! They were amateurish! Neil arrived, grabbing some fellows from me, leaving my right arm free! "Hey, cop this, another one bites the dust and yet another." Then I took hold of another as his mates beat retreat like Custer's final stand! "Pal, let me entertain you."

"Let go!" said this stranger, "and we'll call it a day!"

"Fine by me!"

Blood was gushing from my mouth so I went up the stairs into the road before popping next door into Zigzag's, a nightspot with our security in attendance. I went into a toilet. I had somehow bitten right through my tongue. When I returned, they'd left! The landlord said, "Four people were carried out!" Not too bad for a night's work! Next evening, Neil Charlton worked at Longs wine bar when he noticed a few men from the badger bar the evening prior! They said, "All we done was hit that man, and he was knocking us out! Four of us went to the hospital with broken noses!" I shall say that I was pleased with the overall outcome! My mind resembles a time machine with me travelling back and forth, stopping here and there.

Back in the past, I would say, Barry, Dave and me were similar to the Backstreet Boys. We all wore hand-me-down, short trousers with our Dave pushing polished pram and Baz holding my hand as we marched! At the bottom of our stairs, leading to the garden, was a door consisting of panelled sections. Upper half was two long narrow window panes, however, the right window pane was missing for over a year! I'd cry, "Come on, Tink," and he came flying down the stairs and leapt out through the empty section into our garden. One day, our dad repaired the door, replacing the missing panel with a heavy piece of glass! I shouted, "Come along, Tinker!" He came bounding down the flight of stairs and whoops, the glass panel stopped Tinker in his tracks and nearly killed the silly blodger! If he'd hit the heavy pane of glass any harder, folk would be coming around, singing, "How much is that doggie in the window frame!"

A point of interest! In our security team, I hold the record for confirmed cases of breaking most noses in one day: four at the badger bars! Next in line is Tony Carpenter with three! Now, one evening, at third side, Paul was informed by a female, three men in the lower bar were tipping drinks over girls, then laughing! He called us over for help. Normally, it's only morale support but on this occasion, there were three men causing a fracas. We went down where we confronted them.

Two ladies were absolutely drenched in beer. These chaps were laughing. Two were tall and well developed, and the other ogre was exceptionally tall, I'd say, six-feet seven-inches!

Paul Layton turned to these punks and said, "I'm asking you to stop pouring beer over girls!"

"Who are you?"

"We're the monster mash party!"

"What?"

"Cop this!" Next moment, this fellow's holding his chin, which is out of shape, and he was moaning!

"I like it," said Layton, "You two dear chaps, assist your mate and please get him out of this club." Outside, I could see this person's mouth was, as I faced him, out of alignment! If I left hooked him, common sense suggests, it would require repositioning his jaw, but instead, it appeared to make things worse! Several months passed, then I saw him and reported back to Paul. "This fellow is drinking from a straw!" I was called to the sour-grapes at the triangle.

"A giant was causing trouble on the dance floor, nobody could handle him!" I arrived after midnight. There were two of them. I would say, there wasn't much space between him and the upper interior! On entering this establishment, a doorman stated, he just walked in, didn't say much but looked quiet and shy.

I cried, "Punks leave!" My fist sank into his midriff and "Ouch, that hurt," exclaimed this citizen, and yes, another one bites the dust!

Eventually, they went outside and drifted as a punter remarked, "Elvis has left the building!" Everything relating to bouncing appeared to revolve around me, and I'll say, there certainly was never a dull moment being with the likes of our doormen! One evening, Lorraine put sweets in a bowl. "Tonight, you're not going out, so just leave it to Roger and Paul!"

"Ok, I'll ring them!"

Later, Ken Cooper sent word trouble was brewing at the anchor bar! "Both managers are attending, but you're required!" I reached the Royal Exeter and walked to the seafront but every step of the way, I flatulated! Other doormen from all over Bournemouth converged upon the anchor. I could not understand why my stomach was acting up! Behind me, our staff were creasing themselves. "Sid, you don't need us, you'll blow 'em down like ten-pin bowls!"

"Boss, bowl them over!" We arrived and the storm abated! When I eventually returned to our humble abode, was told by my mother and Lorraine this novel story. She said, "I put flatulent sweets in that bowl; you picked every one! No wonder you were trumpeting."

Prior to home, I stopped at the Godfather for a midnight feast! That's what our children called them! A bit of bother came in whilst I was in there! The owner asked them to leave but they refused! "Gentlemen, you're going home, either you walk, or I'll call an ambulance for you, what will it be?"

A man said, "He's Sid Falconer! We're going!" The proprietor was extremely thankful and presented me with everything from burgers to spare ribs, southern fried chicken, to pizza; later, we had a banquet!

I began Falconer Security at Oscars nightspot, part of the Royal Exeter complex! John Church from London was the proprietor and indeed master of the realm. A good person but manager, Bob Shepherd, held the reins! He gave me permission to run the door but only because I said I'd stay at Thirdside if I didn't run the door, so he agreed and I came along for the ride! As I've stated previously, Bob was a likeable chap but needed controlling! We had a falling out over my pay!

My wage doubled, then I began organising doors elsewhere! Within a week, I'd picked up three places requiring doormen! Trouble in the town was rife and I knew just how to stop it! Police their establishments with a call for assistance. Whenever a fracas started, phone for assistance! I took all the men, bar one, from Oscars and returned as soon as possible after a dispute was over! This worked fine! I organised coverage from each location to converge when required, with consent of their establishment, upon venues in trouble!

Every doorman required a smart black suit and bow-tie, this was standard regulation! Soon, I ran doors everywhere from Poole to Southampton! All due to Bob Shepherd plus my imagination! As our business developed, I recruited two managers, Roger and Paul, to collect and instruct our doormen with our policy which was be extremely polite and open doors for punters! Say, "Hello, good evening and welcome to this fine establishment!" Never get involved in an incident but call for backup! It was our managers job to talk with clientele instead of mixing the business and avoid fighting like the plague! Only when necessary and unavoidable, and yes, the final resort, take the punk out without anybody seeing!

One evening, in Spats wine bar, a chap was out of control, and there was no other option for me, so the only course of action left open was to say, pick up your dukes, and hooked him, then Roger or Paul, I can't remember who, took hold of one arm whilst I had the other, then we escorted him out!

He was barely conscious so customers probably thought this punter was dead drunk!

I don't need trouble, but it always seemed to find me, such as a time we employed Nobby Clark from Kinson at Oscars! He was a big son of a goatherder! Always touching the ladies! One night, his girlfriend came in, an argument began, one minute quiet, then the next, a fracas flashed out of control, ending with Clark assaulting her! I said, "Nobby, stop it!" Don't forget this idiot was employed by me; suddenly, he pushed me intact, I fell over an armchair and a table, which really doesn't matter! Fact, Rambo drew first blood! "That's it, put up your dukes!" He came quite fast but whoopee, I conquered, and before he could say jackflash, I planted a seed right on his conk and unexpectedly, he's fast asleep, extraordinary peacefully, resembling a wall flower, all picturesque-like! Later that evening, I received word Clark was outside, stating he wanted to exact revenge and was waiting redemption. "Come outside."

"Get lost." Now that's a song! I then obliged but when it came to the crunch and I appeared suddenly, he lost his jolly green bottle along with his dear old legs! What a gutless punk? I gather it's ok punching a lady about, but when it comes to fighting a man, well, that's a different story!

I'll never understand tough diamonds battering women, like the time a girl approached me saying downstairs, a Liverpudlian, a scouser, has just knocked her best friend unconscious, and he's dancing around as though it's a joke! Blood is everywhere! I went down and noticed this scouser dancing with his legs astride an unconscious female! I approached and asked him to accompany me upstairs, because I want to talk to him regarding this matter! He duly accepted my invitation but when we arrived at the stairs, he declined my invitation! He turned away from the stairs and didn't notice two bouncers; next, they hoisted him and away they went up to ground level and out onto the road via the exit! Outside, he screamed revenge against me! "Come out!"

"Are you sure?" I remarked.

"Come out, and I'll kill you!" He produced this dirk.

Once again, I said, "Are you sure you want me to come out?"

"I'll murder you, come out!" I've stepped into Stafford road and said, Pick up your dukes, and a flash of thunder from Thor, and another one bites the dust. "Bobby George, what would you say?"

"Lubbly jubbly!"

One night, I was sitting with Josie, the proprietor in Zigzags night spot, when Roger Paul and Tony arrived, saying, Dave Martin, who works at a nightspot we call Ron Wade's old place, wouldn't let them in and said he'd do the same thing to me! When we finally arrived, Tony rang the bell. Ding dong and Martin opened the door, saying, "I've already told you, and he most certainly wasn't expecting me!

"Hello, Davy Crockett, I presume," says I in this old pirate tone. 'Have ye got a kind word for ya old mucker?" One time, I employed shameful David, back a few years prior, at the Sour Grapes in the triangle! He got the push! The old heave-ho! Got caught on camera banging out two little boys! Naughty-like and made a name for himself! Thought he could take on a big boy, did our Martin! "'Ere I be, shipmate!" cried I.

Suddenly, David replied, "As I told them, you're not welcome here!" Davy took a swing! I returned, full complement! Instantly, another one bit the dust! Blood covered a deck as I stood back to give Roger a turn! He stepped inside, "Anybody else want a piece of the action?"

"Any takers?" said Paul, standing beside his pal, ready for battle! The other doormen thought twice before mixing the business with my compadres. "Now, cat weasel, it was most certainly the right time for me but the wrong place for them!"

David, maybe, once upon a time, you were sane but now ye live in cloud-cuckoo-land hey, what! "Immature, our Davy, to think he could take on a boxing machine!"

"What's going on?" remarked a fellow from behind us. "Nothing!" said I.

"We're the CID."

"EI Cid, get out of the way, I'm coming through." And I wasn't in a mood for a couple of nosey prats claiming to be plain-closed officers who hadn't seen anything; actually, I'd seen these two coppers before! A pair of liars! They weren't CID but ordinary run-of-the-mill policemen; mind you, most of the police were trustworthy unlike these lying toe rags!

As we walked away, one said "I'll have you!"

Paul turned quickly and faced them both saying, "Suckers, wanna fight? I am here; I'll take on the pair of you!" Chicken refused his invitation, and I wonder why? Later, I received an official letter to attend crown court, charged with grievous bodily harm! An assault upon tough guy David Martin, can you believe, hey what? He actually threw his fist at me, initiating this whole incident, then when it's back fired, he resorted to this level! How low can one sink? "What a guttersnipe!" It won't do any good, the truth will prevail, and the day arrived, and I attended court! "May I speak with the jury?"

"You may," came the reply from a judge!

"Martin, the gutless swine, once worked for me, but I sacked him for bashing two men without cause or provocation! He threw a right hand clenched fist in my direction; had I not moved, it would've struck me! According to the law, I am allowed to protect myself using minimal force! What is minimal against an assailant ready to inflict bodily harm or maybe worse, possibly, it's quite plausible, even death!"

I had the jury in the palm of my hand and I was going to close it tighter than a can of sardines! "The manager and the other three bouncers inside this club have stated, in writing, David Martin threw the first punch and Falconer defended himself, so why am I here, attending court? Answer: these two lying toerags claiming to be CID." My solicitor, Mister Keith O'Neil from Andrew McQueen's said this was a trump up charge!

"Not guilty," cried the jury foreman!

"Have a good day," I replied, leaving the dock!

"Morning, grasshopper, it's nice to see you."

"Jumping jeepers, Sid, I see jackrabbits are butchering cabbage munchers!"

"You're joking?"

"Nope, the flat-footed fleabags are spilling blood and guts all over Headache!

"This is the wrong book, get back from whence you come!" Now, let's drift back to Berlin! There were four areas, one was the Russian, another American, third, French and British. Somehow, I was in the American sector without my pals! I must've gone to a toilet or something but when I turned around, they were gone, and I was alone and didn't have a clue where to go and locate them! That's what I must do! Next, I'm at a bar, asking a young German girl if she'd seen my friends! A smart American soldier came over to me. I was dressed in civvies and wasn't looking for any trouble, least of all here with an American army! The place was chock-a-block with us uniforms but before one could vacate these premises, this tall redneck jerk invited me outside. I was being friendly, but he accused me of chatting his fiancée! How this day came to pass? God only knows, yet here I was facing a general court martial, or so it appeared! This is a sharp reminder to our troops: don't get lost in enemy territory!

I said, "I'm looking for my mates and I've only enquired if she had noticed anyone fitting their description," but this GI wasn't bothered one iota! He wanted a tussle, and I'm in the wrong place! Still, never mind, I'll go down boxing these kippers! He took a shot but it backfired, and he wasn't expecting what came next; neither did I and never in a million years expected what came next for I knocked a sack of salt out of him; suddenly, another one bit the dust. "Know what I mean?"

"Lovely jubbly," said old Delboy.

Maybe a couple of years later, two soldiers from the Prince of Wales regiment told me they'd seen this action! They were at the pub in the American sector when hellfire broke loose, and they thought I was a German civilian; well, it is nice to know someone can vouch this did occur!

Down the road from Montgomery Barracks, Berlin was the PK public bar and on the corner was Alfred's bar! One afternoon, I recall a fracas occurred following a heated discussion! Passmore, a slender chap, was sitting with his new girlfriend, a nice German lass. Should I say was, because he had gone to the lavatory; on his return, he was confronted by a massive stranger occupying a seat he'd just vacated next to his girl! "Excuse me, that's my saddle!" (part of a bench seating) "Could you go and park elsewhere?"

"I'm happy here!" said the citizen. There was no need for this; punk was taking an absolute liberty! A total bully! Worse kind of human, a bloody skunk! "Excuse me, pal, get out of his seat!" I think one of his associates recognised me as he spoke to him all kind of hushed! Next, this gopher apologised and sat elsewhere! Later, I left the pub; outside, chaps, including the one I'd had words with, were waiting for me; suddenly, out from the old public house emerged half a dozen Germans! Pepe, my pal, had watched them leave and this was the result! Well, these English louts took a jolly good old fashioned pasting by German army! It was like watching an uproarious football match: Germany one, England nil. Would you believe the creeps were PWO?

"NO," they most certainly were.

Back to the badger bars! I was in pain and sitting on a counter at the end of the main bar! A young person was standing next to where I was sitting. A brawl between the barman and a customer erupted, and as I moved, this fellow kicked me right in the cobblers! I keeled over ever so slightly, simultaneously striking out, catching him, taking out his glasses, smashing one upon cobbled floor, and another one bit the dukes! A short time later, I went outside! By this time, there were at least twelve of them! This person I'd dropped turned out to be the groom! Somebody shouted, "That shyster knocked our pal out and smashed his glasses!" He was lucky I didn't knock his head off!

Gutless rat was supposed to be getting married; well, they came and I lifted a few before they turned tail! In the lower bar, I'd done nothing to warrant this violent attack, so he got less than he actually bargained for or deserved! What agent I am, don't you agree?

Now, Spats wine bar! Two brothers were selling dope in the toilets but instead of calling the police, I asked them politely to leave, but instead, they told me in no uncertain terms what I could do. Well, I said, "Pick up thy dukes!" A second, possibly, and one was on the deck! I turned a bit as the elder brother pleaded for mercy! Jim Dudley, one of my doormen, was standing by a door, keeping folk out! I talked to this ugly man and again asked him to take his brother and leave; then, unbeknown to me, his kin had gotten up and grabbed my legs! I went backwards and lost my balance, and over went I, with a bang, and him, still attached to me! Next, I'm being kicked whilst poor Dudley, being afraid, just watched, then in came a second security officer, Rod Rickard, who at least said, "Come on, let him go!" Except for this, he did nothing. Finally, I got up, but by this time, had sustained an injury to my hand then Wim, the proprietor, said, "Sid, let them go!" I was about to slaughter these useless shitehawks! Outside, these punks gave a bit of bravado. Pistol Pete, what I'd have given to have left those two gutless pigs in the gutter with blood flowing from the nostrils and bleeding profusely and broken teeth but instead, complied with Wim's request! Another occasion, Ken Cooper was on duty at the Branksome Arms in the Triangle, Bournemouth! Around nine pm, Roger, Paul and I were playing pool upstairs which we normally did on Friday and Saturday evening when it was booked for us and our security team! This particular night, five gents in their late twenties or possibly early thirties decided to ridicule the doorman, goad him, give this door attendant some grief. Mike, the pub manager, came upstairs and told us Ken was having problems with some tough-looking dudes and didn't think he could handle the situation!

I said, "Whilst you're playing, I'll take a peek!" Kenneth saw me, then asked one fellow to leave! He blatantly refused, next, Mister Cooper put his arm around this buffoon then hoisted him off a seat, nice and easy! Ken surprised me! Yes, he knew I was there as backup, physical support but fair play to him, they were very large blokes, possibly, anything could happen and he was doing a great job, full credit to him then he escorted this brute outside into a moonlit night, thus reminding me of old Mexico and that infamous speedy Gonzalez!

Outside, I took over! A thought crossed my mind! There were four of them still inside! I said, "If you behave, I'll let you go back in but if you start any shenanigans, we'll turf you out, understand?" I didn't know the tough guys inside were planning to have a dust up!

Mike told them who we were but they said, "We're rugby players, and can sort them!" Out they came surrounding Kenny and I! "Do you know where an intensive care unit is?" shouted their leader.

"Why?" replied I.

"Because I'm gonna knock your blooming lights out!"

"Pal, I'm Sid Falconer," but before I could say jackrabbit like, pick up your dukes, he attacked, and I automatically hooked him, and over he sailed, and his head split like a ripe tomato! They moved! I said, "Anyone else?" Yes, another one bit the dust, but I wasn't amused but concerned with his health! I said, "Call an ambulance." Instead, his mates just picked him up and off down the road they went! Late evening, the police arrived and took statements, why? Seeing nobody ever reported this incident! A constable asked me to accompany him to the police station, and I replied, "Get your facts right and statements from those involved before inviting me, for I only defended myself! He was just a cop with no evidence whatsoever, so why the invitation? Answer, there are many marvellous chickens in a coop but there is always one rotten egg in every basket. Why? Johnny Boucher is a man with the heart of a lion, Terry Downes from South Africa, Ivor Evans and Jimmy Redman ran the door at Sour Grapes! Luckily, we hardly got calls from this quarter! One evening at the Branksome, Roger, Paul and, of course, yours truly heard an almighty racket erupting outside in the road, and it sounded like a riot! We looked out from the upstairs window and across the way, I'd say, there were eighty or more national front campaigners—an organised body arousing public interest! This was reminiscent of a military operation, and my word, they were going hammer and tongs, swearing abuse, directing all their anger towards the Branksome Arms public house! The national front movement apparently suspected, or were led to believe, this old public bar was full of gay folk which I suspect wasn't true; anyway, did it really matter? A small number in this massive group attacked the main door! Mister Cooper, meanwhile, put a pool cue in a position which prevented the front door opening except by heavy force! This kept the rioters at bay! We came down the stairs as the window exploded and stood at the bar in case them political knobheads entered; suddenly, I said, "God, I feel ill."

Paul replied, "No wonder, look down!" On the ground, directly in front of us, was this gas canister discharging its content! Water filled my eye sockets! Unexpectedly, a loud explosion and a stream of fluid cascaded downward like a river flows! This may sound theatrical, but this is the only way I can explain how I felt at that particular time! Half an hour later, the police cordoned off the upper road but didn't attempt to intervene! An inspector invited us to enter the Pembroke Shades where, many years prior, our boxing gym was situated, to identify ring leaders. This remark from the law enforcement was utterly ridiculous! Quite improper, actually, to suggest our lads do their job so I suggested his constables move into the bar whilst we'll stay outside and when his officers fetch suspects outside, we will point to instigators! Policemen went inside then came back with skinheads, and we picked the obvious ringleaders out! There were umpteen arrests that evening but many eluded capture because they were not inside the shades at that one moment in time; however, later, Tony Carpenter and I were walking, I'll say, back to the Branksome Arms when we reached a gents toilet. He decided to go inside for a leak, meantime, across the road, a young skin-headed woman came up the main road with two comrades as Tony came out of the public urinals instantly recognising her from outside the Branksome earlier! She was definitely one of the ringleaders. "Excuse me, miss, weren't you involved in an incident?"

"Yes," came her reply!

"Well, in that case, I'm making a citizen's arrest!" What happened next was most amusing and quite enjoyable, so get a cuppa and keep reading. Unbeknown to my mate, two other rioters, whom, I must say, were giants, came up behind my pal to do him harm! Words were exchanged, and they were very aggressive towards my comrade!

One was, I'd say, colossal, so I interrupted, "Pardon me but I don't like to say this; my associate has made an arrest and if you wish to leave, do so but I've a sneaky feeling you're looking for some action, am I right? If so, you've come to the right gent!"

"Spot on!"

"In that case, you thumping, great oaf, pick up your dukes!" In a couple of ticks, I've chopped this absolute monstrosity down like felling an enormous redwood and another one bites the dust, would you believe, when I'd turned around, guess what? A police van with several coppers climbing out!

"Amigo," said this sergeant. "Full marks, magnifico!" Well, the other officers clapped their hands and clapped them in irons, just joking. "Gentlemen," remarked this officer, "we'll take it from here, and I'll say goodnight to you. Pick them up! Lady, I am arresting you for inciting a riot!"

I just hate hitting folk because I know the outcome and nobody can ever call me a bully! Now, when I was working at the Chelsea Village in Bournemouth, Johnny Radcliffe, a former professional boxer, came on duty wearing a beautiful shiner! John weighed in the region of ten stone or maybe eleven but not much more! A gutsy fighter, like a little leopard! I said, "Johnny, what damn well happened to you?

"I got in a wee pickle last evening."

"Who watched your back?" Then this situation developed on the dance floor, and all hell broke out! "Leave them twerps to me!" There were door staff standing with Radcliffe and I at the main bar! "Stay here, and watch me do the business, and don't move." There were three raised dance areas plus a lower level section covering most of the club, leading to the stage! Umpteen characters were fighting! It was like a massive battle being staged before my eyes; suddenly, they paired! This was my opportunity! I marched down, took two pillocks by their long hair and knocked heads together, then I banged another set until everywhere men were holding their heads or blooming well crying! Served them right for causing a fracas! I returned to the bar! "That's how things should be done, lads, evict them." The next day, I saw the notorious Ginger Potter! I caught his eye, because he went across old Christchurch Road! "Hey, Ginger, what's up?" Knowing I'd obviously seen him, came over! "I heard on the grapevine, did you knock-out sixteen men last night in the Chelsea?" "Not quite," said I and laughed! "About ten!" I hadn't KOed any! "Sid, word around these parts travels fast." Ginger was a lovely guy, as far as I was concerned! Now, back in 1985, Potter and another chap came into our nightclub in Christchurch, unfortunately, carrying a bag etc, and purchased a drink then before leaving, showed me its content! I don't know why but inside was dope and money, around ten thousand pounds! I said, "Ginger, get out of here, and take him with you!" They went down the fire-escape at the rear into a car park then drove off! God, they're both half-sloshed, so I shot down the front stairs and along the road, hopefully to stop these drunks, then I witnessed this police car chase after them! The very next evening, a woman visited me in the club and asked if Ginger had left anything in my club! I said he hadn't! She told me Potter and his mate were dead! They'd been chased by the old bill. "Yes, I know, I'd seen a patrol vehicle go after them but I thought there was only one officer in the police car!" Apparently, along Matchams Lane, he'd veered off the road and struck a tree! Several years later, his son, Paul, introduced a few good disc jockeys at my nightspot and set my club buzzing and Valentines became the number one club along the south coast, all thanks to Paul Potter! Now, I believe he is a top DJ in the Caribbean, which brings joy to my heart!

Bumbles Nightclub on Poole Hill, Bournemouth, springs into my mind, gracefully cavorting back and forth just like a hophead, drunkard or horny frog leaping to and fro, here and there! Roger, Paul and I, with Tony taking up the rear! This evening was steadily drawing upon the midnight hour when we reached our final port of call! In this establishment were two splendid lounges, each with a bar! A top and lower section! We chose the upper! Paul led the way, followed by Roger, me and last of all, tail-end Tony bringing up the rear! I became aware of a hefty hunk instantly when I entered the lounge. As Paul was passing, this brute intentionally, although somewhat clumsily, barged into him! Instinctively, Layton turned, reared, ready to strike with deadly accuracy! This ogre moved away, all apologetic-like. A few seconds passed before Roger passed by, and the same type of situation occurred; then, it was my turn but he decided against this course of action and subsequently side-stepped me but there was still one more, Tony! And yes, I'm patiently watching each microscopic detail but now! I turned my back away, leaving one's pal to face this monster alone! Moments passed then this goon accused him of bumping into him! "Outside," cried this enormous giant. I don't know if I've mentioned this fact but when I boxed in the army, I never had more than four days training before fighting soldiers like the paratroopers, who trained fifty-two weeks a year, and I still managed to give them a real belting!

Tony knocked my foot but I took no notice, and again came heavy foot-tapping, eventually, I turned, then gave an almighty laugh! Everyone in the top bar turned towards me! I put my hand in front of Mister Carpenter and moved him back! "Now, son of a goatherder, I'll tell you a wee tale!" I felt a sudden coolness approach and a stilled-silence in the air, a kind of hush all over the place, and thought, silence is golden! "Pig face, my pal, Paul, walked in and you knocked him, Roger entered, and you did the same but bypassed me, then your chance approached, yes, the icing on the cake, Tony came onto the scene! Let me explain, he's, one would say, around five feet nine inches tall, not stocky built. I would put you somewhere in the region of six two, broad at the shoulder, narrow at the hip! A typical twat, now pick on one of my friends, and ya pick on me! You're leaving Roger, take his glass!" I escorted him to the main entrance but halfway down the steps is a wee landing, and an echo rang-out, signalling another one bites the dust! I forgot to mention, I said, "Pick up ya dukes," and knocked him unconscious.

A few minutes passed, then door staff carried this character out and left him lying in a gutter; later came heavy pounding on the main entrance doors. Eventually, I went downstairs to enquire where all this noise was coming from! The security staff said, "It's that bloody geek you knocked out banging on the door!"

"Why don't you open the door?"

"We don't want any trouble."

"For crying sake, open it!" I said, "What's wrong?"

"I want a beer!"

"Ok, fair play, it's your round."

"Sure enough, governor!

"This doorman wants a pint!"

"Whatever!" Back upstairs we went!

"Roger, Paul, Tony, this chap would like to buy a round for us all but first, you must apologise for your ungentlemanly conduct!"

"Sorry, wanna drink?" I respect Liverpudlians but everywhere in this world, there is good and bad! After two months of constant fracas involving scousers, I hung a notice on the main window, aimed solely at the few trouble shooters. One evening, when I was patrolling in the lower level, our manager, Lee Beeston, informed me saying, "There are eight Liverpudlians outside, calling, offering to kick my head in, now, that's not very nice or polite, is it?" Let's not forget I could be maimed for life or murdered, hey, what! What would you do, call for help? Telephone the constabulary or next best thing, call an ambulance? Well, I'd put a letter on the window! Now, I must stand up and be counted and face the consequence! Outside I went! "I accept your invite! Lads, it's showtime!" They were a wild bad bunch and I'm a mean son of? Cowpoke! "Pick up ya dukes!" Pest one flew over the cuckoo's nest and rest did their best and put me to the test then legged it as another, "deputy dog, one bit the dust!"

Back in the late seventies, eighties, and early part of the nineties, we ran the doors of many fine establishments and had a lot of door staff who were under strict orders to call for assistance and never get involved in a confrontation! This was my strict code of conduct! Bumbles was owned by Fidel, a fabulous friend who, in 1974, worked with me at La Maximes! His club was getting a lot of bad publicity! Incidents occurring regularly inside and outside involving gypsies! I went along to his local premises to stop the fracas, let's say, nip them in the bud! Once word gets around to the hard men that Bumbles is a no-go area, then I could return to running our door business, but for now, I was going under cover, back to the very heart of my roots! Standing at the main entrance one evening, club doorman Gary said, "We've got problems!"

Malcolm Tottle, my pal, said, "Why?"

"Bow Murphy is pulling up outside, and he's trouble!"

"We'll handle it, you go upstairs!" A gypsy, along with a female, came up to us! "Good evening," said I, "are you members?"

"Yes," called Bow.

"Mal, could you go upstairs and fetch the membership register, please!"

A few moments passed, then he returned. The manager was with him! "You know, I'm not a member," said Murphy. "I always come here!"

"I'm sorry but I've never seen you before and why tell me blatant lies?"

He turned to his lady, "You go back to the pickup! I'll sort this chap!" She went down a few steps, five or six at the most, leaving Murphy without his bow. "This tale's a real cracker," said Jimmy Cricket! "Murphy, you can't come in."

"You're Sid Falconer?"

"That, I am!"

"Let's go outside, and sort it out, man to man?" With this, he went down the main stairs! "Come outside?"

"Now, that's a song!" said Cricket.

"Are you sure?" He repeated his invite! Now, people were stopping, watching this fracas unfold! It was early and the sun was hot and the weather forecast, 'mainly bright!' I stepped outside and said, "I say, Bow, you punch me in the stomach, and I'll put my hands round your neck, if you can't hurt me, then it'll be my turn! One tickle on your weak chin!" With this I positioned, interlocking hands clenched tight around his neck and he began pounding away! "Is that the best you can do?" Now, he developed a cold sweat! "You're not very fit." Finally, he gave up the ghost! "You're knackered, it's my turn, cop this! Next instant, he's unconscious, with his head resting gently against the back wheel of his pickup, and once again, all together, "Another one bites the dust!" Around town, Bow was the man, now I've established that mantle! "Anyone barred from a club or pub in my small empire is banished from our entire establishments! Word passed from clubs to wine bars but when I walked into Little Peters at the Crest Hotel, Bow Murphy was there! "Punk, get out!" He left but later, we, Paul, Roger and I, went over to Spats wine bar; he was there with his pals! He saw me, then walked outside! I went after him! "Bow Murphy, don't cause any more trouble in my establishments, and you can stay in, ok?"

"Fair enough, pal!"

"Now then, return to your mates!" I never had any complaints, and indeed, an everlasting friendship developed.

A doorman from Little Peters bar at the Crest Hotel, Lansdowne, came across to Spats to inform me Keith Perkins, former manager of Adrianos nightspot, in Holdenhurst road is back in town and he's gonna show everybody Falconer ain't the hardest man in Bournemouth! (Does it matter?) Tony and I were enjoying a glass of red wine! "I'll be over in a short while!"

We carried on drinking, and I totally forgot about the threat! Later, we went inside the Crest Hotel, spoke to management then via a public restaurant, entered Little Peters! At the bar was Ben, an old friend, and Keith Perkins, of course, he's wanting a fracas, and he'd come to the right place! I approached, "Hi, Ben and Mister Perkins, how the devil are you?" With a second or two, he attempted to head butt me but I moved back! Now, would you believe it, the only empty glass on the floor and I caught my foot right on top? Now, that's funny, ha-ha, next, I've gone, tumbling backward, towards a leather seat then, I'm sat down and he's hammering away! I'm just sitting there, without a care in the world!

This badger was an amateur! Wasting his energy, and I'm simply trapping his fiery shots with my arms or catching his punches with my hands! Next moment, Tony rolled him, and I'm up on my feet! Customers had moved away! Security officer Brendan Gear approached! "Bren Gun, I'll sort it!" Perkins stood up! By this time, I moved into an open space! "Pick up ya dukes, sodger!" He came but I conquered! An uppercut lifted him and a hook finished the job! He went sailing like Rod Stewart's song, into the air, then he's horizontal and all together, "Another one bites the dust!" Well, all these folks clapped, obviously, they loved it! Tony went to the toilet, and when Keith awoke, lay him outside on all fours where a couple of tables were situated, then I went back inside! There was a glass window in this establishment which everybody was looking through.

Outside, Perkins began to call me out, so I obliged! He was making idle threats as I clambered onto a table top to entertain the audience! Carpenter appeared, then laughed! "I don't know why you are laughing because when I've finished with him, I'm gonna have you, ok?" stated Perkins.

I did a quick jig to entertain the ladies then climbed off the table and moved in his direction, and he backed away! "Punk, don't let me catch you in Bournemouth again, understand?" He began to leave, then the constabulary arrived and led him away! The next occasion I met Keith Perkins was at the West Hants tennis club! I was having a coffee with coach Graham Holden when he appeared saying, "I don't want any trouble and I'm sorry for that bout at Little Petes, can we be friends?"

"Keith, that's ok by me!"

We were in Crater City, Aden. On the top of Barclays Bank! Positioned inside a sandbag bunker or fortified sentry post with this loaded GPMG, general purpose machine gun, sited ready if and when required to open fire! Two of us were surveying every road and alleyways for any unfriendly activity. The bank managers living in quarters within this building were awarded servants! We'd go and ask for refreshments, and a Somalian female would fetch us food and drink! This pretty young lady slept in accommodation beneath the roof where a vent was situated. It was hot at night and the troops would sneak a peek! Totally out of order! She was a lovely person, sweet and innocent! Whenever we were stationed there, she'd bring us food etc, and never complained, just simply smiled then went away! One day, when I was on patrol in Crater, she approached and presented me with a choc-ice! What a nice gesture, don't you think?

Philip Webb was my best pal in Aden until I left B company, then he drifted away! His father, Sergeant Webb, trained us at Strensall, near York. Those were the days, my friends, now doesn't that remind you of a song? In the cantonment area, we'd go to the pictures and for a pint or a game of bowls! A long way from home but one night, in this restricted encampment guarded by local soldiers, I bumped into a mate from Manchester Road, Bradford, Yorkshire, Johnny Wilcox. His dad owned a sweetshop, now he was stationed in the rat. In Bradford, Johnny Winterbottom, another friend, came out of prison which turned him into a real tough guy, well at least, that's what he thought! We were mates but neither me or my best friend at that time thought he could fight!

Now, Keith Sharkey he was a true live hard nut for anyone who fancied a crack! His strength was truly beyond paranormal! An absolutely remarkable chap, also, Peter Scully! Pete's dad took us out collecting cardboard etc from tomato ketchup factories. God, the smell creased me, vomit came quickly! Never went again, you could stuff that right up your jumper! At fourteen, I was five feet, ten inches tall! Back then, I looked eighteen! My brother Barry and buddies went to the pub! One night, I was at the bar when constabulary arrived, so I turned away with a pint in each hand! They walked across to my brother who was eighteen! Asked for identification from everyone sitting down but never looked in my direction, man, that was good, "What a gas."

Well, we flew out from Berlin, Germany, and I was homeward bound with our duty free! Everyone was opening their bottles, including me! At Kings Cross station, I took a train to Foster Square station, Bradford via Leeds! This train was pulling several coaches containing compartments! Inside were seats for eight people! We entered one, with four pretty girls approximately our age!

Looking at the females, I could see they were intelligent and respectable! A big hunky soldier who I'd never seen before began to insult these wenches! Eventually, I got mad, then I can't remember anything more until arriving home! According to mum, apparently, I arrived and awoke half the neighbourhood! My suitcase was missing but eventually located at the lost property office in Leeds' lost property office. After leave, I returned to Roman Barracks, Colchester, and was informed I'd knocked this soldier unconscious, and another one bit the dust! Was arrested by an officer on the train then eventually he let me off at Leeds! Last occasion they saw me, I was walking along the main line towards Bradford! Days later, I bumped into the guy I'd knocked out, and he was still sporting black eyes! Well, that's another one bites the dust! He apologised for causing fracas! I was pleased as punch with myself because it turned out that he was one of the hard chaps from D Company, along with the likes of Eddie Kilkenny!

Eddie was the chosen one and could box a bit as well! Won not only the army championships but also included the (MELF) middle east land forces! Boxed like Mohammad Ali but looked a bit like me, white, except I turned professional! My manager, Jack Turner, asked Eddie to turn pro! Would have made a profitable living on the game, would Mister Kilkenny, ha-ha, just jesting! He's a great pal, lives in Hull with his wife, Christine, son, Sean, and lovely daughters, Lisa and Leanne!

We visit them occasionally but should go more often! We enjoy karaoke and go to their markets! Believe me, Eddie sings like Dean Martin and I could kill him with my jealously! Amazingly, Christine has voice of a saint, but Leanne! Her voice is like an archangel! Simon Cowell, I firmly believe you've never heard a voice like this! Lord gave her, by jove, this magic tone! Just hear and you will become a true believer! She sings Hallelujah just like Eddie, anybody remember that song?

Talk of the town was a nightspot in Bournemouth that I used to frequent with my buddy and professional middleweight boxer, Mike Evans! One evening, I arrived and noticed a fracas at the till! The manageress asked him to leave but this guy refused! I advised him to depart, and he left without any further nonsense, then I entered the main bar! It was dark and my eyes hadn't focused, next instant, my natural sense moved into action, automatically, I raised my hand then both arms covering an attack upon myself! Whosoever it was seemed amateurish in every meaning of the word! He was getting frustrated, agitated! Knowing he'd picked the wrong fellow to mess with then came a gap! I let rip with an uppercut, and he keeled over like the titanic on her final throes, and I recognised this insidious mug, Wally Durant! A wally medallion, sums him up! One tummy tuck and over he went. Outside it was raining cats and dogs, so I advised him to go! He must've got absolutely soaked! Mike said he had picked a fight with him! He said, "Fat prat was heavy, and you appeared, so I stated fight him he's more your size!" Well I sorted it! I'd inflicted pain and took the wind out of his sails, and he'd got a belly ache!

Why did I ever box for the Prince of Wales regiment? Answer, prestige, that's why! Because I could! When the most I trained was four days! Sergeant Garrigan could honestly vouch for this! Now, that was a man, courageous in every sense of the word. He fought with blood flowing and boxed his heart out, only to be robbed by this blind ref! This was against the paratroops, what a shambles that night in Colchester! We were totally gutted, utterly disgraceful, diabolical decisions, fragrant abuse by an awful bent referee! A typical shitehawk! That's Arabic shitehouse! I won't lower myself to his standard any longer, end of that story, amen. Nicest thing about boxing is, there's no rank once you enter the ring, like an evening I fought a corporal from the old Green Howards! I was using adroit footwork and cutting him to pieces with my left jab. Not too bad for four days training! I was slipping, then stepping gracefully in ducking and diving! Dad taught me well and I followed in his footprint, which I'm quite proud of! Met some well-known folk, celebrities unfortunately, some ain't worth a mention! Well, here I go! Peter Starsted was great entertainment at the Studland Hotel. Alum Chine! Tony Carpenter and I were called in as his minders! He was the perfect host, pure gold! Back at the Third side, in Bournemouth's triangle, in the late seventies, I met the fabulous Windsor Davies! Whilst this is still fresh in my mind! When our dad fought young Johnny Williams, as I've stated prior in this saga, Williams was led to his corner seat then came an announcement! I don't know the facts because I wasn't there but my imagination tells me it went something like this! The referee announced, "Williams cannot continue, he has suffered an injury relating to whatever and Sid Falconer has not been disqualified but on a technical merit, this bout is awarded to 23-year-old Williams!" This entire event was staged and a disgraceful episode by a bent referee. Eventually, the governing body introduced ringside judges but still, many referees have total authority of a boxing match.

I state, based on my experience, this stinks even worse than underground sewerage! Corruption reigns. "God save one's moral fibre!"

News flash, Tim Witherspoon former Heavyweight Champion of the world, apparently admitted in his book throwing his bout against Bonecrusher Smith to get out of his contract and the clutches of his manager Don King; well, in my opinion, I think he's a disgrace to himself, the general public and boxing. To lose a fight on purpose, people should boycott his book! Many pugilists would have given their right arm to have an important person like Don King as their manager and given the opportunity to get out of the gutter and become rich superstars! What an ungrateful man Tim Witherspoon was and this crook wasn't concerned one iota for his supporters! I have no sympathy for this creep, unlike John Conteh, who was fragrantly abused by top promoters in London when Light-heavyweight Champion of the world! He deserved one hundred thousand for defending his title rather than the paltry twenty-five thousand they demanded he took, and because he refused their offer, they paid up, but his reasonable argument over money unfortunately cost him his title!

Now, the Chelsea Village, Glenfern Road is where I met the Bachelors but only briefly and found them to be a great trio, laughing, quite jovial, happy go lucky and just entertaining types! I admitted them, and that's the end! Noddy Holder was another big character! Freddie Starr came in the main entrance with two tall blonds and I said, "You two ladies, go down stairs, Freddie won't be far behind!" They did what I commanded and without any fuss! "Freddie, this young female in the kiosk is Sally!" They exchanged formal greetings then, I said, "I'd like you to sing some Elvis songs for us." He began, obviously, without any music and sang some latest hits from ballads to rock-n-roll then after approximately half an hour, he finished, then off he went to find the girls! How many folks can honestly say the legendary Freddie Starr sang songs for them! He was truly unbelievable, and I never got his autograph, would you believe?

Our gymnasium on Bournemouth Road was officially opened by the minister of sport, Dennis Howe. A few celebrities were present including Don McClean and Lenny Henry! He loves talking, period, no, only joking about boxing, and I was the top doggie in this field around these parts! Lenny picked up our son and placed Sidney upon his shoulders while Lorraine took a movie! One night, Roger, Paul, me and another doorman went in the Henry Tudor wine bar owned by Tilio Jones! Seated near the bar was Jim Davison with a couple of gents! I approached him and politely introduced myself and asked him, extremely gracefully, "Jimmy, where's your show being staged?"

Before he could utter a word, his manager said, "There's no free tickets!"

"Rodney, what a plonker," says Del Boy. I was extremely annoyed by his remark! These people have no right to treat us with disrespect just because they are managers of a celebrity who is in the lime-light! He required a lesson in politeness, decorum! "I am talking to the organ-grinder, not his monkey, so shut it!" This room suddenly went quiet! A song springs to mind! There's a kind of hush all over the place! Next, I got upon my high horse and spat a few words of my own! "Davison, I asked you a simple question, do you understand my English?"

Shaken and stirred by my statement, he replied, "I'm performing at the pavilion!"

"Next time, make sure that stupid prat doesn't open his gob, ok?" Several fleeting seconds passed, finally, he sheepishly replied, "Sorry, Sid!" I turned away and went to the bar and told a few jokes! A week later, Jim Davison and his lady went along to the Poole Registry Office! Registrar, Mrs Jean Lovell, discussed relevance matters, then my mother said, "I understand you met my son at the Henry Tudor wine bar?"

"Who's your son?"

"Sid Falconer!"

"My God, not him, I could not get a word in edgeways!"

Jim, I'm the comedian in this neck of the woods, thanks! By the way, Jimmy, if I was in your wee boots I'd kick that sod of a manager into touch, oh yes, titter, titter.

Now, to the one and only, Jimmy Tarbuck! Roger, Paul, me, plus eight doormen drove along to Madison Joes nightspot in Bournemouth square! I asked our drivers to park our cars then come on in! We entered and inside, by the main till, was Jimmy Tarbuck! I introduced myself along with the normal procedure of introducing pals and a bit of general patter! Casually, I said, "A couple of minutes prior, I'd been speaking about you!"

"Sure you was," came his reply but the tone in his voice suggested untruth!

I said, "Tarbuck, I am not a liar! Stand in that corner, and if you move, I'll turn ya lights out!" I was shocked by his attitude! Absolutely gobsmacked! "Roger, inform me if he moves, ok?"

"Will do!" Two or three minutes passed, before our drivers appeared!

I asked, "What was we talking about?"

"Number plates," came a reply! "What number plate did I mention?" "C,O,M,I,C! Tarbuck's plate."

"My old number," said Tarby! I replied, "Had you been talking to another guy, your teeth may have popped out, lucky for you, I'm in a good mood! I turned to a cashier saying, "These thugs are with me." We ascended the stairs with Paul seething at the leash, wanting to return to chastise Tarbuck, reprimand this oaf for insulting me! We entered the lounge.

Roger said, "Look, a red carpet and reserve signs for Jimmy Tarbuck and his entourage! A braid of red twisted rope attached to two posts formed a cordon preventing access! "Please, unfasten them!" We moved inside, called the head doorman! A true gent whose wage really didn't match his status! Knowing approximately how much payment he received, I asked him for a wee bit of service! This security officer was definitely management material! He swung into action; within maybe one or two minutes, a female waitress was taking our requirements when Tarby entered! He stood there, watching us and I could feel his devilish red eyes penetrating my body like Satan himself; suddenly, Kenny Lynch promptly appeared with two long-legged blondes! They discussed matters relating to yours truly, then I called to him, and finally, he made his way over in our general direction, then stopped as though asking me for an invitation, permission, to come aboard!

"Mister Lynch, would you please join our company?" He accepted my invitation and sat down! Tarbuck went away but later returned with the club owner, Joe Lucy. By the way, his dad was once the professional boxing champion of Great Britain!

I was talking to Roger at this precise moment and asked if he could keep on talking whilst I clocked their conversation! Tarby said, "Look, they've taken seating reserved for me and my company!"

Joe replied, "Sorry, Mister Tarbuck, it appears Sid Falconer has commandeered your seats and I'm afraid there's nothing I can do!" "Bye-bye-baby, goodbye!" We certainly enjoyed it when Tarby eventually forsook this sinking ship! Give him this, he tried but didn't conquer! Kenny spent the rest of this night in our company, finally, Lynch duly paid his regards then absconded with those tasty tarts! That's according to our bunch of rugged minders! Tarbuck won't forget poor old Sid, because I drive the fastest storyline in the west! He'll never forget me, but you ask him, and I'd bet, for love and money, he can't recall but I and Joe Lucy remember only too well! Occasionally, celebrities need pulling down a peg or two! I'm not saying I'm a saint, but I always treat folk with respect and dignity! There are plenty of well-known people, and this man is no exception! Freddie Starr, Lenny Henry and Windsor Davies are simply the best! Davies came to the Thirdside and I opened the door but lest I forget a short appraisal! The constabulary, whether on official business or enjoying off duty, they are the bosses, governors, kingpins in their field. If you remember this fact, you won't go far wrong! In actual fact, you'll be better off long term. In my back yard, I do all the planting, get this drift, understand me lingo, it means, "bashing plonkers!" (Update) Referees, until recently, were judge and sole jury but because of bad decisions the governing body (in layman's language) introduced circuit judges—a professional band of people trained in the noble art of whatever sport it maybe! To award an honest judgement, yes to the best of their ability based upon what they've witnessed. Back to the past, I opened the front door! "Hello, Windsor Davies!" I formally introduced myself, "I'm Sid Falconer, come in! Are you working at the pier approach?"

"I am."

"Okey dokey!" One of the owners was sitting behind the till! He awarded this celebrity a membership, then I escorted him to the bar for a beverage, purchased a beer and after I'd had a quick natter, returned to duty. Literally everybody in the bar flooded to him, and like Moses parting the red sea, Windsor was completely in his natural environment! He laughed and joked throughout the evening, then I went downstairs and when I returned, he'd left, saying he'd enjoyed a fabulous night and hoped to return soon! Twenty years later, give or take, Lorraine and I went across the road from our nightclub on the corner of old Christchurch Road and Stafford Road into a restaurant to celebrate her birthday, and Windsor came in! I approached him at the bar! "Excuse me."

"Hi, Sid, how are you?" Would one believe it? After all those years!

I was shell-shocked! "Would you join us?"

"I'd love to!" This was magic, to have such a wonderful person in our company! I invited Windsor to have a meal, which he accepted! His table manners were impeccable! He made us laugh then insisted on paying the bill, which I duly accepted, and for his kindness, invited him over to Valentines, eventually, he said goodbye then off he went happy as a sandlark! A week later, he returned with a few guests but unfortunately, we were in Wales! Windsor Davies, thank you for a great evening which gives us a memory we will treasure! (Bradford, 1963) I was on leave spending day with my dad when we entered a selected bar at the bottom of Manchester Road. This bar was situated on the second or third floor! Two doors swung open like an old western type saloon! No other person was in when I approached the barman, a stout chap with a broad smile! Dad went into the gentleman's toilets! The bartender called out, "What's your beverage?"

"Two pints of Yorkshire bitter, please!"

Behind me, I heard this distinctive squeak as the double doors swung open! A person shouted, "Usual, Bill," and two people approached the counter and stood to my right, looked at me and turned to face the bar.

The publican poured two pints of Tetley's then passed them across to the new arrivals without any consideration! "Excuse me, but they're my beers!"

"Keep shut, kid!" said beer-pusher.

"Sorry, but they're other."

"What's going on?"

"These two gentlemen, far as I'm concerned, purchased Tetley's Yorkshire brew after I, so rightly those drinks are ours, don't you agree?"

"Kid, shut it!" remarked the bartender!

"Want a bit of trouble, lad?" cried the nearest dude! These punks are gonna get it but they don't know it! "Shut up, you pair of idiots," shouted Sid senior!

I exclaimed, intervening, "Pick up ya dukes!" Two punches passed me from dad's direction and they weren't counting sheep but sound asleep.

"Sweet dreams," said papa, dragging them out through these saloon swing doors and dumping them there before returning! "I say, landlord are the beers ours?"

"Sir, take them!"

"Son, did you pay?"

"Nope."

"Sidney, they'll be complimentary!"

"Cheers, Dad."

"Down the hatch!"

"Well, this is turning out a grand night!"

"I think it certainly is but…"

"But what?"

"Dad, you're having all the fun, next time, allow me some practise for you don't need any training, I do!"

"Okey dokey, the next one's on the house! Let's pop up to the fountain!"

"That sounds truly promising!"

"A splendid public house in Manchester road with a colourful reputation!" By the way, my father was a parachutist in the army in 1937, long before the parachute regiment was formed in 1954.

When I was thirteen, Keith Sharkey, myself and our pal named Patrick went up to Ingleby street off Thornton Road in Bradford. Keith had arranged to meet his girlfriend, Joan Samson! Along came a group of yobs saying I'd been bragging to Tom, Dick or maybe even Harry! Reckoned I'd threatened to clobber him! I explained I've never seen or spoken to anyone concerning a fight and didn't haven't a clue what he was referring to! These locals, tough young hard cases, came all tooled up, just looking for trouble, which at this moment, we never knew, eventually, our pal, Patrick, I could see, was getting ready to rumble, and Sharkey, who was sitting on a low wall with Joan, stood up! I asked the leader who was standing in the centre of this pack consisting of at least ten teds (teddy boys) if he was aware we were the devil's disciples from Manchester Road! Patrick, a tough strong Irish Navvy, had seen and heard enough, decided this was the right moment to intervene! "I'm a man of me word, and I've half a brain that's truth! Here's how I've seen this picture, you scumbags come looking for trouble, well, you've got ten seconds to vamoose, one, two, six, ten!" Next moment, he's chopped one down. "Who's next?" said Pat! They moved away, except the leader, who'd squared up to the wrong guy! Our Keith had stepped in front of me, plunged his fist into this challenger's stomach! He keeled over like a great big bag of manure but simultaneously, this fellow thrust his hand out and I saw a flash, glint of white light created by sunlight, striking a flick-knife catching Keith across the bridge of his nose, red blood exploded! This cut-throat razor closed as this twerp stood back, and his bunch of dim-witted lunatics legged it! "Enjoyable," said Patrick, looking somewhat confused! This lad, realising what he'd done, turned then ran away. What a nasty piece of human excrement. "Grip your nose, bridge that gap! Push it tightly together."

"We've got to call an ambulance," cried Pat!

"What for?" exclaimed Sharkey, laughing! "It's only a scratch! I've suffered far worse!" He didn't see what we could. Keith became blind, and me, I'm concerned for my pal's safety! When we eventually arrived at the hospital, a man arranged for a surgeon to fix him up! We waited while they operated, later, a nurse came out! She said they had saved his eyesight but only just! A blink of an eyelid, and hey presto, he'd be totally blind! I felt sick to my stomach; what a cowardly act by so called teds! Writing this tale brings memories flooding and tears flow down like that notorious Mississippi! Each line brought the same reaction even after fifty-two plus years! I ring Keith, and today, I will call him again, that is for sure! Keith and Joan Sampson got married but I wasn't in their wedding photographs as I was now on active service stationed at Waterloo Lines in Aden!

Keith and Joan have three children, all grown up, Darren, Wayne and Michelle, now, that brings a song to my mind by the Beatles and the Overlanders, which I sing! I've a voice in a million so landlords reckon and often say, "Sid, can you sing Faraway or Silent Night?" Especially at the weekend. One publican offered me a regular spot! He said, "If you could sing last song of the evening, I'll pay you five pounds."

"Mate," replied I, "you've got a deal."

"Great."

"Why?" stated I, inquisitively!

"It's the quickest way to get punters to leave, ha-ha-ha." Joan Sharkey passed away unexpectedly. My wife and I attended her funeral to celebrate her life; rest in peace, friend. I remember the first day we met Joan, aged 12, approaching 13! A bonny lassie with blond hair and a smile which generated like a flower in full blossom, what a sweet girl, and Keith was indeed the luckiest young fellow alive and their love like a fairy-story where the knight in shining armour arrived to sweep her off her feet never faded from that day one iota.

Albert Cunningham, John Sharkey, our Barry and I went to a pub in Ivesgate, looking for some action, dancing with the fairer sex, except, when we arrived, a man was sitting on this chair all by his lonesome in the centre of a big room with a bar! His head hung over and blood poured onto a wooden floor. "Put his head back!" I shouted and raised it aloft! My God, someone had stuck a broken pint glass into both eyes and they were sliced in sections! We duly left in a hurry! Some godforsaken pig had done that to another human being, what a crazy world. Barry moved down south to Poole in Dorset! Mum and Jack followed, thereafter, I arrived at London airport with our Dave apparently our aeroplane caught fire before landing at Rome. WE stayed in the airport for hours before setting off and eventually, arrived then we got a taxi home twenty-six hours late! Jack and mum came to the airport and were informed by an officer that we had departed Aden the day before but they couldn't get any information from officials and eventually, they returned to Poole, unaware of our predicament! We were brown as berries and walked through Poole high street in shirt sleeve order for months whilst locals covered up and we stood proud and certainly pleased as punch!

One day, I was working for Lindley Parkinson on the Arndale Centre in Poole, which has recently been renamed the Dolphin Centre! I was absent from the army! Our Baz was working for Conways, an Irish company with umpteen grand lads! Seeing our Barry was self-employed, I used his national employment card under the name of Barry Lee! My elder brother's father was shot by a sniper in the second world war, then mum met dad who already had a son from a previous marriage! One morning, this coloured fellow, Sid Brown, said he was a professional boxer, saying, "I'd like you to meet my manager, Jack Turner!" I was in the Ansty Arms public bar when Turner arrived and invited me along for a training session, so I went to the Brunswick in Charminster and trained! I was a dumper driver at Parkinson then joined our Barry at Conways! The work was tough, we'd loosen metal props holding rows of hundred-weight panels on which concrete, with steel inlaid, had set rock hard, then we'd pull the props and run!

The money was much better than Parkinson where I loved driving and loading gear, unloading, fill sand and offloading, a couple of yards of concrete but now, I'm moving away to the Globetrotters nightclub in Library road, Poole where hearsay was ripe and I heard most of it! This married couple used to frequent, regular-like but this lady had a bit of a reputation with the men! One night, she left the club with a man, and he certainly wasn't her spouse! They popped along to Poole quay up the road! This tale goes, her husband went along to the quay then noticed a car was parked only ten feet from the water's edge! Lucky for him, the old handbrake lever wasn't engaged, so he crept up behind the vehicle and over into the brink it went! A man inside this car attempted to climb out an open window but failed; apparently, he was halfway out when an ocean's salt water filled his lungs! This case remains an unsolved murder but I assure you, the husband told me it was him who'd committed the act but who'd believe me?

Poole hardman Brian Gibbs claimed he was toughest guy in town etc! He was married to an attractive female and they, I believe, had four children; what a life for Brian but he required more and a girl kept him company when lady love wasn't present! One night, at the globetrotters, after I'd departed, apparently, Barbara, our club manageress, was heading home when he stopped his car and suggested he'd give her a ride, no strings attached! There were other lads in the vehicle, so she accepted his offer but instead of taking her straight home, dropped his comrades off then along to Poole park where she refused his generous offer of sex! Eventually, without getting his bacon ration, other words, oats, dropped, her home now that's what I call gentlemanly conduct! Next evening, in the nightclub, came Gibbs' ignorant pals like a pack of wolves, hunting for sweet Barbara, shouting at her, saying, "Our mate had you last night, how about us tonight!" She told me what happened! I saw our Gibbo enter the toilets, so I followed inside and asked him most politely to stop his mates, literally, put them on leash but he refused my request; eventually I said, "Pick up ya dukes!" Next instant, he's under the sinks, out cold, and another one bites the dust, and in temper, I struck three sinks and Jericho, the walls came tumbling down, not quite, three white basins fell upon him and red blood came quick so I went out into the bar and told his entourage to quieten down and aid their mate now no longer the hard nut who'd just been cracked but a gentle acorn sleeping it off in the gents lavatory! "Bravo." His wife entered the scene and immediately called the local constabulary to have innocent me arrested for belting her poor husband still sleeping it off in the latrines, what a shame but little did she know the tale behind this fracas! A police sergeant arrived with a constable and I was questioned! Informed the police of the position and Barbara reported the incident evening prior to Gibb's spouse!

Half an hour later, she refused to press any charges and the matter was officially squashed, then about four weeks later, big Geordie Cooper, all mouth in trousers popped into the globetrotter and caused a disturbance! Yes, you got it, another basher bloggs, ruddy tough guy! "Hey, pal, here we go, again. I've been informed," said I, "you'll fight anybody at any time?"

"Anywhere," replied this idiot! Now, this was comic relief month, I'm sure! "Come along to my boxing gymnasium with me where we can have a contest with or without the old boxing gloves?"

He said, "Come over to the ship cafe across Poole bridge tomorrow at five pm, and I'll come down to your gym!"

That evening, for some unknown reason, he remained quiet! I think he was thinking things over, well, the next day, at five pm, I was inside this gaff and asked a waitress where King-Kong was! He wasn't in, as promised, so I challenged him in his absence in front of umpteen witnesses to a wee bout of fisticuffs under strict Queensbury rules, just joking! A duel of an era! Poole's lunatic asylum seeker against a pugilist!

Next morning, I was working on multi-story car park behind bus-station when my work colleague, Johnny Tilson, informed me Geordies, Cooper and Long, a pug-nosed creep, were waiting for me across road! Over I went, but Cooper was absent, but Long was sitting in a car! I shouted, "Put your hands on the steering wheel, and if I see them come off, I'll bang ya ruddy head in, understand?" He complied with my request! George arrived, clutching a newspaper rolled up into a ball!
"Lookin' for me, was ye?" I just love pirate lingo!

"Comrade. pick up your dukes!" One fist connected, and that's all it took, that's all, and a flip of a coin, he's unconscious, and that's another one bites the dust! I think this story is getting to be a tad violent and a regular occurrence, don't you think? Well, that was that, short and sweet! One day, Cooper was in the new London public bar when I popped in and he popped out! Outside, I asked him to return. "Geordie, take this!" and gave him a litre bottle of navy rum!

There's a saying, drink brings out the devil in us! What's he doing there in the first place? I say, if one can't hold their liqueur, don't consume it! In my job, I meet some unsavoury characters, Geordie Cooper, was the typical bully type but he changed dramatically. I was riding my Vespa scooter down the high street, which has now become pedestrian! He stopped me and asked if I could him and his mate a lift! I duly obliged! Can you imagine, three up on a scooter! My folks were walking home and I'd had a fight cancelled! Well, I passed them! Later, when I got home, they said all they saw was six legs jutting out! Next moment, a police siren and I'm off along the road, turned right, and headed towards the old George Hotel! God's truth, I was only giving them a lift, for Christ almighty!

Dropped them off, next, I've gone out of a car park and turned left into Longfleet Road, turned left again and across Denmark road then, they were up my tail. At the end was this tall wall where I've done a broadside and caught the brickwork, then drove along a wee narrow path! The distinct sound of brakes, wheels locking, then I've turned! The chasing police car was an inch from disaster! "Good bit of driving, officer!" And I've driven away like cat had got cream but did I? Thinking I'd pop into the back of the maternity hospital and stay there awhile before tripping down to Parkstone Road via Hillside Road and coming back from that direction, well never underestimate the old bill, I tell you, believe me, they were just sitting, patiently waiting for me, nosey sods, the plods! Too intelligent for my liking. "Ha-ha-ha, well what happened?" Clever me should've stayed put in the grounds for maybe half an hour then drove across the road, and blow me down, those twisted blighters were right up behind me and there was no escaping this occasion. "Fair game, constable, I give up!" They took me to Poole police station where the old dungeons are! Every padded cell was full chock-a-block with drunks and the main lock-up, which normally holds, I'd say, four dozen prisoners, was empty except for a man lying down on an old mattress or something similar! "Sarge," called a constable, "every cell is full!"

I said, "What about this one?" pointing to the large room with only one occupant!

"You cannot go in there, he's an animal!"

I realised it was Georgie! "I'll go in there and if he wakes up and causes a disturbance, I'll just kick his butt, ok?" Well, they laughed and said, "If he kicks off, hellfire will surely explode!"

"Sergeant, what shall I do?"

"I'm getting rather sick of this; bring him back up, the world cup is on!" I went back. "Want a cuppa, sunshine?" said the duty sarge!

"A cup of coffee would be much appreciated!"

"In future, don't give strangers a lift?"

"Sarge, whatever you say."

"Lad, sit down and enjoy a cuppa, and watch the world cup!"

"Cheers!"

"Tom, we've a celeb in our presence, our Sid is a professional boxer!" Later, they breathalysed me, and of course, it registered no alcohol and finally, they released me without any charge! Who can fault the Poole police? Not me! I suppose, I've been very fortunate but truly folks, I am the good guy out there, because sometimes, it's an outrageous jungle which one really detests! I loathe hitting people but when it's necessary and there isn't any other course of action left open, then what can I do? It's them or me.

There have been many rewarding moments in my life and one of them was my wife and I taking our Sidney aged twelve to Dover. He was meeting Sue Peglar and the deaf tennis squad! They were going to Lille, in France, to participate in some selected singles and doubles matches! We were at Brighton, travelling a coastal road, and everything was magic and we had plenty of time! We approached a set of traffic lights which was blatantly green; my intention was to pass safely through whilst the signals were in our favour, thus, giving us the right of way! Next moment, a car came from the right, rushing across our path! I applied footbrakes but there simply was no place to manoeuvre or time to execute a skilful movement! Both cars collided! I moved our car to the edge of the road for safety procedure! We approached the party involved! They were an elderly couple and he muttered something about following a hearse, being late, then I realised what had occurred! This couple were well behind a funeral car, and they were attempting to catch it! I'd earlier seen the hearse go across the signals when they were on red but the lights changed at least one minute or maybe even longer ago! Police arrived! A woman patrol officer took detailed statement then after speaking, went to the elderly fellow next his wife who'd meanwhile gone missing, surprisingly, reappeared, stating I was at fault, her daughter said! This policewoman asked where her daughter was. "In Hove," came her reply! She then said, "I was speaking to her on the phone," dog and bone, telephone!

This situation was absolutely mental. "My daughter has stated," I couldn't believe this silly woman, "on the phone that the car involved in collision was travelling to fast."

"Well, I'm afraid," said this police office, "she is wrong and we'll let court decide, ok?" A taxi-driver arrived and explained to the law that he actually witnessed the collision and he was stationary at the lights waiting to cross over for these signals to change but the lights were on red! This was the evidence that I required to prove they were in the wrong! She wasn't telling the truth! This taxi-driver said he'd gone home, told his wife what he'd seen and she'd said go back, these people may need your evidence, thank goodness for this pleasant lady! Before this incident, I was driving along merrily and had plenty of time until the boat set sail, metaphorically speaking; now, we were late and with little money, right in the quagmire! "Where were you travelling to?" enquired this taxi-driver.

"To Dover, but now we will have to wait for the (rae) recovery unit!

"I'll pop home then take you there, wanna come?"

"We haven't a couple of dimes to spare between us!"

"I trust you!" Well, believe me, I thanked him from the bottom of my heart, and we sent him a cheque! He took us to his house and we met his wife and off up to Dover. We arrived in time, saw him board, then back to our car in Brighton! The RAC arrived and took us home! Thank God for watching and protecting us from harm and for this taxi-driver, his wife and the royal automobile club.

Another occasion, I was driving up Poole Hill in Bournemouth when this car did a U-turn directly into ones pathway, causing me to swerve automatically and instinctively to avoid an unavoidable collision and ended up in front of an on-coming bus; luckily, for me, we both managed to stop! An old gent with a poorly attitude got out of his car, screaming abuse, like a raging bull! "What in God's name were you doing, couldn't you see a flashing indicator?" Lucky for me, God was clearly watching this whole affair just sitting up there, laughing, I wouldn't be surprised, because he sent this copper over to intervene who said, "I was standing on the corner of the middle of this road watching all the pretty little fair ladies passing by and I was enjoying being alive, until!" Inspector Ciouseau for some moments paused as if searching for correct words! The sun was baking me like a carrot cake, sweltering heat was getting out of control! All one needed was a car crash but that was exactly what occurred! This policeman continued, "A man, without looking or warning indicator, turned into traffic!" I wasn't at fault, and lucky for me, this police officer was present and came to my rescue! Now, who can knock the constabulary, certainly not me!

One evening, I was driving along Barrack Road toward Iford roundabout when I noticed a stationary police patrol car situated by a pub, and no sooner we'd passed, it pulled out! I was in company. My wife, Richard and Louise Payne, two influential people. This police vehicle's headlights went off as we drove along, I'd say, approximately a mile, maybe even further, then on went his lights followed by a blue flasher! It was an exceptionally dark evening and the moon was shaded by clouds, obscuring whatever paleness was in the sky! I was well inside the speed limit, watching them behind, and I'd not been drinking, except for a glass of water! Inspector Morse was driving quite fast; finally, we stopped, and he emerged from his vehicle and seconds later, another, much younger patrolman appeared by his side! I got out and said, "I saw you turn off your lights and observed you following us!" I knew they were from Christchurch where our nightclub was at this time situated. This inspector saw us leave a restaurant and recognised me on sight. That was why they were tailing me and they made it plain fact by their awkward attitude!

"Have you been drinking?"

"Officer, I've had a glass of alcoholic water!"

"In that case, you'll have to wait for twenty minutes before I'm allowed to breathalyse you!" That ranks amongst the most stupid statements I've ever heard.

"This is crap!"

"Sir, that's the law which I abide!"

Richard Payne called from our car! "Inspector, why have you stopped us?"

The officer replied, "Be quiet, it's nothing to do with you!"

Richard said, "1 would like to point out, do you know the chief constable is a personal friend and should we be detained much longer, I will call him for you to answer for your action this evening, what do you say, shall I phone him?" He showed inspector muppet his mobile and said, "Look, here's the chief constable's private number, would you like me to dial?"

"Sir, I am sorry for any inconvenience, good night!" He was literally shaken and stirred and like demons in the night, took flight and were gone with the wind and so ended this saga.

La-Maximes, 1974! This night, I was speaking to a customer when Mick, a Londoner, arrived and I could see from his expression, something wasn't right! His face was a picture, and if looks could kill, someone was going to die this evening! An elderly gent with six students sat close by, and rain beat hard against the rear door like a backdrop filling a scene with a touch of serenity reminding me of a serenata, serenade waltz, and my mind tiptoed stealthily into a fantasia; next instant, I became aware of Mick! Like a jerboa, small rodent, challenging this group who'd mocked his dancing! I intervened saying, "I'm sorry, pal, for their mockery but insist you maintain the peace whilst inside this audacious establishment!"

Mick was far beyond any reasoning and plainly didn't care, now, these mortals were going to pay for insulting him! I attempted to calm him but to no avail! He was like Avatar, (Hindu mythology, descent of a deity, god or goddess.) Finally, I said, "Au revoir," simultaneously, opening a door and leading outside. He turned towards me and raised both hands! This was enough to warrant my wrath!

Blow hesitation, I swung into action and in a micro-second, Mick lay fast asleep, and another one bites the dust! I picked him up, carried his lifeless torso outside into this parking bay situated at the rear and drove my vehicle to Queen's Road, in Pokesdown, Southbourne, where he lived and still unconscious, I took him up to his front door then left him!

Now, the Neptune Bars on Bascombe beach sea front belongs to the Bournemouth Council, an establishment with a bad reputation! Asked the general manager for a job! "We don't employ many doormen!" I knew this club's past history; recently, four young assailants were awarded four years' imprisonment for glassing four security, and at this precise time, this venue had no bouncers! Who would work in a place with such a renowned character? Only one foolish moron required this job, yes, me! "Mister Chapman," said I, "don't extract the urine." I was annoyed! They couldn't get anyone to operate security and exclaimed, "If you don't want me, that's fair enough but don't insult my intelligence; by the way, governor, I'm a professional boxer, and if I can't handle any situation, nobody will."

"When can you start?"

"Tonight, providing the money is right!"

"The council pay six pounds a day!"

"God, no wonder you can't get men when they could get slashed, throat cut or even worse, for a few miserable quid, that's ridiculous!"

"After six weeks, you'll get a raise!"

"Ok, that'll do me!" The first evening, everything went as clockwork! The general was real pleased, and I worked for six weeks without any security, talking to customers, getting to know all the ins and outs! One night, I approached the manager saying, "I am well aware there were four doormen working here prior, consequently, I'm doing their job which is wrong and could you sort a bit of extra money!"

"I'll see what I can do!" A few weeks sailed past but no pay increase! Every night, I was risking my own life for six pounds; funny thing is, when I think of the Neptune Bars, my blood boils at the poor wages I received, and I'd like to see those yellow, good-for-nothing, guttersnipe councillors do my job!

Bournemouth councillors were the pits of society, toffee-nosed snakes who speak with a plum in their mouth! Gutless people who wouldn't have the bottle to work an evening at the Neptune bars and never had to scratch a living. Born with a smile on their face and a silver spoon in their gob! They wouldn't pay me additional wages, yet, I alone was running two doors, one at each end of this mighty building! Two thousand plus more holiday makers at two locations, an upstairs bar and the lower bar! I was running around like this stuffed bear and nobody helped me! Come to think of it, a fracas began with bikers in the upstairs bar! A female bartender was in a pickle when I arrived and without hesitation or thought, knocked one out, then calmly said, "Anyone like a slice of the action?" Luckily, for me, there were no takers, and yes, another one bites the dust! "Take him outside!" Can you just imagine this scene? It was the end of summertime, and we were packed to the rafters. I said to Chapman, "That is it, I've had enough! I knocked out a biker and there are another hundred and fifty still up there, and if they kick off, I'm off, ok?" Mister Chapman didn't offer me a dime extra, only Jesus Christ could handle these riders from hell, and I'm on my own, with hundreds of raging lunatics! Time passed and I'm going up and down like a yo-yo, running between two bars in Boscombe in the middle of August, 1970, and asked, "Where's our mentor?"

"Probably in the toilet!" remarked a bartender, and by the way, this general manager was in the lavatory! My money didn't rise, so I introduced my friends, Dudley Garwood, a former heavyweight professional boxer and Jeff Fellows to Chapman who employed them and a council worker and what a load of rubbish he turned out to be, and yes, stunk the place out! When trouble was in store, guess where this council employee was? That's correct, you're right, in the latrines like the rest of those Bournemouth councillors! Well, our summer went, and it was December when daredevil Jeff Fellows drove his car without stopping across Owl road from Saint Johns road and a car struck our vehicle, and I became paralysed! Never did go back as I was in bed suffering pain, 24/7, but Dudley told me fights came and he was off along with Jeff Fellows and that council worker left the next evening, and after this incident, they employed eight or more door staff; just think, I did that place on my tod Jack Jones for months, I'd like to see major-domo councillors do that! I say, "Put the lot in a coalmine!"

"What a dim-witted bunch of mongrels!" When I think of these times, it makes me feel happy. I've done things which are truly unbelievable and stood against an entire rugby team and a football team in Oscars! One evening, a group who'd just been playing at Dean Park arrived! At the time, I was attending to an incident at the far end! When eventually I returned, there was a racket, loud noise, by the bar! I said, "Quieten down, gentlemen, you're disturbing clientele."

"It's ok," exclaimed a footballer, "it's Ian Botham!"

"Sorry, Ian but any more ruction, and I'll knock your heads together, understand?" Maybe words to such an effect! Botham and his merry crew turned, then all went quiet like a mouse, and I calmly walked away, patiently waiting for their response! When I got home and told my wife of an incident involving Ian Botham, I exaggerated this meeting! I am sorry for that night, I'd have loved a formal meeting with a cricket legend, and I should have shown a bit of decorum! For years, my wife and I would see this Spencer Clark! He's the image of Ian Botham, and he'd wave and smile and I conned my wife many times as Spencer drove past, and Lorraine would say, "Wasn't that Ian Botham?"

"Yes, dear," eventually, I said, "That person was not Ian Botham but Spencer Clark, a lookalike and in his heyday, an amateur boxer." Well, this storyline has run its course so I'm heading off to new pastures!

When I was between the age of eleven and twelve, we moved up to number thirty-three the bank in Eccleshill, in Bradford, where I met Richard Rhodes, and he became a true pal in that region. Now, he lived in a fine house with this raised garden at the rear, leading to these mighty woods where red squirrels dwell! One morning, he climbed up to a grey squirrel's nest and took a young one which he reared, nurtured, what a lovely little creature! Richard knew the area well, and we'd go down to Greengates and Applybridge, walk by the canal and dive off the lock! One day, this lad dived off the lock but the water was low and smashed his head and died almost instantaneously! Never went back! Applybridge river was deep in parts and a farmer emptied sand at one location for folks to swim in comparative safety. In the summertime, we'd go down to the stream and lark around for ages or lay in the hay with the sun baking our skin like frying bacon over a hot stove! Many a time, we'd arrive home burnt to a cinder then outcome the old lotion! Baz met a fabulous looking blond girl called Deleis! One evening, she went to a fish-shop on the back of a motor bike, then it began to rain but instead of taking her back to this party, took her to Barry Rhodes where they raped her! In those days, it was taboo for a young female to call the police, and our Barry never got over this and became wild like.

Baz was a fantastic brother but I'm making no excuses for him whatsoever, his behaviour, but after this incident, he changed. Went back to his old haunt and mixed with bad company, robbing stores and ended in custody! Drifted around and moved far away from his first true love! Initially, he went in prison in Armley jail, in Leeds then, Wormwood Scrubs, in London. and Dartmoor prison where he met Mitchell, the Axeman! Each day, Frank, a fitness fanatic, did one-hundred one-arm push-ups before breakfast! Strong as a bull, said Barry, finally, he moved to Poole in Dorset then Summerset, logging timber, and eventually, Barry drifted away and we lost touch. After eight years without a single letter, out of the blue, he came home to twenty-seven Chatsworth road! End of 1972, we purchased old bangers, worthless cars, and repaired them quite badly with our young assistant, David Onion, from next door! He was a clever lad and certainly knew his cars. One evening, late in March 1973, I took him to meet my old mate, Dublin Bob, and they got on champion, like an house on fire, continually telling jokes until finally, time came to head home!

Barry drove his car and I, mine! I clambered from my jalopy then he climbed out from his! "Did you have a nice evening?" Barry's reply was all mixed up! Was he ok?" His answer was nonsense, meaningless words, all jumbled literature! I called mum!

She said, "Take him to the hospital." At the A&E in Poole, we waited for a doctor! Baz was in a terrible state, blabbing incoherently!

This old sergeant approached, saying, "If that drunk doesn't quieten down, I'll lock him in a cell!"

I stated, "There is something terribly wrong with my brother!" He suddenly collapsed in my arms then this nurse called, and we assisted our Barry to a cubicle where he was seen by a doctor! Later, I was informed of Barry's condition! He had a tumour in his head which had burst, and this doctor said he didn't think he'd last the night! I went home, mother was patiently waiting! I said, Barry will be fine! They are keeping him overnight for tests! He died six weeks later on 29/03/1973.

For one year, I'd regularly break down; thankfully, Dee Scourse, a dear friend, allowed me access to a room where I laid undisturbed until I'd recover! Her place was my refuge, a sanctuary, whatever, and I am forever grateful for her kindness! She had daily problems herself, organising this nursing home and general chores like raising a family, last thing she needed at that present time was me, what a wonderful woman! It is hell, losing family, especially one's brother! Barry was twenty-nine years and five months when he passed away! This devastated me, and I never got over that evening in Poole hospital! 1973.

Lest I forget, when stationed at Roman Barracks in 1967, a pinhead corporal, that is what he must've been, came into my billet and said, "Your name Falconer?"

I said, "Yes," he commanded I clean the toilets out but the words he used, one cannot repeat! I'll explain in simple layman's terms, the time was seven thirty-five am! I am entitled the same as our colonel to breakfast, and that, I had already done, my room task, swept, bumped my bedside and tidied my bed and now, I intended going to the cookhouse after which I'd clean the urinals but this corporal, who I'd never seen before, insisted I attend to this task immediately! I'd already told him twice. I said, "I'm going to breakfast, and I won't repeat this again!" He insisted I do this chore, now remember who was this punk? There was zero time to get to breakfast so I said, "Corporal, pick up ya dukes!"

A clenched fist sailed through the cool air, connecting flush on his jaw, sending him halfway to paradise, now that's what I call music, then I went across to breakfast! What a complete dumbo this corporal must have been, fancy coming in, asking for trouble; well, idiot, got it. Later, I was sitting at a table by myself enjoying breakfast; apparently, this gutless swine reported me and in came the regimental police! Next, I received this tap on the back of my shoulder which I must state did not help their cause! I turned my head slightly in their direction, with my knife and fork waving, and saying, "What the blooming heck is going on?" There were four of them. "What do you want?"

This (RP) regimental police with two stripes upon his sleeve, a full corporal, said, "You are under-arrest?"

I said, "Very sorry, pal but I'm eating, call back later?"

"On your feet, soldier!" What polite manners.

I replied, "I'm hungry and I'm not one happy chapple, and if I were you twerps, I'd be on my way before I let this tiger out of his tank, understand me?"

"What?"

"Leave me alone, I'll see you later, good-bye." Well, blow me down with a feather, off they went with their tail tucked neatly between their legs! For one moment, I wanted to beat the living daylights out of them! Very bloodthirsty, this book, but I knew inside I'm in for the high jump, yes in the cart again! When I returned to the billet, there they were, sitting on my bed!

"Ready, soldier?"

"Ok."

"Quick march, left right!" Next day, I went before Colonel Todd! Explained my entitlement and why I've defended myself in the line of duty!

"This big thug, like a giant, attacked me, and I'm willing to attend a court-martial!" If I remember correctly, I was acquitted! Not bad, think he believed me? Neither do I. Sunday morning prior, I had given Toddy a tasty bone for his lovely dog, covered in munchie meat; ain't I intelligent, don't you agree? Our colonel was simply the best!

We operated security at the Royal Exeter hotel complex which consisted of the Exeter's main bar and rooms, Oscars nightclub two bars and the Bowl. One bar which was situated at front of the Exeter, this bar was on the lower level! One evening, Ray, a former magistrate, called me upstairs as he was experiencing some difficulty! He'd asked an American negro to leave the bar, and he'd refused! Dave Fish, Nigel Drew and I were working at Oscars, and it was chock-a-block so they stayed whilst I sorted this small problem! I accompanied Ray up a set of stairs leading into the upstairs lounge bar! Behind the counter stood a very tall barman! This side was the huge thick-set man! "Sir, you've been asked by the duty manager to leave this building!" At this moment, I can't remember his reply but eventually offered him outside! We walked towards a double door, leading to stairs but both of us couldn't walk through together, so I went first and stepped down a stairway until reaching the bottom, then I walked away!

He said, "What's up?"

I replied, "I've done the job, good night!" This gent commanded I explain! "You're out of the Exeter's bar and they've just closed, end of!" I walked back into Oscars! Moments passed before he's at the door wanting to enter but being refused; now, I lost my patience, end of, "Let's go and do the business in the car park where we won't be disturbed!" Outside, I said, "Pick up ya dukes," and hit him like one dart, Peter Manley! Onto his chin and muchas gracias, sleepy-baby (son et lumiere) the night's entertainment was officially over and I returned to the nightclub! After a while, I became concerned as to his welfare and asked Davy to take a peek!

He reported back! "I can't find him, it's pitch-black out there!" We all went into the car park to search for a missing body and found him beside a car where I'd planted him, finally, when he recovered, he said, "I've fallen down the stairs." Well, we laughed, he left, and another one bites the dust!

We ran the door of Bumbles Buccaneer bar, Corkers, in Poole, Hollies, Moordown, Poets corner, Bournemouth! Jeff Fisher, was the owner at this time, what a noteworthy man, and Matchams Lodge owned by Major John Hancock! One couldn't fail to admire him; now, Dave Partridge, once a professional footballer who played for Blackpool with incredible talent! Now, let me say, his son, Rodney, was magical but never had the backing, was never lacking in skill just like his dad went inside Matchams Chalet Motel to have a game of pool whilst I discussed matters of importance with John Hancock! Alan Spurlock was on duty as head of security! Everything inside and out was running smooth as silk like clockwork, and I was enjoying John's company! Later, David said, "I'll tell you a little story! I was playing a game of pool with big Al earlier when Spurlock remarked, 'I see the boss has come in!' 'Yes,; I exclaimed, Alan replied, 'Mighty puncher, our Sid,' to which I casually stated, 'The other month, at Spats wine bar, Sonnyjim knocked-out two large chaps supporting gum shields, protectors and a lead cosh! Knocked one's teeth out,' to which he cried, removing his dentures, 'It was me.'" Well, I creased myself and had to go to the toilet!

One evening, quite early, I arrived at Poets' Corner to witness Jim Bowen, a top celebrity, actually queuing to enter a lounge bar situated on first level! Give him respect for this but the doorman should have explained to Bowen what type of establishment this was and ushered him, along with his guests, inside to take a peek! I approached him! "Jim Bowen, let me introduce myself, I'm Sid Falconer, head of the security in these parts." Now, with the formalities over, I said, "I don't think you'd enjoy this place, it's full of young trendies." But I escorted them inside! I was correct. "I'll take you to the Palace Vaults, it's a more select age group!" He never did say thank you, never mind, that's his royal prerogative; incidentally, I've been knocked out recently by pistol, Peter lves, in a dart match! Blodger, absolute toe rag, had the tenacity to ask me to include this fact; now that the good deed of the day is finally done, I'll continue with this account! "Thanks, Pete, for your intellectual humour, it was much appreciated but I appreciate your wife's humour more!"

I was on McCowan's boxing booth, Southampton common, on main stage, bruising the punch bag whilst waiting a challenge from out of an audience gathering around our tent when this smartly attired gent stepped forth! "I'll fight that fellow," pointing towards me! I could see this man was useful by the cut of his cloth, and he looked in fine fettle except for a slight baldness, thus giving him a slightly aged appearance! Mister

Jack Turner came to our dressing room prior commencement of my bout saying, "This gent is Clive Williams, a former top-class professional pugilist!" No mention he'd been his manager, whatsoever.

"Ladies and Gentlemen," said Bernard McCowan, addressing public gallery as he came into the centre of this ring! "This is a three-round contest."

I looked around, folk seemed excited and anxious for blood but I wasn't taking any chances, and as soon as the bell rang, I'm out the gate, and bang goes the weasel! I've gone under his jab and an explosive left hook tagged his jaw! He appeared as if in suspended animation, and next instant, he's on that canvas, spread-eagled, what a crushing blow, and another one bites the dust! This reminds me of another occasion on Southampton common; by the way, I boxed on Christchurch common as well! This exceedingly tall chap came up and challenged me! My word, I was standing on a stage erected to put us on exhibit, a platform of approximately three or more feet from ground level! A real beanpole, I'd say! I climbed through the ropes into the old ring as he strode over the top rope, could you believe it and into this arena! Barry, his younger brother, or maybe, Stewart, entered the ring to a fanfare! "Ladies and gentlemen!" The sound of his voice mingled amongst the crowd! Normally, when I'm fighting on a fairground booth, I give the general public an exhibition! An entertaining show for their cash, sometimes, one stages the entire show performing for our audience by taking one or even two sucker-punches and let's say, perform, Macbeth! Down upon the canvas, I would go to cheers from the assembly of jubilation for their man who appeared in sight of victory as the referee begins the count but I eventually arise, Sir Knight, and like a juggernaut, deliver heavy punishment and knock him out! On this particular occasion, I'm ready to execute a variety of adroit footwork and perform, Madame Butterfly, yes sir, float like a butterfly, sting like a bee, and dance the tango before carrying out the last waltz, and hey, presto, lights out but to my utter surprise, I barely clipped him, bingo, he's unconscious! Jack Turner picked up a microphone and cried, "Anybody with medical experience in the house?" The ring master was as surprised as me; anyway, he awoke and without saying any words, stepped through the ropes then left, and another one bites the dust!

Once again, I'm returning to the saga of Clive Williams; now, maybe two years after this episode on Southampton common where I knocked him unconscious, I bumped into him! Can't remember exactly where but he told me he'd come to the booth to gee with me! Now, Turner never told me this but instead, advised me to attack with the intention of destroying him!

It turned out Clive was, once upon a time, managed by Jack! A gee is two colleagues giving a crowd pure entertainment, exhibition, over three rounds! It's a con! Local hard men usually stay clear of boxing booths but not all the time like on Basingstoke common where I met trumpet player, Kenny Ball! Midnight in Moscow springs to mind; actually Johnny Jagger and I used to play this music and Johnny was brilliant! Both of us played cornets, and of course, we read music! I used to transpose music i.e. write in a different key for each instrument except for the drum! I'm going off the subject! Now, let's go back to the second occasion I met Clive Williams! I must say this, he was one of the best; well, he told me things referring to that night which, obviously, I never knew! He'd spoken to Turner and agreed to box an exhibition! We know what happened, yes, absolutely disgraceful, what a carve up! Later, Clive trained with me at the local gym and sparred with me, and we became great friends! Turned out, Clive was born with one lung, and that night, on the fairground, Jack gave me an unfair advantage! Williams came towards me, expecting, in our terms, non-hostile aggression but I instinctively attacked with utmost force and caught him flush on the jaw, and another one bites the dust; sorry, pal, I wish I'd known and could turn back time!

The Badger inn, Beer Keller bars, back in 1974. I was working late one night when an eerie sound began to bite, then in came this monster mash party! Dennis and his son, Tony, were performing German accordion music! These ogres sat on wooden benches and seemed to enjoy the swell entertainment! This evening, the pub was chock-a-block, yes, crammed full; suddenly, those creeps began flicking drink over young girls on the next bench who were wearing long, fancy traditional costumes and were accompanied by male escorts! These brutes became rowdy, finally, their ringleader went to the gentleman's toilet! I followed, as it was time to sort this out and where better than the privacy of the privy (lavatory) where we'd be less disturbed. Guess what this goon was holding?

I said, "You geezers are out of order, so leave the bar or else!" This idiot, said, "F-k off before I finish this, ok?" I saw Dick and said, "Pick up ya dukes," after he'd finished, and the next instant, hooked him, and another one bites the dust! Back in the bar, I asked his pal, saying, "Comrades, pop out and pick up your leader, and carry your pal outside; apparently, he had a mishap in the men's toilets!" Well, they went to the men's and never came back!

This incident reminds me of a time when on the outskirts of Leeds, our father, Barry and I were having a drink at the infamous Star and Garter! I was fifteen and working at New Boulds on the flower gang at the time, and this evening, dad was at the bar, ordering more drinks! Barry was standing beside me to my right when two heavies, local Teddy Boys, brushed against Baz, spilling his drink onto my brother's clothes; Barry automatically said, "Sorry, pal." These two geezers turned quite nasty with their tongues but walked away!

I said, "Barry, they knocked you and your beer splashed your clothes, not their suits!" "Let it go, Sid, we don't need any trouble!" What I didn't know at this very moment was Barry didn't want dad involved! I watched these uglies, overweight bananas, for my moment and indeed, a short time lapsed, and expectedly, they required a leak, and well, guess what? Sure enough, before I could utter those immortal words, runts need a piddle, they were off and entered the lavatories! I said, "I must go to the men's powder room and walked quickly but quietly over to the latrines."

When Sid senior returned, he apparently remarked, "Barry, where's our Sidney?"

"Gone to the wash-place!"

"Sunshine, he's been in there a long time! What's going on?"

I'd gone over into the ablutions where those two Teds had entered a couple of minutes prior and shouted, "Hey guys, pick up ya dukes." Instead, they just stood up against the urinal, holding, guess what? That's the correct answer, their winkles; well, back in those days and against ginormous giants, one didn't give away an opportunity or advantage, so I said, tally-ho, amigos and hooked them, punching one, then the other, and my, what a sweet treat! They fell asleep and stopped urinating then a few seconds later, simultaneously peed, freely all over their lovely trousers and my goodness, what large bladders, titter-titter, say no more and two pissed Teds, ho-ho-ho, were out for the count! When dad and Barry arrived, I was combing my black, Elvis Presley style hair into the old quiff, and these two twats were still sound asleep, and yes, another two bit the dust! We went back to the bar where, I believe, Al Martino sang Spanish Eyes; funny, never, even saw them characters leave the toilet, could still be inside but I think it's probably been knocked down like most places! This venue was a landmark, national treasure! Dad was pleased as punch but he was extremely disappointed and very concerned because they were tough nutcrackers for one nut to crack, but I drew first blood! "What if them guys weren't knocked unconscious and a situation developed, then the outcome could have been different! We'll never know but next time, make sure you've got our back-up; anyway, that was a majestic performance, well-done!"

Back in the latter stage of the sixties or early seventies, I worked at the Georgian nightclub at the far end of Dear Hay lane in Poole. Blond Bunty was the manageress with three bouncers, Pete Mitchell, Tom Money, including me. Well, years later, Tommy said, "Pete always stated he felt safe working with Sid Falconer." Now, ain't that one ginormous compliment, especially coming from a work colleague! Tom boxed at middle weight on the fairgrounds alongside me! One night, this man challenged him! Unbeknown to us, he was an ex-professional pugilist! The bout commenced with Tom suddenly unleashing a combination of punches, then overcame a haymaker striking the target full on, and sweet home Alabama, for that gent, and this was Tom's finest hour!

Later, I worked at Thimbles Coffee Lounge in the high street which was grand because I mixed with some very nice people indeed, and the two owners were great, and the staff, majestic, then I went into security full time and ran the door at the New Fox in Bournemouth but I can't recall an occasion when trouble arose!

The last thing I want to do is bore the pants off you with idle statements about daily stuff like going to the gymnasium and taking Sidney, and of course Matthew, to local West Hants tennis club or spending hours with top coaches Graham Holden, Roger and Mike Booth! Going over to Christchurch where I came across a right cropper on a ski-slope! Nearly killed myself, both our children came rushing down to my rescue! "Dad, you all right?" I was in pain, took a tumble, and my hand went into an artificial surface and banged each part of my body like many others before me.

I'd hazard a guess, well, I exclaimed, "I'm fine!" They just laughed, and so, I went back up and sailed down the slope! Later, took them horse riding near Hurn Airport! Some horseplay and a horse toppled me over the top, well, they both laughed, and I, say, no more felt great! I'd staged the entire episode, hey what, and what an excellent bit of acting, wouldn't you agree? Over in Christchurch was a putting green with an amusement park and Arcade! Sidney mounted this small bumper car, a child's ride! Lorraine paid and the owner pushed a big black button on the machine which automatically operated the bike and hey presto, off he went around; when the car stopped, Sidney pressed the button and off he went again. Later, we went inside this penny arcade where Basil Brush, another ride, was situated but this time, a twenty pence was required to operate the machine! First, place coin in a slot, then turn clockwise, and Bob's your uncle, he's off; eventually, it stopped, he pressed a black button but it wouldn't restart, finally, he gave up!

We occasionally have parties and I play darts with some of the best! Won a few matches and lost some, funny, nobody has been knocked out yet, and that can't be bad, can it? In the past years, I've become accustomed to this peaceful style! I suppose some would say boring, still, at least, I'm not walking around punching teeth lose! Now, I let someone else do it! The police don't call much these days, what a shame! Ian Swarbrick and inspector Roger Pierce were amongst many splendid policemen whom I haven't mentioned but are remembered with warm feeling inside my old mind, along with all my other pleasant memories; well, this story is mainly short and sweet! Now, before I go, there is an audacious finale! After I finished working at the Badger Bars, I popped out the back door and entered the old Chelsea village where I attended an area inside main entrance! This evening, whilst working at the badger, a couple just married came in! Well, at the end of the evening, I suggested they go around to the Chelsea village! "Tell my brother I'd sent you!" They left and I shot out the back door and across to the main entrance! This couple duly arrived! "Good evening," said I. Well, they just stared at me! He scratched his head!

"Haven't we seen you in the Badger bar?"

"Nope, you've met Sid, my brother, I'm Dave, his twin!" One could have laughed at their expressions!

A couple of seconds passed. "Sid said you'd let us in."

"I'm sorry but you're both wearing jeans, and we don't allow them, company policy."

"Sid told us to tell you we're just married!"

"Why didn't you say?"

"I have."

"That makes all the difference!"

"Sally, give them a ticket, now, go and have a good time!"

They were going downstairs as this young bouncer, David Thompson, said, "Hey, you, you're wearing jeans, get out!"

I walked down a wide flight of steps then said, "Thompson, your language is awful," then I knocked him out, my goodness, a tad violent, don't you agree? Here I go again, yes, weirdly innocent, that's me, and another one bites the dust!

There was a lot of trouble at the Park Inn lower triangle, back of M&S, Bournemouth! Landlady called me, requesting security! Her door staff had left her high and dry, and so, we ran the door! After a few weeks, her head doorman came out of hospital and was reinstated! No longer did she require us! A couple of weeks later, she rang me, needing door staff! We returned! Three months passed, finally, stated her team could manage without us! Once again, we left, then a call came from the establishment but now, they could stew! A pub in Westbourne required security!

We ran the door for over two months and everything in this joint was running nice and smoothly, then one evening, I was actually talking to the manageress when an incident occurred! This chap who'd been barred decided nobody in this establishment was stopping him coming in and hit one of our security personnel in the face! The door was shut and bolted, and outside, he was having a field day, kicking, head butting, banging and threatening folk near the doorway!

I walked over to the entrance, "Why is the door shut? Open it!" I walked out and stated, "You've been barred, now, go away and stop causing an affray, a breach of the peace!" Next moment, up came his dukes! "Good night." Instantly, I tagged him sweet then caught his head and laid him out on old stone cobbled floor! Two doormen carried him around the back then dumped him and another one bit the dust!

Macawbers wine bar was part of the Criterion public house in old Christchurch road where we ran the door of this entire complex! Gary Daley, Tom Webb and Sid Brown worked for me back then, also, our Terry Henderson from Kinson! Many of their names I've forgotten over the years but never forgotten their ugly mugs, that's for sure, just joking. I recall Philip House from Christchurch and Ian Doe! It's nice, remembering these tough gents! We had many recorded incidents back then but we have been extremely lucky, no fatalities! There was plenty of trouble at the Guildhall, Southampton. Influence of alcohol, for this creates idiots who won't take no!

There were many reasons why I left the army back in 1968 but I've only managed to outline just a few! RSM Ben Campey was a good regimental sergeant major at first! He was our regimental sergeant major at the junior leaders, Strensall barracks, where he chastised me many times, why? God only knows, maybe I was rebellious, and scumbag Warrant Officer Dennis repeatedly caused problems. Yes, I may have a tendency to rebel as I was only fifteen! Older soldiers in camp were evil thugs, and the morning we arrived at Strensall, Johnny Jagger was beaten-up by Seth Adams! Why?

When I joined the regiment in Berlin, my reputation for defying lawful authority preceded me! Firstly, band staff-sergeant Reily gave me grief until I sorted him, and the day I arrived at Colchester, this bedding staff-sergeant, a man I'd never seen in my life, said, "My mate Sergeant Swales told me about you and…" the rest has faded from my mind!

I believe there was a conspiracy against me, maybe not intentional but even in the armed forces, there are gangs, would you believe? Ben Campey, Brian Swales and plenty of others whose names I can't remember, but they were bad apples. When

I left the regiment, they went back on active service to Aden, after which I became an official deserter, facing a general court martial, a judicial court for trying members of the armed services. On the 6th of January 1970, I returned to Colchester and was awarded this six-month detention, now ain't that nice of them in a military training centre just across from our camp, real penal servitude in the local penitentiary!

At Madera Road, police station, Bournemouth, back in the eighties and early nineties, there was a wanted poster with three mug shots, photographs of me and muckers, Roger and Paul situated in the constable's rest room, stating, get these thugs at all cost! Actually, I do believe this is against the law or maybe, I'm wrong, am I? Well, I've really lived a colourful life but never ever extorted money or did anything unlawful, so why this? Yet, I've still managed to retain a few friends in the police force until today! Inspector Roger Pierce, Ian Swarbrick, Duncan Harrison and, "there's more," stated Jimmy Cricket! Would you believe? Seldom do officers visit us now but occasionally, I do bump into John, an ex-copper from regional crime office, and yes, he's plain magic! A pleasure to know. My friend, Bob Peelo, once said, "Sid, when you write a novel, tell the readers about the time you knocked out Johnny the grass from Blandford who informed on several gypsies and the one from Somerford who battered women! An informer who ratted on car dealer in Hampshire, yes, from Somerford in Christchurch!" Well, I must say Bob was correct; now, here goes, I fried him good and proper! This saga began when John Lilley, one of our older security officers, approached me saying he picked up a female passenger in his taxi at the local hospital. She had three broken ribs and a face like Jekyll and Hyde! When asked, this woman said, "My lodger did this!"

"Why?" remarked Mister Lilley. The tale goes something like this! Her parents were killed in this road incident, leaving this girl with a mortgage! She got a second debt over a long period to cover the property, then met a man who moved in! At some point, their relationship ended, and he became an independent lodger! Time drifted slowly, then, one day, he said he was moving in with his brother and wanted £2000 from her!

The story deepens now, the cutting edge of this novel was and she refused, so he inflicted actual bodily harm! The constabulary said, "This is a domestic!" Six months later, he broke her bones and in a wild rage, rearranged the face, leaving a few broken teeth! What a nice chap, get my drift? Well, I met up with this person! She was now staying at her sister's while he lived alone, rent free, with no intention of vacating occupancy! The night was young, and birds twittered gaily, when I arrived at the house and lights shone bright! Next moment, I opened a door and called out, "Johnny!"

"Who is it down there?" came an instant reply! I went upstairs, and big John was in bed!

"Get up, pal, you're leaving."

"Who says?" What a thicko; I slapped him with a gauntlet!

"I say." I should've hit boyo with my tickling stick!

He got up and cried, "Get out of this house!"

"I hear you want two thousand pounds."

"Lady owes me!" I asked Mister Obstreperous to go before I extract his teeth! This was to frighten him but instead, this giant oaf picked up his dukes, and in self-defence, I knocked him unconscious, then waited for him to regain full consciousness. Finally, he awoke, then roared like a lion and attacked me! Mother of dear God, believe me, another punch connected, then poor old Johnny sailed into Merryland. My word, this large lodger was on dope! Blodger was high as a kite! Twenty minutes passed, eventually, vociferous being awoke again, I politely asked him to pack his clothes and leave! He packed two cases, then I turned away from him for only a few seconds but long enough for him to pick up this baseball bat I hadn't noticed, well, what an idiot this lunatic was as he attempted to strike me but failed, end of, so I KOed him, and yes, my friends, another one bit the dust!

Let me state, there came to pass two occasions which were the most happiest, these being the birth of our children, Sidney and Matthew! Those happy days are behind us, yet these great memories linger and are still vivid! Roger, Paul, and Ken Cooper visit occasionally along with Paul Lody, and of course, Malcolm Tottle. We go across to Tony Carpenter at Bascombe Conservative Club. Now this story is becoming extremely bland, not much more to say!

This noteworthy tale, I hope, has been jovial, and most probably, "a tad violent," exclaimed Glory Jagger.

"Titter-titter," remarked myself using my elder Frankie Howard impersonation!

"Want a Carver-style haircut, heir Falconer, for a shilling?" interrupted an audacious Johnny (madcap) Jagger! Now, going back one last time to the Sour Grapes, Roger, Paul and I were drinking at the bar when a knocking disturbed us! Robert Roberts was, on this particular occasion, attending to the main door! I said, "I'll see what all this hullabaloo is!" Walked to the entrance! "Bob, what's going on?"

"There's a chap outside who I refused entry and I'm not letting him come in!"

"That's fair, still, we can't have all that noise, open the door, and ask him to stop kicking the door!"

"Idiot, I suggest you refrain from booting the door," said Roberts as he shut it! Again, two distinct, heavy thuds echoed inside this club! Next, one of the club's clients came over, then asked if someone could possibly quieten it down a touch! This prominent banging was certainly out of control! Bob opened the door again!

"Ok, Robert, I'll take it from here, thanks!"

The night was cool with a slight breeze, and outside this establishment, a tall, heavy-built person who tossed a dis-organised haymaker heavy-handedly across, consequently, I ducked, bobbed and weaved, then let one of my fist tickle his chin, sending him into the gutter! "Ok, mate, want a bit of slap and tickle?" Other folks were gathering, and now wasn't a good time to extract this ogre's teeth, possibly, another time and another place! I walked inside! Little John, a big fellow who worked alongside Bob Roberts, walked up from the main dance area!

"Sid, there's two chaps messing around, can Roger or Paul give me a hand!"

Roger Rider said, "Go along, Paul, call if you require assistance, ok?" Layton was only too eager for a punch up!

"I assure you, I won't need anyone." Next moment, we heard clunk, and Layton suddenly laughed!

"Roger, give him a hand!" Clunk, Rider popped another, like a small light bulb exploding! My word, when will I ever get a chance for some fun. "It ain't fair." Would you believe this, no sooner than my thoughts registered, a distinctive familiar banging echoed throughout this building! I went to the main door entrance, knowing this massive bug was back! I said, "Why are you causing such a disturbance?"

He shouted, "F-k off," and I replied, "Pick up your dukes," and zap, laid him on a zebra crossing; would you believe another one bit the dust?

Folk reading this book will presumably think I'm a rough diamond, but I assure you now that I'm the local protector and have never had cause to belt an innocent person. Trouble is, in our game, when thugs cause a fracas, we, that being Roger, Paul, Tony Brooker, Tony Carpenter and I, end it, period.

I'd like to say I approached a company who offered to publish this book and stated it would cost two thousand pounds to produce and promote this book, but no sooner than I agreed, the cost spiralled to approximately five thousand so I asked for my memory stick consisting of the manuscript back, and it returned all gobbledegook, so I'm having to recopy the entire tale, so should anyone send a memory stick, make sure you have a copy. Now, travelling back in time, Tim Wood required a sparring partner so they contacted my manager and I went! I was told to be at the gym, ready to commence at 6:30 pm! Nobody turned up so I did ten rounds on the heavy bag, then just after 7 pm, they turned up and Tim changed, then skipped for three rounds! His coach said we'd box eight rounds, but they called a halt after five or six rounds! Every night was the same with me catching Wood with a left hook and sometimes chopping him down like a big oak tree and so on, then I got this massive blister on the undercarriage of my left foot and was informed my services were no longer required, then I was refused payment! I said, if I'm not paid, I'll bust both manager and boxer! He paid me in full, and I left!

After a week or two, an article appeared in the boxing news stating Tim had sent me packing but I assure you they did not like my ammunition and never gave me the opportunity to avenge a somewhat dubious defeat, don't you agree? Never mind, that's past history! Last but not least, I recall an occasion at the Badger Bars when this man threatened a barmaid with a glass so I knocked him out clean as a whistle, simultaneously his head struck a large brass bell, a metal object in the shape of a deep upturned cup, widening at the lip which once belonged to a ship that had sunk, according to the landlord. Suddenly it went ding-dong, then one evening many years later, he saw me standing at a bar and approached, "Hey you, don't I know you?"

"Funny thing is," said I, "pal, your face does ring a bell," and I don't think he appreciated the pun because this brute walked away, and I've never seen him since so, if anybody sees a gent with a scar across his head just above the ear, ask if he was in the Badger Bar, and tell him Sid said hello. Well, two chaps from Currys, Kevin Allen from Southampton and his assistant Tomas Bysfrainsky, from Slovakia, have arrived to fit a new cooker, so that's it! "Not quite," exclaimed Lorraine!

"I agree, my dear," I replied! Now, many seasoned fighters in the past came from a slum area and were in general regarded as illiterate! Several former amateur boxing stars who won the world title such as Ricky Hatton, Amir Khan, Joe Frazier, Mohammad Ali and of course, last but not least, our British, European, commonwealth champion, Henry Cooper! These dedicated men employed a well-established ghost writer to record their heroic biography! I did not aspire to their greatness but I am truly grateful to almighty God for blessing me with an audacious family, enchanting friends, great neighbours and what a wonderful town to live; also, the icing on the cake is, I've overcome many obstacles thrust upon me and achieved my goals.

Became a professional gladiator and fought quality pugilists. "It's party time," remarked Finnegan!

"Let's drink, dance and yodel," stated Paddy O'Tool!

"Somebody fetch the potcheen, and storyteller, time to ride a dormouse!"

"Gentlemen, it's great to be back!"

"Not at all," stated O'Marley!

If one reads this book, then all I can say is, well done, Alistair Darling and you have been, joking apart I say no more. 'Cept, that's all folks.